Caught

The sound of footsteps tromping up the stairs rang through the apartment. Chen looked up with a gasp. The stranger snapped his head around, then swore. Following his eyes, Chen saw the blinking red light on a tiny sensor hooked up to the far wall of the living room.

Chen froze, trembling as he gazed at the sensor. "They... they've been monitoring us!"

The stranger grabbed his arm and pulled him toward a bedroom. "Probably because they never found that thing. Come on!" Chen stumbled as he struggled to stay with the stranger. He led Chen across the room to the gaping window, broken glass still scattered on the floor underneath it. Chen slipped the data drive into his pocket, glancing back through the apartment to the front door. The footfalls had reached the hallway outside the apartment.

Halcyon

CATHERINE FITZSIMMONS

For Lizy
Stay nerdy!
Catherine Fitz

Brain Lag

Milton, Ontario
http://www.brain-lag.com/

This is a work of fiction. All of the characters, events, and organizations portrayed in this novel are either products of the author's imagination or are used fictitiously.

Brain Lag Publishing
Milton, Ontario
http://www.brain-lag.com/

Cover artwork by Andre Podolsky

Fitzsimmons, Catherine, 1981-
    Halcyon / Catherine Fitzsimmons.

ISBN 978-0-9866493-5-6

    I. Title.

PS3606.I887H35 2012   813'.6   C2012-900907-5

Acknowledgments

Thanks first and foremost go to Andre, this book's biggest fan from its clunky first draft. This is for all the sketches, renders and conversations it spawned, from the engineering challenges in a tiered city to hilariously tragic modes of death.

Big thanks to Jason Lamey for his information on computer viruses and how to stop them. Any errors in the following are my own.

Once again, the Office of Letters and Light for putting on National Novel Writing Month (www.nanowrimo.org) and giving me an excellent excuse to write the first draft of this book.

The usual suspects for your support—Ryan Harron, Heather Milne, Lizy Miceli, Stephanie Haas and anyone else I may have forgotten.

And of course, Ryan, my idea bouncer, plot hole filler, character definer, fact checker, first and last proofreader and toughest critic. And, you know, those other things, like baby sitter, sanity maintainer and bread winner.

0

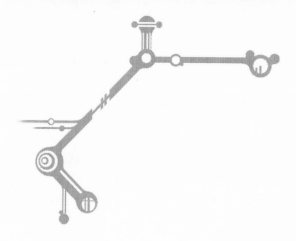

chapter.ONE

HE WAS DEAD by the time Zander arrived.

Zander had expected that. What he hadn't expected was the police investigation. Crouching at the living room window, peering in at the forensics team, he caught snippets of conversation and a time of death of 14:08. Not fifteen minutes before he had arrived. Many implants now sent out a lost connection signal when their power source suddenly went dead, but the potential for false alarms usually meant the paramedics didn't arrive right away and Zander had counted on being able to beat the authorities to the scene.

Worse, Carlisle was still there when the crime scene unit arrived. Only knowing the victim thirdhand, his story was sketchy at best. The cause of death was beyond question, the man's formatted electronics attested to that, but it was still police duty to do a search. They investigated these deaths more thoroughly than they probably should. They were desperate for answers.

Zander could understand.

He remained on edge as he watched the proceedings within. Carlisle had assured him that he received the data file while Zander was on his way to the victim's home. It was a major break in his own investigation, but only if the police didn't confiscate it first. Where could Carlisle hide the tiny data drive where the police wouldn't look?

Zander ducked away from the window as a head inside spun in

his direction. He sighed, running a hand through his hair. The constant thrum of traffic roared around him over the fence surrounding the building floor. He crouched in a rare patch of bushes in the middle of the city, the earthy smell of real plants filling his nose. The buildings around him still towered into the air, but only one layer of road passed overhead and a greater amount of natural light reflected off the walls overhead to illuminate the complex's lawn than Zander normally saw. The victim must have been fairly well off to be living this close to sky level alone.

Shifting, Zander pulled out his cell phone and held it up to the corner of the window, using its camera to glimpse the inside of the apartment. The officers standing near the entrance to the unit with Carlisle shifted and prepared to leave. Carlisle was not in handcuffs. Zander hoped the police had not searched him. Pocketing the phone, he disentangled himself from the bushes and stood. He crept along the side of the building beneath the row of windows, making his way around the corner and past the side door toward the front entrance.

At the corner along the front wall of the complex, he paused and peered carefully around the wall to watch the main entrance. The police officers and Carlisle came out the front door shortly, still talking.

He knew he shouldn't be here and knew he was in dangerous territory hanging around this close to a crime scene. All it would take was one good look at him and his face could be in the memory banks of every cop in the city. However, when Carlisle messaged to tell him about the victim, he had to come himself. He hadn't expected a hit so soon.

Finally, the officers waved off Carlisle. With a nod, he turned and began walking through the grass toward Zander, hands buried in his jacket pockets. Zander stepped back, but not far enough for Carlisle to keep from nearly running into him as he turned the corner. Carlisle swallowed a yelp as he lurched back.

"Sorry," Zander said. "You got it?"

Carlisle ran a hand through his hair, glancing around. "Man, I haven't had to crank out that much bullshit since high school." Carefully, he lifted his shirt up to his ribs, and fiddling with a patch of skin beside his navel, a pocket twisted open like a car's ash tray. Zander smiled. Known on the streets as a stash hatch, it was a safer way to transport small goods than many other means, and Carlisle's was quality work. Constructed of ballistics-grade plastic to fool a metal detector, the hatch door was integrated seamlessly into his skin and had to have involved expensive and time-consuming surgery to implant it. It wouldn't pass thorough police inspection but most others would miss it.

Reaching into the hatch, Carlisle pulled out a data drive and handed it to Zander. Zander breathed a sigh of relief as he took the drive hardly larger than his small thumb joint.

He glanced up at Carlisle. "This is going to save all of us." Slipping the drive into a pocket, Zander pulled out a handful of bills, which he shoved into Carlisle's palm. "Thank you." The money meant little to Zander. The appreciation did. Carlisle seemed pleased enough to take the cash and slip it into the hatch.

"What are you doing there?" barked a voice nearby.

Swearing, Zander spun and fled, Carlisle following close behind as he jumped the fence at the edge of the property. The officers shouted commands into wrist-mounted radios as they ran after the two men.

Damn it, Zander thought. *I knew I should've just gone home and messaged him later.* Running from the cops was guaranteed to get him followed, but he didn't want to find out if any of his earlier activities had left any outstanding warrants for his arrest. If they confiscated the data drive, all was lost. Cursing himself, he raced down the sidewalk as the officer's voice trailed after him.

"Stop right there or you're under arrest!"

Ignoring him, Zander darted across the street, dodging between traffic. It took little to escape the glimpse of greenery and as soon as his feet met pavement the city swallowed him up again. Buildings towered around him, the fenced-in lawn quickly forgotten in the maze of steel and concrete. The daylight bulbs attached to the underside of roads passing overhead shone down on the crowded streets.

Yelps and curses rang out as Zander darted between people on the sidewalk, the officer's voice yelling out warnings behind him. He had no idea where Carlisle was and couldn't spare the energy to find out. Zander felt guilty about getting him in trouble, since his interview at the victim's apartment meant he would undoubtedly be caught. Zander was hardly safe himself. Police officers were equipped with top-of-the-line machinery to enhance their speed and endurance, as advanced as his own, and escaping would not be easy.

He tore across an intersection just as the light turned red and cars rolled forward behind him, horns bleating. As he spun to cross the road the other way, a flat-bed truck conveying a forklift sped up alongside him. Grabbing the side of the truck, he swung up onto the bed, hoping the forklift would hide him from the driver's view. He grabbed one of the forks to steady himself as the intersection and the police officer diminished behind him. He panted, watching the road fly past as the truck gained speed.

Zander knew he wasn't clear yet. The officers at the scene knew he was there and they probably suspected he had something that had been taken from a suddenly deceased victim. He shook his head, touching the data drive in his pocket. He hadn't wanted to make an escape like that, but all it would take was one scan of the data for the police to take it and Zander couldn't afford that. Time was running out.

As the truck turned a corner several blocks away, Zander could see the officer in the distance finally giving up the chase. He knew that didn't mean he was free. They would put a tracer on the truck and more cops could be anywhere.

At the next red light Zander hopped off the truck. His phone rumbled in its clip on his belt as he jogged over to a nearby elevator. Snatching the phone out of its holster, he answered the call and opened a secure group connection. "Hey."

"Zander, what's going on? Where are you?" He recognized Ryn's voice and realized his follow-up call was late.

"Ran into some trouble." He arrived at the elevator, but the one going down had just closed its doors and the next one going up was another minute away. "I got it, but…" He swore. A block and a half down the street, a police officer rounded the corner and raced toward him. Zander turned toward the platforms where a few people waited for the next elevators.

"Squirrel," he said into the phone as he shoved through the crowd, "a quick exit would be appreciated."

"On my way, chief," another voice replied. Zander pocketed the phone and leaped off the platform into the open air beyond. Shouts and exclamations rang out behind him as he fell. Sliding his hands into his jacket sleeves, he grabbed the cable of the descending elevator. He slid a few feet down the cable before letting go, grunting as he hit the roof of the elevator. The elevator slowed to a stop as it reached the landing for the next layer of the city, and he glanced out at the streets before him. Through the crowds, he could see cops running toward the elevator from two different directions. People waiting for the elevator pointed and gave him strange looks. Zander jumped off and grabbed the counter cable for the up elevator, descending another layer as the shouted commands of the officers rang out above. The street below was noticeably quieter and darker. He was nearing ground level.

Reaching his legs out, he kicked off from the wall and let go, falling half a story before he hit the cracked road. He grunted as he rolled on landing, hitting his shoulder hard. Lunging to his feet, he continued running, knowing the police would be on the elevator on its way down.

He had descended to the first city level, only one layer of road and sidewalk above ground. The surrounding buildings looked seedy and run-down and the streetlamps were of poorer quality. The daylight bulbs were less illuminating, the light more artificial than on higher levels, and a haze of smog, smoke and dust filtering down from higher levels lingered in the air. Tattered bars with flickering neon logos and grocery stores with signs written in foreign languages stuck out between decrepit apartment buildings. Girders and support columns broke up the streets at regular intervals. None of the people occupying the streets seemed to notice him. A fleeting thought crossed Zander's mind that once, long ago, this area had been the domain of the wealthy, before three more city levels were built on top of it. The roads and sidewalks were a patchwork of old and older pavement, the newer sections thrown up hastily to support the second city level when it was originally added. Now this level had nowhere to go but further down.

He turned a corner, hoping he could find some way to evade the police. It didn't help that they would have put out an additional bulletin on him for catching a free elevator ride, unconventional though it was. Stairs between city levels were available but they were few and far between and only modestly maintained. The city liked the revenue from the elevator fares too much to make the stairs more prevalent. In any case, few people wanted to walk ten or more stories between city levels.

Panting, Zander rounded another corner and glanced around as he continued jogging away. Spying the ancient remains of a warehouse nearby, he turned and headed for the entrance.

He paused as he shut the doors quickly but gently behind him, his eyes adjusting to the darkness inside. The floor of the warehouse was still littered with broken pallets and rusting machinery and every high window was shattered. Graffiti marked the walls, though he could barely make out the tags in the darkness. Peering through the broken windows in the metal entrance doors, he sighted the two remaining police officers a block away. They looked around and discussed something amongst themselves before they set out at a slower pace, splitting up as they turned down different streets. He groaned. He had hoped they would give up after this long, but clearly their suspicions of Carlisle had extended onto him. Of course, that was his own fault for running in the first place. He cursed himself again.

Ducking beneath the windows, he crept around the debris deeper into the warehouse. He slid his phone out of his pocket and dialed the last number. Even hushed, his voice rang through the empty building.

"Tell me you're getting close, Squirrel."

"I'll just be another minute, boss," the voice replied through a haze of static. "I'm having a hard time finding you."

Zander ignored the title. "I'm not even sure where I am now. Follow my phone's signal."

"That's—harder. I'm—a good signal. Are you—did you hear me?" The reception was getting worse as Zander moved deeper into the warehouse.

"Squirrel? Squirrel!"

"It's the—did you—I ca—"

The phone cut out. Zander waved it around, but the display screen stubbornly flashed 'No Signal.' Transmitters were not common on the first level and the thousands of tons of concrete and steel above him often blocked out cellular signals. Grumbling, he slid the phone away, hurrying his pace as he continued through the building.

As he moved around the remains of a huge machine, a sharp intake of breath drew his attention to the corner of the decrepit machinery. He spun into a crouch, but as soon as he glimpsed the source of the sound, he paused. His eyes widened.

A woman kneeled in the corner of the machine, tensing as she gazed up at him. Zander blinked, unable to move as he tried to make out her features in the dim light trickling through the warehouse's high windows. Most of her ghostly pale body was covered by a dirty overcoat and cracked leather boots. White-blonde hair tumbled out from beneath an oversized flat cap. She was ragged and filthy but strikingly lovely.

"Sorry," he said quickly, straightening. She said nothing, only stared at him. He squinted, trying to make out her face. "Do... do I know you?" She tilted her head, a flicker of uncertainty touching her eyes.

The doors to the warehouse opened. Zander ducked behind the machine near the woman, thinking that there was no way he would escape cops this determined. The officer's footsteps rang through the cavernous walls of the warehouse, the beam of his industrial flashlight swinging through the air. Zander frowned, feeling guilty about bringing his pursuers to the woman crouching a few paces away. She was clearly homeless and the officers likely wouldn't leave her alone if they found her.

"Sorry about this," he hissed to her. "But I think you'll need to clear out of here. I'll draw his attention, you can sneak out the back door." He nodded in the direction of the rear exit from the warehouse. She inclined her head in return, a tired look crossing her face, but she seemed unsurprised. Zander hesitated a moment as the footfalls came closer.

Nodding to her once more, he crept out from behind the machine, trying to stay out of the police officer's flashlight beam. He knew he had to be noticed to give the woman an opportunity to escape, but he had to avoid being caught as well.

Engrossed in thoughts about the strange pale woman and focused on the officer's movements, he didn't see the broken board lying in his path until he stumbled over it. Immediately, he was illuminated by the flashlight.

"Hold it right there!"

Swearing, Zander broke into a run, maneuvering around the litter covering the floor as he swerved toward an emergency exit on the side of the building. The officer's shouted commands echoed off the walls, sounding like five people at once chasing him. Zander's heart raced from the effort of running and his ears rang from the shouts all around him.

Finally, he reached the emergency exit and flung himself against the doors. The poorly imitated daylight blinded him as he wove between traffic across the street, continuing along the road and wondering how to escape the officer's pursuit.

Then, two more cops rounded the corner ahead of him, guns

out and wrist-mounted recorders alight with activity. Zander threw himself to a stop and turned around. The other officer that had accompanied the one in the warehouse came down the sidewalk from the opposite direction. Panting, Zander glanced between the police officers as the one chasing him through the warehouse emerged, gun out. Bystanders on the sidewalk yelped and darted away as the police closed in on him.

"Freeze! Put your hands on your head now!"

Zander continued scanning the area, hoping to find something to use to his advantage. Standing by the railing on the road with no entrances to other buildings near him, he was trapped. His only way out was down to ground level, not nearly as far a fall as from the upper levels but still farther than he wanted to jump. And on ground level, little machinery still worked and the officers could still chase him longer than he could run. If he didn't get away fast, though, they would get a good picture of his face that they could use to find him later.

"Put your hands up now! This is your last warning!"

Zander swallowed uneasily. The traffic on the street slowed to a crawl as the officer from the warehouse slowly crossed to him, and the people on the sidewalk lingered beyond the other cops, watching the scene with a mixture of curiosity and uneasiness.

Zander's phone suddenly rumbled twice in its holster. He fought to suppress a grin. Inhaling deeply, he lifted his arms, holding his palms out as he faced the officer that had chased him through the warehouse. The officers approached him on all sides, guns and handcuffs held out.

He let his grin show. Moving a hand to his head, he saluted the officers, then jumped off the road.

Grabbing the railing, he swung around beneath the road and dropped down onto the roof of a dark blue van idling directly beneath. The roof of the van bent down as he landed on it, feet and knees stinging from the impact. He slid off the edge of the van, swinging through the open cargo door and collapsing inside.

"Go!" he snapped as soon as he hit the floor of the van. He braced himself as the van lurched forward and sped down the street, bullets following after it. Moving to his knees, Zander grabbed the handle to the cargo door and slid it shut, then crawled forward into the passenger seat.

"Squirrel, your timing is impeccable as always."

The driver grinned without looking away from the road ahead.

"Just doing my job, boss."

Zander turned his head to smirk at Squirrel, a wiry and curly-haired man who reached only to eye level on Zander. "How many times have I told you not to call me that?"

Squirrel's smile never wavered. "More than I can count, boss." Zander chuckled as he settled in to the seat and buckled his seat belt. The radar warning of nearby police officers on the van's dashboard went silent and Zander knew that they would not be tracked now. The van rocked as it weaved between the maze of enormous steel girders supporting the higher levels, the buildings and cracked road around them deserted. The haze was so thick, overlaying the air like a yellowish fog, that he couldn't see more than a quarter mile ahead.

As soon as he was comfortable, his phone came to life with noise, Ryn's voice growing frantic. "Zander, are you there? What happened?"

He grabbed the phone and opened the group connection. "I'm fine, Squirrel got me. And better yet, I got it." His hand dropped to the small bulge of the data drive in his pocket.

"Thank God. We'll see you back at your place, then?"

"Half an hour with Squirrel behind the wheel."

"Alright, see you then."

Suddenly, as Squirrel turned a corner, Zander saw the pale woman from the warehouse, running across the street half a block ahead of them. He gazed at her in surprise, not expecting to see her again after she left in a different direction from the warehouse. She panted, her hair bouncing limply with her gait.

Even as he watched her running, the roar of a speeding motorcycle preceded its turn around a corner a block ahead, following after the woman. Driving it was a tall, well-built man with short, dirty blonde hair. A familiar figure. Zander swore loudly and Squirrel slammed on the brakes, turning sharply down the next side street and revving the engine.

"Oh my God," Zander uttered. He glanced out the rear-view mirrors on the van at the woman being chased by the man on the motorcycle. "It's her."

"Zander?" Squirrel asked.

"Turn around. We've got to follow him."

"Aye aye, sir." There was no question in the driver's voice. Zander braced himself against the door as Squirrel spun the van around and drove back down the street after the woman.

Remembering the phone in his hand, Zander quickly raised the microphone to his mouth.

"Ryn, you guys head back home, we'll catch up with you later."

Ryn's voice came back swiftly, full of worry. "What? What happened? Do you need our help?"

"We can handle it. Something just came up. I'll talk to you later."

"Zander!" cried another voice over the phone before he could disconnect. "You're not coming back? What's going on?"

"It's alright, Chen." A smile spread across Zander's face as Squirrel turned the corner. The motorcycle rounded another corner a few blocks ahead.

"We found Elya."

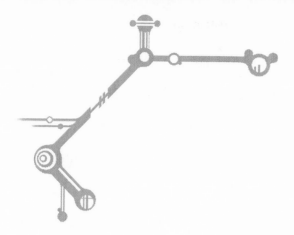

chapter.TWO

Two years ago

DWAYNE LEANED OVER his knees, his foot twitching rapidly as he waited in the silent hall. The stillness was overpowering, every breath he let out and every thump of his foot against the floor ringing in his ears. He ran a hand through his dark, curly hair and glanced down the empty hall, the neutral-colored walls lined with photographs of military vehicles. To his left, two more plastic-backed and nylon-padded chairs sat neatly beside his, a manila folder lying on the nearer one. To his right, only a closed door broke up the hallway. He tried to calm himself down and smoothed out his tie.

Finally, the door opened. Dwayne swiftly rose to his feet as a middle-aged woman stepped out, covered in a sharply tailored army dress uniform. "Dwayne Gillespie. Please come in." Swallowing hard, he picked up his folder, took a steadying breath and stepped inside the room.

The conference room's centerpiece was a heavy cherrywood table, polished to a glossy sheen that reflected the images of those sitting around it. The walls of the room were painted the same shade of taupe as the hall outside, the back wall given to one large window, imitation daylight shining in through the blinds. The woman who joined her companions at the table made seven, each sitting in a high-backed leather chair and clothed in a pressed army uniform, rows of badges pinned above their name tags. *There's more brass in here than a hardware store,* Dwayne thought as he glanced at each of the officers, his hands trembling faintly.

The woman who had admitted him, short dark hair framing a thin face, said, "Thank you for coming, Mr. Gillespie."

He nodded awkwardly as he stepped up to the empty end of the table. "The honor is mine, ma'am."

"I am Colonel Adelaide." She indicated each of the others seated around the table with her. "This is Major Ingolls." A fleshy man with dark eyes behind horn-rimmed glasses nodded. "Lieutenant Colonel Gibson." A balding man with neatly trimmed beard inclined his head. "Major Baron." Her nod was stiff and Dwayne wondered if the tight bun of her auburn hair stretched her face. "Colonel Warrester." Dark-skinned and intense, he steepled his fingers in front of his chin. "Lieutenant Colonel Gurevchek." He actually smiled, and his smooth blonde hair and lightly tanned skin showed he had taken greater advantage of modern technology than his companions. "And General LaCostas." She indicated the man sitting directly across the table from Dwayne, his chair silhouetted by the artificial sunlight.

Dwayne nodded again. "Thank you for taking the time to see me, sirs."

"Professor Chisolm had good things to say about you. You're studying computer science?"

"Yes, ma'am. I've nearly completed my master's and I'm going to start on my PhD in the fall."

Colonel Warrester's baritone voice rang out. "Do you have a specific focus in your studies?"

Dwayne shifted. "My expertise is with systems security, but I've spent a lot of time studying computers."

Major Baron leaned forward. "Do you have any experience with bioengineering, physiology, anatomy?"

"No, ma'am," Dwayne answered briskly, trying to hide his self-consciousness.

"Alright, Mr. Gillespie." Colonel Adelaide twined her fingers together on the table top. "You may present your proposal."

Dwayne inhaled, trying to picture the room of military officials before him as his bathroom mirror, where he had recited his speech a dozen times already.

"It's been nearly fifty years since scientists first successfully integrated computer technology with human tissue. As cybernetic implants have been used to regulate nervous and immune systems and other body functions, we have all but eradicated disease. Yet in spite of this, the most deadly disease we as humans have ever faced has arisen: the computer virus known as Halcyon. It can infect any kind of cybernetic implant and is one hundred percent fatal. The only controlling factor that has ever limited infections is the wireless quarantine the city's been placed under, forcing all incoming and outgoing transmissions to go through land lines. Of course, that means that anyone who has received an implant in the city is at risk.

"The problem with trying to stop Halcyon is that we cannot learn anything from it. Halcyon is cunning and intelligent and as soon as it kills, it deletes itself. We don't even know how it transmits, since it can directly infect implants through wireless connections that can't even access regular networks. The virus then overwrites server log data that could be used to trace the route of infection with garbage. Its attacks are random and the victims have nothing in common.

"This has been the biggest stumbling block in attempts to stop it. The virus uses whatever cybernetics a person has to kill them, swiftly and efficiently, and the victim doesn't even know he's infected until it's too late. It has worked its way around firewalls and highly encrypted connections. All attempts at creating an antivirus have failed. There has been no stopping it."

He set the folder on the table top and opened it up, sliding it toward Lieutenant Colonel Gibson to his right. "After studying Halcyon for the past six months, I have devised a two-step plan for stopping it." Gibson grabbed the proffered folder and looked at the files inside. "The first part is to write an antivirus. The antiviruses that have been attempted so far haven't succeeded for any of a few different reasons. Either the virus mutates and self-replicates, working its way around the antivirus, or it takes over the operational roles of certain files in an implant's operating system so that removing the virus still disables the implant. Or in one case, the virus still causes a fatal attack on the nervous system, since many cybernetic implants are connected to that as a way of informing the user of any malfunctions."

Major Ingolls leaned back in his chair with a creak. "So how do you propose to create an antivirus if none of these other methods work?"

"My plan is to create a retrovirus that assumes the operational role in an implant's software and then deletes the virus."

Lieutenant Colonel Warrester glanced at him from the corner of his eye. "Hasn't that been attempted before?"

Dwayne shifted his weight from one foot to the other. "Yes, this isn't a new idea. The problem with using a retrovirus to stop Halcyon so far has been that it infects so many different types of implants that by the time the antivirus figures out how the affected implant is supposed to operate, the virus has killed the user anyway. Unfortunately, with the operational speed of cybernetic implants, all this happens so quickly that we still have no further information on how the virus operates."

Lieutenant Colonel Gibson looked up from Dwayne's folder. "Can it be detected while dormant?"

Dwayne shook his head. "Some have tried, but no one really knows how Halcyon works and cybernetic software by nature is fluid, so it's been impossible to find any foreign code."

Lieutenant Colonel Gurevchek asked, "But the virus has to enter the implant wirelessly. Can't you just scan server logs for this garbage data that the virus writes?"

"That's also been tried. Not only does it take a tremendous amount of resources to constantly monitor server logs, but there's just enough of a pause before Halcyon overwrites the data that scanning software has already cleared it. The virus is remarkably intelligent."

Colonel Adelaide leaned back. "So how is your retrovirus supposed to work where others haven't?"

Dwayne nodded toward Lieutenant Colonel Gurevchek, who was currently examining the manila folder. "I have outlined a plan to streamline the analysis of implant software so that the retrovirus can resume basic operations until it can be fixed properly.

"Of course, the only way to test an antivirus's effectiveness is through a controlled infection. Since we are unable to obtain a copy of the virus code, there is no way to do this. So the second part of my solution involves, well… creating people."

All eyes fixed on him.

He chuckled nervously. "To ensure that the antivirus works and that it can successfully operate vital cybernetic implants, I propose setting up a computer array to mimic people with implants. That way, when the virus infects it, we can both record a copy of the virus and test the antivirus's effectiveness."

"But the virus infections are random," Major Baron pointed out. "There is no guarantee your computer array will ever be attacked by Halcyon."

Dwayne opened his mouth to respond, but before he could speak, Lieutenant Colonel Gibson said, "Wait, you said this computer array will record a copy of the virus when it's infected? Then why not just wait to create an antivirus based off that, instead of trying to make one now?"

Dwayne shifted. "Well, based on the broad range of implants that Halcyon infects, even those using different operating systems, I don't think there will be… that is, I don't think a more effective solution would present itself just by looking at the virus code."

"But if we were able to use a computer array to capture the virus in that manner," Colonel Warrester replied, "then we could create an antivirus based on that. Why should we need to put the money and manpower into making yours, an untested solution, when we will have all the information we need to write a guaranteed successful antivirus once we've captured Halcyon?"

Seven pairs of eyes bored into Dwayne. His throat constricted and he swallowed. "Well, I've already started the background work on my retrovirus. Professor Chisolm just told me not to start programming it yet for reasons of patent."

"He's a smart man," Colonel Adelaide remarked with a wry smile.

Dwayne cleared his throat. "I just thought that if my proposal was going to be well funded, I should do what I can to make sure it worked."

Major Baron looked unimpressed. "How well funded were you thinking your idea would be?"

He almost winced at his slip. "Well, depending on the software, I figure a high-end server is probably advanced enough to imitate five people at a high enough degree of complexity to fool Halcyon. Given the population that has at least some sort of cybernetic implant and the current rate of infection, if we had enough servers to mimic 10,000 people, then statistically we'd be guaranteed to capture a copy of Halcyon in about six and a half months."

Silence fell over the room.

"That's an awfully big up-front expense for such a delayed

payout." All eyes turned to General LaCostas, who had remained silent throughout Dwayne's presentation. "Especially since the market for the antivirus is limited to people inside the city. Few firms are going to want to accept such a risky business maneuver."

Dwayne shifted. "Well, considering the rate of infections is increasing, we'd be likely to get a hit sooner than that. That's just based on the current rate of infections. And once the quarantine is lifted the market will expand."

Major Baron frowned. "Didn't you read the entire press release when the quarantine was put into effect? They're only going to lift it when Halcyon is gone, not when an antivirus is released. We can't vaccinate the entire world."

Major Ingolls added, "And even if your figures are correct, you're probably being optimistic about the amount of servers we'd be able to procure. It would take even longer than you're estimating."

Dwayne had no answer for him.

"I'm curious about your method of analyzing implants to resume basic operations," Lieutenant Colonel Gurevchek stated. "Many people have medically necessary implants to regulate things like diabetes or high blood pressure, myself included. Do you really think your antivirus will be able to control such delicate and complex bodily processes as easily as, say, an artificial knee before Halcyon can disable it?"

Dwayne held his hands behind his back to keep from fidgeting. "It's more or less a method of analyzing the software in the implant and using general information to create a working replica, no matter how complex it is. The retrovirus isn't going to run the implant, just try to remind it how to run itself."

"But there's still a chance it won't work in time," Lieutenant Colonel Gibson remarked.

"Yes," he answered uneasily, "but the only other way I can think of to maintain the implant's functionality until it can be fixed properly is to have the antivirus access a comprehensive database of implant information and get its information from there. Not only does no such database exist, but in the time it would take to connect to the database, find the proper software, download it and re-install it in the implant, the host would probably be dead anyway."

A few more questions followed, but gradually the pauses grew longer until silence fell once more over the room. The army officials glanced at one another or leaned over and whispered to their neighbors. Colonel Adelaide inhaled as her eyes met those of the other officers, each in turn. After she examined each of them, she nodded to Dwayne. "Thank you for your proposal, Mr. Gillespie." She held up the manila folder. "Can we keep this?"

He waved his approval.

"We'll discuss your ideas and get back to you sometime later this week. Please give Professor Chisolm my regards."

He nodded stiffly. "Thank you for your time, ma'am. Sirs." Turning, he strode out of the room, forcing himself not to look back and gauge their reactions further. The door closed behind him and he let out a shaky breath, his hands trembling. He had never been in a room with so many people of power, and as much as he tried to convince himself that the worst that could happen was that his proposal would be rejected, he couldn't help feeling nervous. He turned his palm up and slid his sleeves back. A display embedded in his wrist flashed the time. His presentation had passed quicker than he had expected, given that he thought he had been inundated with questions for hours. Inhaling deeply, he strode out of the building and returned to his apartment.

His cell phone rang within half an hour of his return home. His heart did a somersault but it was only his classmate Chen.

"So how'd it go?"

"It was terrible," Dwayne moaned as he paced around his apartment. "They tore my proposal to pieces. I'm just glad it's over. I thought they'd never stop poking holes in my idea."

"Don't feel bad," the voice on the other end replied. "You don't know that they've rejected it yet."

Dwayne sank into a chair with a heavy sigh. "Oh, don't worry, I'm pretty sure they weren't interested. I must have sounded like an idiot." The other end of the phone went quiet and Dwayne could almost hear the uncomfortable frown. "Oh well. I'd better get back to studying. Talk to you later."

"'Bye, Dwayne," the voice quickly responded before Dwayne hung up.

The neighbors complained about the noise a few days later when he received the phone call informing him that his proposal had been accepted.

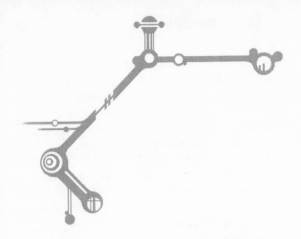

chapter.THREE

SHE RAN.

She had been running for weeks, though she could no longer remember why. Fleeting images lingered in her mind, plain hallways rushing past and a room filled with screens that popped and sparked, but no amount of concentration would restore her memories.

Elya. That was all she knew. That and the need to run, even though she had not seen anyone chasing her in all this time.

This man she hadn't seen before, however. The tall man on the motorcycle with a hungry look on his face as he chased after her, leather jacket flapping in the wind. A small input console with lights blinking was attached above his right ear and one of his eyes had been replaced with an advanced lens. Even in the dense haze on ground level that implant would have no trouble finding her.

Fear drove Elya's feet faster as she watched the motorcycle turn a corner not half a block behind her. He expertly wove the machine between the huge cracks marring the road without ever taking his gaze off her. She darted down the sidewalk toward the remains of a restaurant. On ground level little remained of the building but the structural supports, though as she tore into the room, a few tables still lay about the floor, beaten and broken. She let out a hiss as the motorcycle roared to a stop outside. The restaurant didn't connect to the rest of the building as she had hoped and the emergency doors, the only other exit, would not buy her any additional time. She thought furiously about how she could escape the man outside. If his eye was as advanced as it looked, it probably had various modes of sight. Her greatest concern was thermal imaging. As long as he knew vaguely where she was, few objects, even walls, would be able to hide her heat signature. Struck with an idea, she headed into the restaurant kitchen.

The kitchen had been stripped, the pot hooks on the walls empty and rings showing on counter tops where tins of utensils had once stood. Dust and cobwebs covered every surface and even the stainless steel had succumbed to time, rust flowering in corners and dents marking the scuffed metal counters.

Perhaps too big or too old to be looted, the enormous refrigerator, larger than some elevators between city levels, still sat against the wall not far from the doors. Across the room, a meat freezer connected to the kitchen. Both insulated, both with only one way in or out.

She could hear the man's heavy footfalls pounding through the dining room. Darting across the kitchen, she flung open the doors to the walk-in freezer, then jogged back to the refrigerator, being certain to keep its thick walls between her and the man. She just ducked around to the side of the fridge when he shoved the doors open. There he paused.

"Come out, come out, wherever you are." His rough voice was low and patronizing as though he spoke to a dog. She rolled her eyes at his tone as he stepped across the room toward the walk-in freezer. She carefully crept around the back of the refrigerator as he passed by a few feet in front of her. "This'll go a lot easier for you if you give yourself up." Peering around the corner, she found him nearly at the doors to the walk-in freezer. As he opened the doors, she sneaked out from behind the fridge and tiptoed across the floor toward the swinging doors into the dining room of the restaurant. Heart pounding, she reached for the doors.

The door creaked as it swung outward.

The man snapped his head over just as she darted out the door and his heavy footsteps rang out behind her. His legs were long and his body likely conditioned, and not three seconds passed before he followed her out the swinging doors. She tore across the floor of the restaurant back toward the entrance, fragments of wood turning up under her feet.

In the darkness of the condemned restaurant, she couldn't see the debris that littered the floor well, and a piece of a chair got caught between her ankles. Losing her balance, she tumbled to the floor. She yelped as she fell, but the only sound that came out was a hiss of breath. The man was upon her nearly as soon as she stopped moving. Grabbing a broken piece of the chair, she spun and hurled it up into his face. He grunted and recoiled, and she lunged to her feet and continued toward the entrance.

Flinging the door open, she tore out onto the walkway to the road, running straight toward his motorcycle. She leaped onto the seat and kicked it to life, the machine roaring and rumbling beneath her as the man raced up the walk. Heart pounding, she twisted the throttle. Sparks flew out from the lowered kickstand as the motorcycle rushed forward.

Before she made it out onto the road, the man lunged and grabbed onto the back of the motorcycle. She opened her mouth in another soundless yelp as the additional weight threw her off balance and the bike tipped over. Throwing herself clear of the falling motorcycle, she slammed onto the ground and rolled over a few times, her hat falling off and her coat ripping as it scraped over the cracked asphalt. Warmth ran down the side of her pounding head as several parts of her body burned from the hard landing. She tried to rise and continue fleeing, but the man's ropy arms wrapped around her arms and stomach, pressing her back against him with an iron grip.

She thrashed about, trying to free herself from his grasp, and the heel of her worn boot connected with his ankle. His arms loosened briefly, but before she could wriggle free, he fell to a kneel, pulling her down with him so that she couldn't reach her legs back again. Still she fought, but as soon as she noticed that one of his arms had released her, a thick knife pushed up against her neck. She fell still, eyeing the hunting blade.

"That's it, sweetie," he murmured in her ear. "No more running." She sneered at the tone of his voice. He narrowed his eyes at her. "You'd better not have seriously damaged my bike or I'm going to be pissed."

Then, a jazzy riff rang out.

Twisting her head around, she shot him an odd look. He grinned, the lines of his stubbled jaw deepening. "Comm answer." A light blinked on the panel behind his temple. She could faintly hear another voice answer him, likely through the tiny speaker visible in his ear, but couldn't make out the words. He continued grinning at her as he replied, "Oh yeah, I got her." More mumbling emanated from the speaker in his ear. "Don't worry. She's not going anywhere." She studied her attacker as he continued his conversation. The lines on his face showed him to be in his forties, his muscles thick and sharply defined with only a little fleshiness in his stomach. Beneath his T-shirt, she could see the edge of a tattoo that ended at his neck, a coil of a vine or snake.

"You're just around the corner then. See you in a minute. Comm off." A light on the panel winked out, and he again focused on her. Light glinted off the edge of the knife from the corner of her vision. "You know, we had a hell of a time tracking you down." He chuckled as he slipped the knife into her hair, holding a lock of snowy white strands away from her face. "No wonder. Pretty clever, this. Frankly, I liked the way you looked in the vids better."

She narrowed her eyes at him before twisting her head away. She started struggling in his grip again until the knife returned to her throat.

"Not going to scream for help? After all the trouble you gave us, I was expecting more of a fight."

Her glare grew fiercer, though she didn't face him.

"What's the matter? Cat got your tongue?"

She didn't react.

His grin widened. "So you lost your voice, did you? Well, that'll make our job easier, though I guess Sinclair won't be happy."

A tingle spread quickly through her body. She knew that name. Sinclair. It lingered on the edge of her mind like a forgotten word, but as soon as she focused on it, the memory slipped beyond her grasp, just like the reason why she had been running. The sense of discomfort that the name invoked in her remained, however, and she knew the two were connected.

Before she could remember anything else, a car pulled around the corner and drove down the street toward them. She tried to break free as her attacker's attention turned to the approaching car, but he held fast.

The car pulled to a stop in front of them and the driver's door opened. A woman stepped out, slender and toned and half a dozen years or so younger than her companion, dressed in a snug-fitting

T-shirt and blue jeans. Her blonde hair was cut in a line that fell down to her chin in the front and the base of her skull in the back, below which her head was shaved. On her left arm, five parallel blue LED stripes glowed.

She gave the man a flat stare. "You think this is her?"

He stood, pulling Elya to her feet. "Take a look, Galina. Why do you think we had such a hard time finding her?" He roughly twisted Elya's head around. She stared impassively back as Galina studied her face for a long moment.

Galina jerked her head toward the car. "Get her in."

He dragged Elya around the car toward the passenger seat. She couldn't see through the tinted windows, but when he opened the door, she saw a standard car interior. A short coil of rope lay on the seat. Grabbing it, he bound her wrists together, then shoved her down into the seat. He reached for her legs to lift them into the car, but she pulled her feet in before he could grab her. He grinned at her as he straightened.

From the other side of the car, Galina said, "Gerod."

Looking up, he grabbed a strip of black cloth Galina tossed to him, then reached down to tie it around Elya's face. As darkness shrouded her vision, she could only hear the creak of leather as Gerod straightened.

"You'd better gag her, too. I don't want her screaming the moment we get out."

Elya could hear the grin in Gerod's voice. "No worries about that." Before Elya realized he was close again, he gave her chest a quick squeeze. She inhaled sharply and threw her arms up, but he had already retreated.

"Gerod," Galina admonished.

"See? She won't make a peep."

Elya glared in the direction of his voice, but as soon as she turned her head, the *clump* of the door closing rang out, locking her inside. Then, the driver's side door opened and the car shifted as Galina sat down.

From outside, Gerod said, "See you back at base." Galina didn't respond, only closed the door. The muffled roar of Gerod's motorcycle starting up rang out, then it sped off down the street.

As Galina began driving through the broken roads of ground level, Elya focused on what she could hear and feel, not daring to try to move her hands. She tried to gauge the speed of the car and count the left and right turns to determine where they went, but she lost track before long. She doubted it would have helped. Although she knew the layout of the city in a general sense and occasionally a familiar place had brought an image from her life into her mind, she couldn't remember enough to make a reasonable guess as to where they drove. All she could be certain of was that the car leaned back to travel up two city levels.

The gentle swaying of the car brought the aches of her scrapes to life once more and she could feel warmth drizzling down the side of her head. It took all of her focus to hold her head steady when the car turned suddenly, and to keep from getting sick from the motion. When they pulled to a stop at an intersection, Galina shuffled around and said, "Here." Still blindfolded, Elya could only feel the cloth Galina pressed into her hands. Elya silently raised the cloth with both hands to dab at the wound on her head. It was the only word spoken during the entire drive.

Finally, they pulled to a stop. Galina stepped out of the car and walked around to the passenger door. Elya waited, unmoving. She knew that Galina and Gerod would hold her captive or else hand her over to someone who would, but she didn't fight. The last several weeks had been nothing but danger and she was neither surprised nor distraught that she had been caught at last. She also knew that she was not entirely without hope, and her captors would likelier be caught off guard if they suspected that she had given up, rather than fought them. And with the memory of that large knife held to her throat, she didn't know what these two would do to her if she tried to fight.

The passenger door opened. She began to reach for the blindfold, thinking it unnecessary now that they had arrived at their destination, but before she could pull it off, Galina grabbed her arm. Her grip was firm, not crushing, but her fingers wrapped around one of Elya's scrapes and she let out a hiss. Ignoring the reaction, Galina pulled her out of the car to her feet. She stumbled as she was led around the car. The rumble of Gerod's motorcycle pulled up beside the car before he shut off the engine.

Neither of them spoke as the sound of the engine died away. Elya walked awkwardly beside Galina as the click of a lock unlatching sounded ahead of her, followed by the creak of a door opening. Without another word, the three of them disappeared inside. The door closed and locked behind them and she could hear the hum of a laser defense system start up. Then the blindfold was pulled off her head.

A large, open room lay before her, floored in hardwood and broken up at regular intervals by support columns. The room was furnished, but the furnishings were plain and utilitarian and overshadowed by the rows of guns, rifles, grenades, body armor and other tactical equipment lining the walls. Down the middle of the room sat a large weight training machine, a simple desk with a screen on it, and a sofa in front of a TV. She could see nothing that passed for bedding or kitchen, though there was a bar-size refrigerator at the back of the room and a bathroom was visible in the far corner, beside what looked to be another door out, an access panel on the wall beside it. The walls were bare cement, devoid of decoration, and she could make out the clear plastic coating on the heavy windows that completely obscured all view of the interior from outside. The laser defense system was active over each door and window. There was little here that would help her escape. She frowned as Gerod shoved her forward.

"Get her secure," Galina ordered. "I have to call Sinclair." Elya grimaced and followed as Gerod grabbed her arm and pulled her roughly through the room. He led her toward a cot set up against the wall halfway across the room as Galina dialed a number on a cell phone.

"This is Mollis. We've got Renard."

Elya's eyes shot open as she recognized the name. Galina's conversation faded in her mind as she focused on the word. Renard. It was like something clicked into place in her mind. The word had been on the tip of her tongue for weeks, but it had always eluded her when she tried to find it. It was her name. Elya Renard. Even though she knew nothing else about herself, somehow she felt whole again.

She stumbled as Gerod pushed her forward, her mind returning to the under-furnished room. Galina still talked near the door.

"She's fine, but she can't talk. Yes, of course. We'll meet you at the parking garage on fifty-second. Fourth, on the west side. Eleven-thirty. Yes. We'll see you then, Mr. Sinclair."

As she spoke, Gerod shoved Elya down on the cot and tied a plastic-covered metal wire attached to the floor beside the cot to her wrist. She didn't struggle against Gerod's harsh treatment. Untying the rope holding her wrists together, he yanked her other arm across the cot, pulling the rest of her body with it, and tied a second wire around her other wrist, leaving her sitting up on the cot with her wrists tied as far apart as they could get. The TV and sofa lay just in front of her. She narrowed her eyes at Gerod as he winked at her and retreated to the fridge. The look wasn't just for his treatment of her. It made her uncomfortable to think that Galina and Gerod, and Sinclair, knew who she was when she didn't. Still, just knowing her last name gave her strength. She could get little information on just Elya, but Elya Renard would be a lot easier to find.

"So?" Gerod asked as he opened the refrigerator and pulled out a can of beer.

"We're delivering her tonight." Galina pocketed her phone. "He sounded pleased enough, but I'll be glad to put this assignment behind us. He's been nothing but a thorn in my side since we took this mission. Idiot. If it was as easy to recover her as he thought, then one of the other teams he hired could have found her."

Gerod grunted as he flopped onto the sofa and turned on the TV. "I can already imagine the accusations when we show him her."

Galina fixed her gaze on Elya. Elya returned it steadily, though the intensity in the mercenary's eyes made her uneasy. After a long moment, Galina turned to the desk and brought the screen to life with a flick of her finger, ignoring her prisoner.

Elya twisted her wrists against the cords holding her, but she couldn't move her arms or reach the knots. Her scrapes ached and her head pounded, though the wounds no longer bled openly. Leaning her head back against the hard cement wall, she closed her eyes, listening to Gerod flip through the channels. She sighed, resigned to captivity for the day. Her hope that she could escape later diminished. These two seemed quite thorough in their methods, and from the sound of Galina's conversation they had not been the first people hired to track her down. They would not give up their prey easily. Perhaps she could find a way to get free during the journey to deliver her to Sinclair but that seemed less likely as well. A parking garage would not offer much for hiding places either.

The afternoon and evening ticked away slowly with nothing to pass the time in her confinement. Elya sat still on the cot, growing sore from the uncomfortable seat and unchanging position. Gerod stepped outside to work on his motorcycle at times, but largely continued watching television throughout the afternoon, occasionally making a smart remark or laughing at some inappropriate joke. Galina never responded with more than a roll of her eyes, her time mostly spent reading something on her screen with occasional breaks to exercise. Gradually, the daylight lamps outside faded until the halogen streetlamps flared to life in the deepening dusk. Elya grew hungry and thirsty, her arms aching from being held out over the cot and hands falling asleep from the tight cords around her wrists. Never had she suspected she might miss being on the streets scavenging for food, but being inside and warm offered her no comfort here. She wished she could remember who Sinclair was and dreaded the meeting to occur later that evening even as she tried to figure out a way to escape. She stared at the wall across the room, lost in thought, until she gradually drifted to sleep.

Suddenly, the power cut out. The click of machines turning off and abrupt silence woke her, but she had barely opened her eyes when the doors on either side of the room burst open, gunshots cracking through the darkness. She gasped and tried to duck down on the cot as the lights turned back on with the drone of a generator whirring in the corner. Crashes and shuffling rang out in every direction with the barrage of bullets ripping through the room. Elya pressed herself up against the wall, pulling at her bonds so much that the cords dug into her wrists.

By the time her eyes adjusted to the renewed light, she found two men crouching behind Galina's desk, turned onto its side near her. They reached around the desk top to fire at Galina, who ducked behind the weight training machine and shot back at them. One of the men was dark-skinned with ropy muscles, dreadlocks swaying around his face as he dodged and fired. The other man was shorter and much younger, still a teenager by the looks of it. Brown-skinned, he sported dark clothes and single strands of fiber optic cable interspersed in his spiky black hair, glowing in shifting shades of blue, green, red, orange and violet. Across the room, a third man who had broken in through the far door crouched in the bathroom, firing out through the crack between door and wall at Gerod, who ducked beneath the couch, pulled toward the wall to keep him safe from both groups of assailants.

"You!" Galina snapped over the reports ripping through the air.

"Come on now, kidnapping?" replied the man in the bathroom. Elya's eyes widened as she recognized the voice of the man she had seen in the warehouse that afternoon. "That's illegal."

Elya saw Galina's teeth clench, but before she could answer,

Gerod called back, "Big words coming from someone whose description was just on the news as a 'person of interest' in a homicide. And this is your second B&E."

"That we know of," Galina added.

Gerod smirked. "And I do believe this counts as assault."

"We're just evening up the score on that one," retorted the man from the warehouse.

A hail of bullets cut off any further response and Elya cringed and tried to duck, though the shots weren't aimed in her direction. Opening her eyes, she saw Galina dart behind a stack of metal cases, the two men behind the desk firing after her.

Elya's eyes darted across the room as Gerod glanced over at Galina. In that moment, the man from the warehouse charged out of the bathroom, firing repeatedly at Gerod as he ran forward. Swearing, Gerod ducked down behind the couch instinctively, but held up his gun and tried to shoot through the fabric. In seconds, the man from the warehouse vaulted over the couch, his foot swinging around toward Gerod's hands. Gerod pulled himself out of the way from the blow, but immediately released a hand from his pistol as he blocked the punch the man from the warehouse threw at him upon landing. In the light, Elya saw him clearly for the first time, the plain overhead bulbs illuminating blood red hair combed back over his head with locks of ebony hanging over his forehead. He looked about her age. He maneuvered quickly and carefully in his leather jacket and jeans, he and Gerod moving too fast to aim the guns they still held.

Then, an enormous report boomed through the room and the two other men yelped as the desk they crouched behind jumped from the impact. Turning, Elya found Galina cocking a shotgun, an empty shell spiraling out of the chamber as the next round sprang in. The two men peered around the table briefly before darting behind it again, and the second shot cracked against the desk, wood chips spraying into the air.

Elya's eyes darted back and forth across the room, watching the two separate battles escalate to either side of her. The fox-haired man had seemed genuinely concerned for her safety that afternoon and interested in her welfare now, but why? He and his companions looked more intent on fighting with Galina and Gerod than in paying her any attention. She had been struck at first by the thought of being rescued until she realized they wouldn't risk themselves like this if they didn't want something from her as well, something that wouldn't be served by having the police handle this instead. She tried to press herself as far back against the wall as she could, unable to do anything more.

"Guys!" fox-hair yelled out as he grappled with Gerod. "Get Elya out of here!"

She glanced at him as he spoke her name. Gerod drove a knee into fox-hair's stomach and twisted his arm. Another shotgun blast ripped through the room, drawing her attention back to the other side of the battle. The dark-skinned man yelped as he grasped his side and fell back against the wall. Thin beams of light streamed through a spray of pin-sized holes in the table's surface.

"Deadeye!" cried the man with the fiber optic strands in his hair. He glanced anxiously between his companion, the desk, and Elya while Galina reloaded her shotgun. He peered around the desk, gun held in one unsteady hand, but Galina fired back with her own pistol as soon as his head appeared. He leaped behind the desk with a yelp as the man with the dreadlocks fired back.

Turning, the brown-skinned youth pointed his gun in Elya's direction. She gasped and turned aside, lifting her legs up onto the cot. Three shots fired off and ricocheted off the floor before the wire holding her wrist trembled. It rocked two more times before the man with the dreadlocks barked, "Shad! Charge!"

Grabbing the edges of the desk, the two men lifted it as they stood and charged toward Galina. The desk smashed into pieces as it crashed down on the metal cases that Galina hid behind, and the two men leaped over the broken shards as they attacked her. More bullets tore through the room haphazardly, some striking the ceiling above Elya.

She yelped soundlessly as cement flakes and dust drifted down onto her hair and clothes, crashes rocking the room as the two men fought with Galina and fox-hair continued to battle Gerod. Elya grasped the wires holding her down and pulled at the one that had been shot, the plastic cover stretching as she yanked at it. The man with the fiber optic cables grunted as Galina kicked him into a pile of ammunition boxes, then she spun to face the dark-skinned man.

Suddenly, Gerod landed a kick on fox-hair that sent him sprawling across the room to tumble beside Elya's cot. Over the edge of the cot, she could see flecks of red spray against the floor as he coughed. He groaned, shifting, but didn't rise.

Gerod chuckled as he crouched down and picked up his fallen pistol, striding forward beside Elya's cot to aim it at fox-hair's head. "So long."

Horrified, Elya yanked on the wire with enough force to snap it at its weakened point. The cable flailed as her arm threw around from the force of her pull, and the exposed wire slashed across Gerod's face. He shouted and recoiled and his shot flew wide, the bullet hitting the wall above fox-hair's head. Elya tumbled over the side of the cot from the force of her pull as Gerod pressed his free hand over his eye, blood streaming over his fingers. She blinked, finding herself face-to-face with fox-hair. He gave her a brief grin before gathering his strength. Sliding around her, he lunged forward, driving his fist into Gerod's gut just as the larger man turned. Elya worked at the knot around her other wrist as fox-hair spun, kicking Gerod backward. Losing his balance, Gerod crashed into and knocked over the TV stand, collapsing in a heap only a few paces from where Galina grappled with the other intruders.

Fox-hair swayed in place as he turned to help Elya with the knot around her wrist. "Get out of here," he said, his tongue stained red. Momentarily, they loosened the knot and Elya slipped her wrist out of the loops of cable. Needing no further encouragement, she bolted for the door, fox-hair close on her heels. Yelps and gunshots rang out behind her as they crossed the room. Elya untied the severed cable still hanging from her right wrist and tossed it aside.

She soon reached the door, still hanging open from when fox-hair crashed inside, but the faint buzz of electricity hummed from the laser defense grid active over the doorway. Reaching out, she accessed the control screen for the security grid and soon disabled it.

A shuffling sound emanated behind her and Gerod's running footsteps pounded across the floor. She shot a glance over her shoulder, heart racing. Calmly, fox-hair raised his pistol and fired repeatedly. Gerod lunged out of the way and ducked behind the bar fridge as blue and red lights began flashing against the walls through the windows.

Turning around, Elya shoved through the doorway and into the adjoining hall, the corridor open and quiet. A woman with shoulder-length auburn hair approaching the door pulled up short with a gasp as fox-hair followed Elya out.

"Go," fox-hair said to her, then yelled back through the doorway, "Guys! Get out of there now!" He touched Elya's shoulder, seeming to have regained some strength, and they and the woman raced down the hall and out the front door of the building.

As they stepped out onto the wide sidewalk leading to the road, sirens assaulted their ears. Red and blue flashing lights lit up the buildings a block away, rapidly growing brighter.

"This way!" the woman cried over the noise and raced down the street. Uncertain what else to do, Elya followed after fox-hair and the woman. As they passed by the alley on the other side of the building, the two other men burst out the door and ran down the street with them.

Around the corner, they came upon a plain blue van parked against the curb, its rear door facing them and engine running. The three men and woman overtook Elya as they climbed into the van, but she hesitated.

Turning around, fox-hair held a hand out to her. "It's okay, Elya. We're with Chen."

She frowned. The name did not mean anything to her, though the way fox-hair spoke it suggested that it should. The desire to know who she was overpowered her, like a hunger she couldn't sate.

The sirens drew close around the corner, and with a frantic look, the young man with fiber optic strands in his hair grabbed her arm and yelped, "Come on!"

Elya exhaled sharply and slammed her hand against his arm. Wresting free, she turned and fled down the street.

"Elya!" fox-hair yelled after her.

At the next corner she paused, glancing back at him. He stood outside the van, gazing at her, an arm held out to keep anyone else from following her. He turned at something called to him from inside the van, and then spun around as the sirens drew closer. He turned back to her with a frown. After a moment, he nodded and climbed into the van.

Giving him a regretful look, she turned and continued running away and the van sped off down the street behind her.

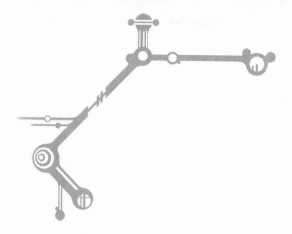

chapter.FOUR

THE SILENCE FOLLOWING Zander's update had Chen too distracted to work. Code still swirled through his head, but he couldn't connect strings and variables with the thought that Zander had found Elya. He paced around the room anxiously, desperate for updates but forcing himself not to call Zander. They would be back soon enough.

On some of his passes, he tidied his desk, moving data drives and piles of notes to drawers in his desk below his tablet computer, but mostly he simply crossed the living room back and forth, awaiting news. He loosened and retied his ponytail. He removed and cleaned his glasses. He straightened the pictures on the wall. He watered the small blue spruce growing out of a plastic pot in the corner. Eventually, he sat back down and distractedly browsed the internet, even though the connection dragged as it passed through the wireless quarantine around the city on old land lines. Outside, the daylight lamps faded and the halogen streetlights flickered on.

Finally, he began working again, but not much time passed before he heard the lock rattle in the front door. He rose from his chair with a start as the door opened. Zander walked in with an unreadable look and an ice pack on his face, followed by the others. Deadeye clutched his side, his dark face grimacing as he moved, and Ryn helped him over to the couch, where she crouched to inspect a hastily dressed wound. Shad quietly followed them in last.

Chen glanced between them curiously as Zander shut the door behind him. "What happened? Where's Elya?" Shad hunched his shoulders with a guilty frown, the fiber optic strands in his hair glowing silently.

"She escaped," Zander answered.

Chen's eyes widened. "Escaped? What do you mean 'escaped'?"

Shad groaned. "It's my fault, alright?"

"Shad," Ryn attempted, reaching a hand out to touch his arm. He flinched away from the touch.

"Look, what's done is done," Zander cut in calmly. "Right now, we just need to focus on finding her again."

"Wait, wait, wait," Chen cut in. "What happened?" He listened intently as Zander related the events of the evening to him.

"I just didn't want the cops to catch us," Shad said with a bewildered shrug. "I didn't think she'd freak out like that."

Chen shook his head, baffled. "I don't understand, you were getting her out of there. Why did she run from you?"

"She was scared," Ryn replied, her eyes narrowing. "You guys burst in there with guns blazing, it's no wonder she didn't trust us."

Zander nodded in agreement. "We have to look at it from her point of view. Sinclair betrayed her, the army betrayed her."

"She didn't even know us," Deadeye piped in.

"She's been living on the streets for months," Ryn added.

Zander nodded again. "Yes, we were trying to free her, but from the way we barged in, she had no way of knowing that." He glanced mildly at Shad. "And we'd've been hard-pressed to get her to, no matter what we did." Shad looked away, seemingly unconvinced.

Chen swallowed, absorbing their words. "Well... you can still find her, right?" He gazed desperately at Zander.

"We can't force her to help us. It'll just push her away."

"You have to find her," Chen pleaded.

"Chen," Ryn reprimanded.

"We'll find her," Zander said, cutting her off. "But we can't push her. She's not an animal. She has to make her own decision. I am *not* going to kidnap her like those mercs."

Chen grasped his computer desk, trying to settle the uneasy feeling that rose in his stomach. "So what do we do?" Zander shook his head as if to clear it, and Chen leaned forward hopefully as he saw the determined glint in his eyes.

"She can't move too fast on foot." Zander turned. "Shad, can you tap into the feeds from the city train surveillance cameras?"

Shad's eyes widened. "It'll take a while, and there's no way I'll be able to watch all of them to find her…"

"Focus on the area where we were, and see if Tiger can write up a protocol to search for her image in the footage. Keep an eye on nearby elevators, too, if you can." They all watched Zander intently as he spoke.

"Do you really think she'll go on the train or elevator?" Ryn asked.

"No, but it's good to cover our bases, just in case."

"I'd be more worried about those mercs finding her again if she doesn't go far," Deadeye spoke up as he brushed a dreadlock over his head.

"I doubt it," Shad replied, finally seeming calmer. "With all the weaponry they had in that place, the cops are going to be patrolling the area for a while."

Zander nodded. "I don't think they're dumb enough to risk going back there anytime soon, even to find Elya."

"So how're we gonna find her?" Deadeye asked.

"We'll figure that out later. Right now, it's late, and we all have lives to return to." Zander pulled the ice pack away to reveal a black eye beneath it. He touched it gingerly. "I hope this doesn't interfere with mine." He turned to Shad. "Keep an eye on those feeds and call me immediately if you see her." Shad nodded meekly as Deadeye and Ryn stood and headed for the door.

Shad glanced at them, then shot Zander a frown. "I'm sorry, Zan."

Zander shook his head. "Don't worry about it. I was pretty worried about the cops catching us, too." Shad gave him and Chen a brief smile as he stepped out the door behind Ryn. Sighing, Zander closed the door behind him and locked the deadbolt before pressing the ice pack against his face once more.

"So what's eating you? You're even more mopey than usual."

Chen glanced up hastily to find Zander examining him. "Nothing. I just really wish you'd brought Elya back."

Zander sighed as he strolled over to the couch. "Me too. But when I saw the look on her face when she ran away the last time…" He shook his head. "I couldn't go after her. We wouldn't have been any better than those mercs." Reaching into his pocket, he pulled out a data drive. "Besides, we still have the next biggest missing piece of the puzzle right here."

Chen sank into the chair in front of his computer desk with a soft groan. "You don't understand, Zander. I'll never be able to reprogram the antivirus. She has the only remaining copy of Dwayne's work. If I can't get it from her, we have no hope."

Zander leaned his head back against the back of the couch, gazing up at the ceiling. "You told me right from the start that we couldn't finish without her. We'll find her, Chen, don't worry. It'll just take a little more time."

Chen glanced distractedly at his computer. "I don't know how much time we have." Silence fell as they each remained lost in their thoughts. Chen swallowed uncomfortably. "Your boss called while you were out." He saw Zander raise his head from the corner of his eye, but didn't face him. Chen shifted. "One of your coworkers was infected with Halcyon last night." He heard Zander lean his head back against the couch and sigh. "Mary… something. He said she usually worked in gardening."

"I've seen her in the lunch room a couple times. Didn't really know her well, we usually had different schedules." Another pause sounded.

Chen ran a faintly trembling hand over his head. "I'm trying to figure out Dwayne's practices but I just don't understand most of this stuff. His research was so thorough that I don't know how I can improve on it, and this biology stuff is way over my head." His anxiety poured out as he spoke, even though his throat grew thick from saying it. "It's all just so much more advanced than anything I can do. I'm doing the best I can but I'm just not as smart as Dwayne."

Chen had only just registered the sound of Zander rising from the couch when he set the data drive down on the desk next to Chen. Zander turned and approached his bedroom, the ice pack hanging from his hand.

"You'll only be doing your best when you stop selling yourself short."

Chen watched silently as Zander retreated into his bedroom and closed the door without looking back.

Chen turned to the data drive with a sigh. Zander was right, the information on the drive provided a huge step in the right direction for them. It had been weeks since they sent out requests online for people to attach data drives to themselves, wearing them around the clock in case they were infected by Halcyon. His own had become a familiar presence, removed along with his glasses only when he showered or slept.

The drives could do nothing to stop Halcyon from infecting them. All it did was record an image file from the afflicted before the virus deleted itself. Dozens of people had volunteered to wear the data drives knowing that they would only be helping if they died. Now someone had.

Chen frowned as he raised the drive. With luck, it contained information on how Halcyon infected cybernetic implants, giving him vital clues to finish the antivirus. However, he still needed the antivirus. Although he had all of Dwayne's notes on how he had planned to program the antivirus and everything he had learned along the way, it had still taken him over a year to write the code that only Elya still had, time Chen was certain they didn't have.

Setting the data drive back on the desk, Chen turned to his computer and opened up a test program he had written a few days ago. He leaned back in his chair and looked at the code arrayed before him on the screen. Zander often tried to assure him that he had the skills necessary to complete the antivirus as Dwayne had envisioned, but he didn't believe it. His specialty in college had been different from Dwayne's and he had only completed a two-year degree. Since he had obtained Dwayne's notes he had spent nearly as much time studying Dwayne's methodologies as actually reprogramming the antivirus. And he still had no knowledge whatsoever of biology, which he needed to improve upon Dwayne's work and finish it.

Chen glanced at the corner of his desk where a small, framed photograph sat. The creased picture showed Dwayne grinning broadly as he stood on a beach, tall and dark-haired and flashing a well-used smile. His arm was around Elya, leaning against him and also flashing the camera a wide smile even as she squinted against the brilliant sunlight. She was stunning, her olive skin and golden brown curls shining in the sunlight. He couldn't even imagine her as Zander had described her, with deathly pale skin and stringy white hair. What had happened to her that night two months ago?

And Dwayne, looking so vigorous and full of life, his eyes glinting happily, his image showed no apprehension or idea what would happen in only a few short months.

A lump formed in Chen's throat as he examined the picture. Letting out a heavy sigh, he turned back to his computer and began testing his program again.

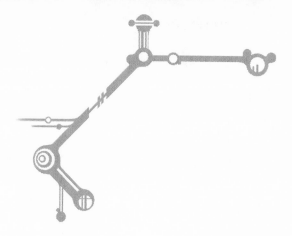

chapter.FIVE

Eighteen months ago

DWAYNE GLANCED UP from his computer as the door opened. Colonel Adelaide, the dark-haired woman who had been present for his proposal, stepped into the lab. He quickly got to his feet as a portly, gray-haired man in a suit and tie walked in after her, a security badge marked "Visitor" clipped to his suit jacket. Dwayne stumbled over some computer parts lying on the floor of the untidy lab as he approached the door. Colonel Adelaide raised an eyebrow, pausing a step into the room.

Dwayne coughed. "Ah, sorry, I haven't organized the equipment that came in yesterday. I'll take care of it today, I promise."

Colonel Adelaide's stoic countenance broke for a moment with a faint grin. "No matter." She stood straighter and held a hand out to the man in the suit. "I wanted to introduce you to Rudy Sinclair, the president and CEO of Integrated Prosthetic Designs, the company that won the contract for the project. Mr. Sinclair, this is Dwayne Gillespie, the founder and lead engineer for Project Requiem."

Dwayne shook Sinclair's hand. "It's a pleasure to meet you, sir."

Sinclair smiled. "The pleasure's all mine, Mr. Gillespie. It's an honor for my company to be selected for this project. How far along have you come?"

"Well, we're still in the pre-development phase, most of our work right now…"

"Is classified," Adelaide cut in. "I'm sorry, Mr. Sinclair, but much of this project is still strictly confidential and we'll need to get you the proper security protocols to discuss it in depth."

Sinclair waved a hand dismissively. "No, don't bother, I won't be working on the project. Although, I suppose you should explain the procedures to my lovely assistant."

Dwayne turned and his eyes widened as a young woman wearing another visitor's badge walked into the room. Her long legs moved fluidly in the short skirt of her navy blue business suit as she approached him. Her whole countenance exuded confidence and femininity, from her poised stance in black pumps to her misty green eyes and buoyant bronze hair. She smiled, holding out her hand. "Hi, I'm Elya Renard."

"Nice to meet you." Dwayne shook her hand, steadying his voice. "I'm Dwayne Gillespie."

"So I heard," she replied with a grin. Dwayne chuckled awkwardly.

Before he could respond, Sinclair stated, "Elya's going to be working on the project with you, Mr. Gillespie. She's been interning at IPD, but she's decided to take a more proactive role in her involvement with the company." Sinclair smiled as he slipped his hands in his pockets. "She's going to test your antivirus for you."

Dwayne's eyes widened. "Oh. Really?"

Elya nodded. "That's right. My implants are going to be updated starting in a couple weeks."

He had almost forgotten about his proposal to test the antivirus safely and effectively. A few months had already passed since he suggested a test subject's implants be set up with redundancies in the software and additional logging capabilities to allow the user a greater chance of surviving the infection and giving him the data he needed to fine-tune the retrovirus. He cleared his throat. "Well, that's great." He tilted his head aside. "Have they told you much about the project?"

She grinned wryly. "I should hope so. I volunteered for it."

His eyes enlarged again. "You did?"

"That's right. It sounds like you really have a chance to beat Halcyon and I'm thrilled to be able to make a difference."

Dwayne hesitated. "Have you…" He shook his head. "Never

mind. Anyway, welcome aboard. It's good to have you on the project."

"Thanks. I'm glad to be here, and I look forward to working with you."

"Me, too." He found it hard to look away from those eyes.

Colonel Adelaide stepped forward and Dwayne finally tore his gaze away from Elya. "We need to fill out the forms for her permanent badge. She'll be coming in with the engineers from IPD tomorrow morning."

Dwayne nodded. "Okay."

The colonel held a hand out toward the door. "Mr. Sinclair, Miss Renard, if you would, please?"

Sinclair reached forward to shake Dwayne's hand again. "Keep up the good work, son. This project will be brilliant."

Elya waved over her shoulder as she turned to follow Colonel Adelaide. "See you soon, Mr. Gillespie."

Before he realized he said it, Dwayne heard himself say, "Please, call me Dwayne."

Elya grinned. "Goodnight, Dwayne."

He held up a hand with a smile as she stepped out of the lab. "'Night, Elya."

Dwayne leaned back in his chair and stretched, the lab still a mess. It was dark outside and the nighttime halogen streetlamps flared their pale light onto the roads.

The day was shot. He had spent so much time explaining the project to the engineers from IPD and discussing ideas for the software to create ghost people with cybernetic implants that he hardly got any work done. Yawning, he stood and walked out of the room toward the kitchenette down the hall from the lab, hoping some coffee would keep him alert while he continued working late.

To his surprise, as he walked into the kitchen he saw Elya standing by the sink.

"Oh, you're still here?"

She turned around and smiled as she met his eyes, now dressed in a pair of brown slacks and a sleeveless, creamy gold blouse. Even having only seen her twice, Dwayne couldn't help admiring how her clothes complemented her so well, the glimmer of the silk blouse accenting the radiance of her hair. "Yeah, I wanted to have a look around. I'd like to get to know the project as well as I can before we begin." She grinned wryly. "After all, it is my body we're hooking up to the virus."

Dwayne chuckled uncertainly. "Yeah, I guess that's true." As he approached her, he found her facing a photograph of a sleek jet on the wall, its glossy white paint glimmering in the sunlight. The sky around it was dark, studded with stars, though the sunlight lit up the plane brilliantly.

He leaned forward, examining the framed picture. "Is that a Wolfhound?"

She turned back to the picture. "An S-26 Titan. One of the first spaceplanes able to stay orbital for thirty-six hours at a time."

He cocked his head in interest. "I didn't realize you were a plane buff."

"Neither did I." She chuckled at his baffled look. "My grandfather used to fly them. I grew up on his stories of what it was like to see the Earth so far below and nothing but empty, open space in every other direction." Her gaze grew distant. "He told me he fought his superiors tooth and nail when they wanted to put him in a spaceplane program, but once he flew one he never looked back. It always seemed magical the way he described the Earth, massive beneath him even when he was so far away already." Dwayne stared at the photograph as she spoke, picturing the stories from her grandfather as if it was his own telling them. "It took him forty minutes to fly up to orbit, with the Earth like an almost infinite carpet below, and yet utterly insignificant with open space all around. It really gave him a sense of how minute we are in the universe, and how little our problems really matter. It was beautiful the way he described it. I wanted to be an astronaut for most of my childhood." She laughed, focusing again on Dwayne, and he blinked as he returned his attention to her. "Somehow, I ended up in bioengineering."

Dwayne laughed along with her. "Well, you're just what I needed." She shot him a coy look. When he realized what he said, he coughed. "For the project, I mean."

She chuckled. "I'm glad to be of help."

He cleared his throat. "So did you know someone who..."

"Died from Halcyon?" she finished for him. She shook her head. "No, fortunately. But a friend of mine lost her cousin a few years ago. They were like sisters to each other."

"I'm sorry to hear that."

"So was I. She's doing better these days." She glanced at him, tossing her hair over her shoulder. "How about you? What got you so interested in starting up Halcyon?"

Dwayne shrugged. "Nothing, really. I just kind of spend a lot of my time problem-solving and I started thinking about creating an antivirus when I saw a news report on it."

Murmuring, she turned to lean against the sink beside him. "You like solving problems, hm?"

He half-grinned at her. "Techie's mind, you know." A chuckle escaped. "I kept getting into trouble as a kid for sticking my hands in broken electronics, trying to fix them."

She smiled in return, though it soon turned pensive. "It's frightening. Halcyon. Almost everybody I know has a medical implant, however small."

He nodded slowly. "Yeah, same here. Do you...?"

She nodded. "Asthma." Grinning, she brushed a lock of hair over her shoulder. "Plus some cosmetic implants to keep my tan and highlights fresh."

His eyebrows raised with a smile. "You mean that's not your natural hair color and skin tone?"

She laughed. "I wish I were so lucky. How about you?"

"Oh, I'm definitely not as lucky as you." At her wry look, he tapped his chest. "Arrhythmia." She murmured sympathetically and he shrugged. "It's funny, ten years ago something that would have been life-threatening two generations ago wasn't even a concern. Now we're all in danger."

She gave him a hopeful look. "Well, that's why we're here."

A frown crossed his face. "I just hope my antivirus will work."

"I don't think the army, or IPD, would have funded Requiem if they didn't believe so."

"Yeah, that's true." Sobering, he glanced at the clock embedded in his wrist. "Well, er, are you hungry?"

Leaning her head back, she gazed up at him in interest. "I am a bit."

"You want to go grab a bite to eat? My treat."

She cocked her head to the side. "Are you asking me out to dinner?"

He blinked, then smiled. "I suppose I am. Are you interested?"

Her smile widened. "Sure."

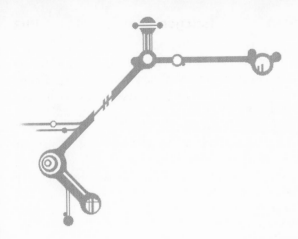

chapter.SIX

AMÉLIE YAWNED AS she stepped outside the elevator onto the fifth story above street level. She strode down the sidewalk along a row of townhouses filling the block all the way up to the next city level, small streetlamps lighting her way. Reaching a house one unit away from the edge of the complex, she moved down the walkway as she dug her keys out of her purse. Identifying herself to the alarm system through the communicator beside the door, she unlocked and opened the front door.

The lights within flicked on as she stepped inside, illuminating the living room opening up directly within. A calico cat rose and stretched from where it curled up on the back of the couch, meowing as it hopped down and strode over to her. Setting her purse on the side table next to the door, Amélie disabled the alarm system.

"Hey there, Miso," she greeted as she bent down to scratch the top of the cat's head. The calico purred loudly in response, shutting its eyes as it pressed its head against her fingers. "You didn't get into trouble today, did you?" Miso meowed, following Amélie as she strode into the kitchen at the back of the tiny townhouse. The cat's insistence weighed down her own weariness from the long day at work. Miso coiled around her legs and meowed as she opened a can of cat food and emptied it onto the cat's dish. The calico nosed furiously into the dish as Amélie set it on the floor. She petted the cat with a smile, then rose and retreated into the living room, looking forward to dinner herself.

Pulling her cell phone out of her pocket, she synchronized the phone to the communicator on the living room wall and played back the messages she had received through the day. She pulled off her scrubs as the first one played.

"Hey baby," the first message began. Amélie smiled as she recognized her boyfriend's voice. "Give me a call if you're still free this evening. I thought we could go out to dinner tonight." She patted Miso, who hopped up onto the arm of the sofa, and grabbed the phone to call him. After a long day, nothing sounded more appealing than a restful evening and dinner out. The next message began to play as she scrolled through the contacts list on her phone and dialed Jason's number.

"Ryn, please call me as soon as you're available." Her smile dropped away as she recognized Zander's voice. She held the phone absently to her ear, the ringing on the other end barely registering behind Zander's message.

"We're going to look for Elya tonight and we could really use your help. Call me as soon as you can. Thanks."

A click sounded on the other end of the phone just as the message stopped playing and Jason said, "Hey baby! How's it going?"

"Hi," Amélie replied hesitantly.

"So you want to go out for dinner tonight? I was thinking Mario's."

Her stomach grumbled as she thought of the fare at her favorite Italian restaurant. The disappointed frown was clear in her voice. "Listen, baby, something's come up…"

Jason groaned over the phone. "Again? I was really hoping I could see you tonight. We've hardly seen each other in a month."

"I know," she answered tiredly as she sank onto the couch. She considered not returning Zander's call and going out with Jason instead. Glancing to the side, she saw her scrubs lying on the couch and her expression fell. Three bodies of people who had died from Halcyon had come through the hospital doors during her shift that day.

"Are you sure you can't postpone?" Jason pressed.

Amélie shut her eyes, the indecision fading from her voice. "I'm sure. I'm sorry, honey. I'll make it up to you soon, I promise."

Jason sighed, failing to entirely hide the irritation and

disappointment in his voice. "Alright, well, take it easy, babe."

"Love you," she answered and ended the call. She sat silently for a moment, hands curled into fists on her lap.

After a moment, Miso meowed and reached out to rub a cheek against her knuckles. Rising, Amélie accessed Zander's message again and called the sender. The display lagged briefly as a program Shad's friend Tiger wrote scrambled the number in the phone's records. She stepped into the kitchen while it dialed.

Squirrel didn't take long to arrive at the first story landing for her townhouse complex and she barely had enough time to eat a simple dinner before she left her house behind in the dark of night once more. Dressed in a button-up green shirt and jeans, she quickly applied a layer of makeup over the dark circles under her eyes. She was the last to step into the van, Zander, Shad and Deadeye already waiting for her inside.

Setting aside her qualms, she took a seat next to Zander. His black eye had faded and the evidence was difficult to see in the dimness of the van. Leaning forward, Shad asked, "So what's the plan?"

The vehicle started rolling out of the visitor's parking lot as Zander braced himself against the van wall. "Alright, Tiger told me that he didn't find any sign of Elya on the trains or elevators today. It's not conclusive and he didn't start the search protocol until about two hours after we left last night, but considering how well she's kept herself hidden, I'd say it's a pretty safe bet she's stayed on foot." Amélie glanced around at the others, all listening intently.

"Shad, I want you to check homeless shelters or any other place in the area that would take her in where she wouldn't look too conspicuous." Zander turned to Amélie. "Ryn, you stay in the van with Squirrel and patrol the area. Deadeye, we're going canvassing." Amélie couldn't help but admire the focused look in Zander's eyes and remembered why she chose to risk her life, let alone her job and her boyfriend, to help him.

She found herself unexpectedly relieved when they neared the area of the gunfight with the mercenaries and Zander hopped out of the van, along with Shad and Deadeye. Sighing, she climbed up into the passenger seat beside Squirrel and buckled the seat belt.

"Well, guess it's just us now," the driver remarked nonchalantly as he put the van into gear. "Any thoughts about the patrol route?"

Amélie shook her head. "You know this part of town better than I do. You can navigate, I'll just keep watch."

"No problem."

She remained silent as they passed through the roads, eyes roaming in search of the pale woman. Occasionally, Shad called in updates over the group connection and Zander would report that he and Deadeye had found no sign of Elya yet, either. Amélie leaned her head against the window and gazed out at the streets beyond, lit up by the nighttime halogen lamps, as rain began to drizzle down the buildings in the gap between roads. It had been a while since she had seen rain, having little use to travel to the upper levels, especially in the middle of a storm. There was something she found calming about rain and she lamented the detachment of the lower level buildings, sheltered from the storm by layers of road and dozens of stories of building rising overhead.

Weariness weighed on her and at one point she nodded off, only to jolt herself awake and find that Squirrel had parked the van in front of a café. Gratefully ordering a coffee, she continued her vigil, her thoughts returning to Elya. She wondered what it must have been like for the pale woman. The sounds of the shootout alone had been enough to make Amélie glad that she had stayed out of it. Deadeye had recognized the brand of generator from the logo outside the mercenaries' apartment, which would kick in and restart the laser defense grid over the doors within one and a half seconds of a power loss. She had been elected to cut the power while the rest of them barged inside in their brief window of opportunity. It was a dangerous enough rescue as it was even without the shootout that proceeded inside. The idea of what would happen if her timing had been even slightly off was nerve-wracking and she was glad her job had been successful, though she wasn't surprised Elya fled.

How had Elya kept herself so well hidden these past two months? How had she survived? What had she eaten? That she was clever was obvious from the way she had managed to avoid capture by both the army and IPD. Despite how exhausted and famished Elya looked, she had still kept herself alive all this time and her resourcefulness impressed Amélie. Staying on ground level kept her difficult to detect and provided her countless abandoned buildings in which to find shelter, though she would have to venture up at least one city level to find palatable food. It had been a delicate play for her and only sheer luck had brought Zander, and possibly the mercenaries as well, to find her. Why, Amélie wondered, hadn't she simply gone to someone she knew? They had approached Elya's parents not long after Amélie met Zander. Her mother had been nearly hysterical with grief, believing her daughter dead, even though the army had told them there was no proof of it. Certainly, Elya must want to contact someone.

The thought had just crossed Amélie's mind when her gaze fixed on a building outside the van window. Lifting her head from her hand, she watched the entrance as the van rolled past.

"Hold it, stop," she said, her head twisting around to look at the building. They were several blocks away and one city level down from the mercenaries' apartment and the drive to get there had been convoluted and winding. Squirrel obediently pulled the van over to the curb.

"You see something?" he asked.

She opened the door nearly as soon as the van stopped. "Just checking something." Shutting the door, she strode down the sidewalk toward the entrance, swiping a payment card against a scanner to enter the building.

Music pounded out the doors as she stepped inside. A dance floor dominated the main room inside, pulsing with glowing lights that flickered in time with the heavy music. Staggered mezzanines rising around the room showed more dancers on higher levels, as well as people playing arcade games and virtual sports, sparring in small arenas, and performing complicated maneuvers with sensors on gloves to create laser light shows around their bodies. A long bar stretched along the back wall on ground level, crowded with people placing orders at the robotic dispensers that mixed up cocktails by request, a pair of bartenders servicing the machines and cutting off patrons as needed. Every floor and mezzanine was crowded with people, bodies swaying and twisting in every direction, and colored lights shone everywhere. Club employees delivering drink orders to the mezzanines threaded through the crowds, their identifying uniforms lighting up with a distinctive flashing pattern of green and orange stripes.

The atmosphere was electric, the air charged with the constant movement of the club's patrons, the thrum of energy and welcoming almost pushing Amélie out onto the dance floor. The outside world seemed forgotten and far away as soon as she stepped inside. Even in the limited space she could see into the throng of bodies, she saw people comfortably and eagerly introducing themselves to complete strangers, cultivating relationships that may never exist outside the club. As she gazed around at the people who had altered their cybernetics to highlight uniqueness in unusual hairstyles or colors, holographic tattoos, patterned skin and other more bizarre traits, she thought many of these people likely looked little like they did outside the club. It was a place where people came to escape the world, a place where an unusual appearance was encouraged, and it was a place where one could hide in the obscurity of numbers.

Amélie considered the crowd on the dance floor as she gazed around at the various levels of entertainment in the building. One other thing the club boasted was network stations, available for patrons looking for rest from the dance floor or a more relaxed outing. Striding over to a nearby staircase, Amélie climbed up to the first mezzanine, studying the crowd on the dance floor as she ascended. The dimness of the club lighting mixing with the flashing lights illuminating the dance floor and the writhing of the crowd made it difficult to make out anyone, and she picked out a few people who looked pale, but as she suspected, none of them was Elya.

As she passed by a smaller dance floor on the first level mezzanine, Amélie paused and glanced at the crowd filling the square area, the floor beneath her feet trembling from the movements of the dancers. This level was dedicated to couples dancing, with more space allowed per person so that partners wouldn't be separated from the movement as easily. Most of the small tables ringing the dance floor were in use by other couples resting or waiting for more room to open up. On the dance floor, couples spun and swayed together and more than a few pressed up closer together than most people would outside. Amélie even saw a pair of women riddled with piercings glinting in the flashing lights dancing so close together that they were constantly touching, and their lips met with each measure in the music. Amélie thought of Jason and nearly grabbed her cell phone to call him. Turning away from the dance floor, she climbed the stairs to the next mezzanine.

After slipping around a maze of a laser tag arena, crossing a bridge to a second, smaller bar, and climbing another level past a group of karaoke singers and musicians, she came to a much calmer area lined up with tables and screens, most of them in use. She peered at the people sitting at the screens, but most of them neglected to turn on the personal lights set up at each unit, and the light was hardly better than on the other levels. She strolled slowly down the lanes of screens, passing people playing video games, chatting, browsing the internet or performing more mundane tasks.

Finally, as she came to the end of a row, she spotted Elya in the far corner. Swallowing, Amélie approached, hoping she wouldn't startle Elya. She chided herself as she drew near for thinking of Elya as the others had, like an abused stray animal.

Elya didn't notice Amélie's presence until she pulled out the empty chair next to her. The pale woman turned with a start, and she leaned her head back as she recognized Amélie.

"Hi," Amélie said over the music and sat down. Elya said nothing in response, only watched her. Up close, Elya looked much more striking than she had appeared the last night, disheveled, distraught and panicked. Now, though suspicion glinted in her eyes, she was much more calm and poised. Her perfectly proportioned body was not outlined in voluptuous curves but was long and shapely, equal parts feminine and toned. The tattered overcoat and a narrow-brimmed hat hung over the back of her chair, her jeans and black and white patterned blouse flattering her physique. She had clipped her hair up at the back of her head, its waves looking less obviously messy, and reaching up at the top of her head, Amélie saw Elya's most distinguishing implant. A pair of tan-colored cat ears rose through her hair, the synthetic fur covering them now a few shades darker than her skin and hair, shifting minutely as Elya gazed at Amélie.

Amélie opened her mouth to introduce herself, but paused. When she met Zander, he had insisted that she not give them her real name, so that if ever they were caught they could not unintentionally give her up, and she supposed he would want the same treatment for Elya. As she looked into Elya's hesitant eyes, however, it seemed unfair to her that Amélie give her only an alias.

"I'm Amélie," she stated, leaning on the table next to Elya. "I'm a nurse." Elya only nodded faintly in acknowledgment. Amélie shifted with a frown. "Look, I'm sorry about what happened last night. So are the others. They didn't mean to hurt you."

The movement was almost imperceptible, Elya's nod even smaller than the previous.

Amélie cleared her throat. "Anyway, I just wanted to see if you were okay." She waited for a response from Elya, but none came. "Are you hurt?" Elya closed her eyes and shook her head, the uncertainty not fading from her face.

"Well," Amélie continued, "I know you don't really have any reason to trust me, but we really are only trying to help you." She reached a hand over to Elya's table. "We're with Chen. He's got Dwayne's notes. We're trying to finish Requiem." Elya glanced away, looking thoughtful. Amélie hoped Elya would trust her. Afraid that she wouldn't, she continued, "Believe me, we have nothing to do with either the army or IPD. In fact, we've had some close brush-ins with both of them I'd sooner not repeat. I promise Zander and Chen will keep you safe."

Elya turned back to the screen in front of her, seemingly ignoring Amélie. Amélie hesitated a moment, then leaned over to look at the screen. A curious look crossed her face.

A short news article was open on the screen.

Mysterious accident leaves two dead

An unexplained accident at the McLelland Building on Regalia Avenue at 46th, third level, has left two people dead. Witnesses reported what sounded like an explosion, but a spokesperson for the office, which is owned by a division of the armed forces, has issued a statement claiming that a power spike caused a surge in a computer bank in the office, and the deaths were the result of infection by Halcyon.

The victims have been identified as Dwayne Gillespie, 23, of the Chatters, and Elya Renard, 25, from Morrow Heights.

Amélie had seen the article. Zander showed it to all of them, though they had since come to learn that the army was keeping more things secret than what actually happened. Elya could have gone to the police to clear up the misunderstanding, but she had allowed the rest of the world to believe her dead. Amélie turned to face Elya once more. "What happened at the lab when Dwayne died?"

Elya reached out to the keyboard, typing in a response. Amélie watched, unsurprised. From the way Elya had not spoken a word in the time Amélie saw her the last night, and from how Zander, Shad and Deadeye said she never screamed or made any noise when they broke into the mercenaries' apartment, Amélie had suspected that she had lost her voice. She leaned over again to read Elya's response.

I don't remember

"Oh," Amélie replied. "Well, I don't think..." She stopped herself as Elya continued typing.

I don't remember anything.

Amélie blinked, and suddenly everything made sense. "Oh." Before she could say anything more, Elya typed out another message.

You know me.

Amélie frowned. "A little. Chen heard about you from Dwayne, but he never met you before."

What do you want from me?

"It's not..." She paused, considering. "I guess if you don't remember anything, it won't mean anything to you if I say we're just trying to finish Requiem."

Elya shook her head.

Reaching out, Amélie laid her hand on the table in front of Elya's. Elya didn't react. "Look, I'm sorry about what happened last night." She rolled her eyes. "The guys can be a bit heavy-handed at times. You know what it's like with men." That drew a wry smile from the cat-eared woman. "I know you don't have any reason to trust me, but I only want to help you. If you want someplace to stay, you're welcome to use the guest bedroom in my house. Zander and the others don't even have to know."

Elya raised an eyebrow inquisitively.

"I don't want to force you to do anything, or try to trick or guilt-trip you into anything. You should make your own decision. And anyway, if you don't remember anything, there isn't so much Chen and Zander can get from you." Grinning, she leaned closer. "And there's a coffee shop just down the street from my house that makes a double chocolate cheesecake to die for." Elya's smile widened.

Amélie rose. "Anyway, I can leave you my number if you'd like. But if you'd rather be left alone, I'll tell the guys I never saw you." She waited a moment, watching as Elya turned back to the screen, studying the news article again. Finally, she turned and began to walk back to the stairs off the platform.

Before she had gone two steps, however, the scrape of a chair against the floor rang out behind her. Turning, she found Elya standing and tapping the screen to close the news site. Her coat and hat were in her arms. Once the screen had returned to the welcome page, she faced Amélie again.

"Are you sure about this?"

With a weary smile, Elya simply shrugged.

Amélie reached out and touched her arm. "I have some clothes at home that should fit you, if you want." The smile widened and she nodded. Replacing the hat on her head, she gestured to Amélie to continue.

Nodding, Amélie turned and began sifting her way back across the mezzanines toward the front entrance. She forced herself not to constantly glance over her shoulder to make certain that Elya still followed. Elya had given her trust, she had to do the same in return.

The pounding music from the main dance floor followed them out onto the street as the door swung open, shifting shades of red, green and blue lights shining onto the sidewalk outside. Amélie felt her ears relax from the strain of the blaring music as the doors swung shut and only the steady beat thrummed against the pavement under her feet. Turning her head, she found Squirrel's van still parked patiently against the curb down the block. Amélie glanced briefly at Elya, then led her toward the van and opened the cargo door for her.

Glancing through the rear-view mirror, Squirrel smiled as he glimpsed Elya, seemingly unsurprised to find her with Amélie, climbing willingly into the van. He held up a hand in greeting. "Nice to meet you, Miss Renard."

Elya nodded with a smile as she crouched inside the van and sat down on one of the side cushions. Amélie took a seat across from Elya and pulled her cell phone out of her pocket. Dialing Zander's number, she opened the group connection, her voice echoing through Squirrel's phone.

"Zander, I found Elya. She's safe."

Zander's voice responded almost instantly. "Really? That's great!"

"Seriously?" Shad's voice chimed in over the line.

Amélie smiled, hearing the worry in his voice. The cough of the van's engine turning over droned behind her voice. "Yeah, she's here and she's fine." Zander asked the driver to pick up him and Deadeye even as Amélie lowered the phone and asked, "Squirrel, can we go find Zander?"

Squirrel grinned as he swung the van onto the road and raised his own cell phone, tapping in a few keys. "Already on my way, boss."

"Don't call me that," Zander replied over the line, though Amélie could hear the smile in his voice. "Thanks." With that, he closed the connection and Amélie leaned back in her seat.

Soon, the van pulled to a stop and Zander, Deadeye and Shad all climbed inside at once. Zander nodded to Amélie in acknowledgment, then fixed his gaze on Elya as he crouched just inside the van. He smiled warmly at her. "I'm glad to see you're alright. I'm sorry about what happened last night." She only smiled and nodded in return. "Are you okay?" She nodded again.

"Zander." Amélie's voice drew everyone's attention. "It's worse than we thought. She didn't just lose her voice. She has amnesia."

Zander's eyes widened as he glanced at her, the expression mirrored in Shad and Deadeye's faces. Turning back to Elya, Zander asked, "Really?" Elya nodded. "Oh man. I'm sorry." She simply shrugged, seemingly unconcerned with the admission.

Of course, Amélie thought, *she's been living this way for two months. It's nothing new to her.*

"Heading out," Squirrel stated from the driver's seat.

Zander took a seat beside Elya as the van pulled away from the curb. "Well, then I'm extra glad you were willing to trust us." He held out his hand to her, and she shook their hands each in turn as Zander introduced them. "I'm Zander Sarkowski. This is Deadeye."

Deadeye nodded as he shook her hand. "Nice to meet ya."

"This is Shadow Mortal."

"Shadow *Morl*," Shad corrected, eyes narrowed. "It's a hidden boss from *Fallen Gods III*, in the—"

"Yeah, yeah, the dreaded Shadow Mumble," Zander cut across him. Amélie suppressed a grin as Shad fumed. She had heard this exchange before and she suspected Zander intentionally got the name wrong just to rile him. Zander returned his attention to Elya. "We just call him Shad."

Anger fading, Shad gave Elya a guilty look as he shook her hand, looking every bit the inexperienced teenager he was. "I'm really sorry about last night. I didn't mean to scare you." Elya merely waved away the offense, apparently unconcerned.

Continuing with the introductions, Zander gestured to the front of the van. "Behind the wheel is our brilliant Squirrel." Squirrel merely held up a hand in greeting and Elya nodded in return. "And, well, I guess you've already met Ryn." Amélie tried not to look suspicious as Elya turned a level gaze on her, hoping it wasn't obvious that she had given Elya her real name. Without missing a beat, however, the cat-eared woman gave her a nod.

"You'll meet Chen soon." Zander frowned. "Though I guess that doesn't mean much to you." Elya shrugged and shook her head.

"Back to your place, then, boss?" Squirrel asked.

Zander opened his mouth to reply, but Amélie cut in, "Actually, I thought maybe I should take her back to my place first. She can have a shower and I have some clean clothes she can wear."

Glancing between them, Zander nodded. "That's fine with me. Let's drop Shad and Deadeye off first, though."

Zander phoned Chen to let him know what had happened, but Amélie merely leaned her head back against the van wall. As soon as she closed her eyes, she felt weariness settle deep in her muscles and the vehicle's rolling movements lulled her nearly to sleep. She didn't know what she would do about Elya when Jason came over next, but she was too tired to care. Jason had to wait that night anyway, and Elya needed some fresh clothes the others wouldn't be able to provide. Amélie only hoped that her involvement with Zander and Chen would diminish now that they had found Elya and she could return to spending more free time with Jason, and to getting more sufficient sleep than she had in recent weeks. Yet no sooner did the thought cross her mind than she thought of the three shrouded bodies that had passed through the hospital doors during her shift that day.

She hoped for everyone's sake that Zander and Chen were close to finishing the antivirus.

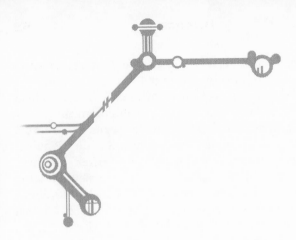

chapter.SEVEN

CHEN WAS SO anxious and relieved to hear the news that it took him most of a minute before he realized the apartment was a mess. He hurried around the living room, dining table and kitchen, picking up strewn clothes, wrappers and computer media.

Just as he dumped the last armful of dirty dishes in the sink, the front door opened. He halted in place as the door swung wide and caught his breath when he saw Elya standing behind it. Her hair was still damp from the shower she had taken at Ryn's house, hanging about her shoulders in fine ringlets. Now dressed in a striped purple sweater, blue jeans and sneakers, she looked perfectly natural and nothing like he expected. From the photos Dwayne had shown him, he couldn't imagine her as Zander and the others had described her. Seeing her now he could certainly see the resemblance, but he still had a hard time believing this pale woman was Elya. Strangely, he found himself unsurprised, if not more than a little dismayed, to learn that she had lost her voice and her memories since Dwayne's death. Nothing remained of the woman she used to be. Still, seeing her filled him with excitement, anticipation and hope. As long as she had the antivirus, everything would work out.

She smiled softly as she met Chen's eyes, the cat ears on top of her head twitching curiously as she scanned the room. Zander stepped inside behind her, carrying her old overcoat. He closed and locked the door. "So this is our home. It's... actually a bit cleaner than I expected. I'm shocked." Zander shot a grin over to Chen.

Hardly able to take his eyes off Elya, Chen cleared his throat and stepped out from the kitchen. "Hi," he began lamely. "My name's Chen Yu. I was in college with Dwayne... well, I guess that doesn't mean much to you." Her smile said it all. There was no recognition in her eyes as she shook his hand. He frowned. "I knew Dwayne pretty well. He was a teacher's assistant for some of my classes. He told me a bit about you... and Requiem." Elya's expression didn't change, a somewhat wistful look in her eyes as she watched him. He cleared his throat and looked away, uncertain what to say.

In the ensuing silence, she glanced around the room. She paused as her eyes fell on the photo on Chen's desk. He watched as she approached the framed picture slowly. Carefully, she picked it up, staring at the image of Dwayne, and herself.

Chen frowned. "He told me a lot about you. I always wanted to meet you someday, just..." He trailed off, not sure where he had been going with the thought. She continued studying the beaten photograph and Zander walked up beside him, arms folded.

"I still think this should have waited until tomorrow," he said in a low voice.

Chen hunched his shoulders. It was nearly midnight, but when he heard that Elya had been found, he had begged Zander to bring her back to their apartment so he could meet her rather than letting her stay at Ryn's house and coming over the next day.

"This is what we've been trying to find for weeks. She has the only remaining copy of Dwayne's antivirus." A lump formed in his throat. "Depending how well it stopped the infection, I could have it finished in just a few weeks."

"You're not planning on doing anything tonight. She's been through a lot and she should sleep." Zander glanced at Chen. "In fact, you look like you need sleep just as much as she does."

"I'm fine."

Zander frowned, but before he could say more, Elya's gaze turned suddenly intense, drawing their attention. Chen took half a step forward. "Did you remember something?" Sighing, she set the photo frame back on the desk and shook her head.

"Well, um, can I take a look at your implants?"

"Chen," Zander warned.

Chen flicked his gaze between Zander and Elya. "I just want to download what she has. And she probably needs a firewall upgrade." Zander frowned, but Elya smiled and nodded in response.

Reaching into a drawer in his computer desk, Chen pulled out a dome-shaped wireless universal synchronizer and set it next to his tablet computer. As the computer blinked out of sleep mode, its projection keyboard glowed blue against the desk. Elya stepped over and laid her hand over the spherical device. Whirs and clicks sounded as the skin on her palm shifted and opened up and the embedded plugs in her hand that linked the synchronizer to her implants emerged and hooked up to the dome.

A tone sounded on Chen's computer as it recognized the connection. His breath sped in excitement. After two long months, he was finally getting Dwayne's antivirus. Studying his work and the status logs on Elya's implants, Chen knew he could improve upon it and make it work as Dwayne had envisioned, in a way he knew he could never program himself. He quickly navigated through the menus and opened up the antivirus on her implants.

His expression fell as he stared at the code. Everything was gibberish. He couldn't make out a single clear command. "It's... it's corrupted." He scrolled down, but it was all the same. "All of it." He scrolled quicker through the hundreds of pages of code, but none of it was intact. Hopelessness washed over him and he sank down in his chair. "It's gone. His work is all gone." He suddenly felt empty inside. "We'll never finish the antivirus now. It's hopeless."

"No it's not." The sharpness of Zander's voice drew Chen's attention, and he found Zander giving him a hard look. "You still have all of Dwayne's research on Requiem, and amnesia or no, we still have Elya." He sent a nod to her.

The knot in Chen's stomach didn't ease. "That hardly means anything without the antivirus."

Zander turned to approach the dining table, but his voice remained firm. "The army and IPD didn't seem to think so, or else they wouldn't have gone after us." He brought back a chair for Elya to sit on and Chen turned back to his tablet. His heart felt heavy. For eight weeks, he had clung to the hope that a copy of the antivirus remained with Elya while all others had been destroyed. But now that they had found her at long last, it turned out that Dwayne's work was gone. He hung his head.

Zander let out an exasperated sigh. "Just because she doesn't have some magic solution doesn't mean that we can't still finish. It may take a while but you can re-create the antivirus. You have everything you need to do it already."

Chen couldn't face him. "I don't know..."

"Yes, you do. We didn't go to all that trouble for nothing."

At a touch, Chen turned. Elya laid a hand on his shoulder and smiled. Even though she looked so different from the photo on his desk, that smile was the same.

He inhaled deeply, his doubt and worry not easing. "I guess I can download your status logs. You should have a lot more info on how the infection affected your implants."

Zander clapped him on the back. "That's the spirit."

Chen blinked as he came across an error message on a status screen. "Oh," he uttered. "The wireless connection on her implants has been disabled."

Zander leaned against Chen's desk, glancing between the tablet screen and Elya. "Well, I guess that's another reason we had such a hard time finding you. The mercenaries too."

"I guess so," Chen answered distractedly as he opened up a status log. Elya leaned over to examine the screen, her hand still over the synchronizer. "Oh, here, let me unplug that." Releasing the connection, the machinery in the sphere retreated into Elya's palm. She rubbed her hand as she pulled it back and Chen moved the synchronizer out of the way. As he did so, he caught a glimpse of the data drive recovered from the dead man the day before, still lying forgotten on his desk.

"Here, Zander, can you have Tiger start analyzing this?" Chen handed Zander the data drive. "We might still find something useful there that isn't in these logs."

Zander pocketed the drive. "No problem, but we should probably get Elya back to Ryn's."

Elya paused, glancing at the status log open on the computer screen, the record of what had happened to her. With a smile, she raised a hand to Zander, all five fingers up.

He hesitated, then chuckled. "Alright. Just let me know when you want to head back." Turning, he retreated into his bedroom, closing the door behind him. Chen turned back to the log and Elya followed his eyes.

"So we're looking for the logs on July fourteenth." He scrolled back through the first file. Despite his disappointment that no intact copy of the antivirus still existed, his curiosity was piqued by the status logs. She studied the screen along with him. He wondered what she was thinking as she read the text. Together, they analyzed the stream of data that had been recorded that night in the lab. Though she had to type out all her thoughts, Chen was surprised to find that all her bioengineering knowledge remained intact while they studied the text. It was difficult making sense of the coded data and whatever had happened had taken several seconds. In computer terms, that meant a lot of logged information.

For all intents and purposes, it did seem as though Halcyon had infected her and yet she had survived the attack. There was no information Chen or Elya could find that gave them any clues how to rewrite the antivirus. But her logs contained a lot of information about what precisely had happened to her. Her implants had maintained basic functions, though much of their controlled or nonessential use had been crippled. Her skin and hair still absorbed sunlight, but she could no longer give them the tone she desired. Her breathing remained normal, but she couldn't speak. The only implant that seemed not to have been disabled in some manner was the cat ears and they assumed that was because it was a strictly cosmetic implant. As for her amnesia, he could only guess that had been a result of shock and trauma. Elya had no way to disagree with him.

She stifled a yawn and as he did the same, he realized he had already seen her do so twice. "Sorry, I should call Squirrel so he can take you back to Ryn's." He reached for his cell phone, but Elya laid a pale hand on his wrist, stopping him. At his curious look, she pointed at the clock in the corner of the tablet screen. "Oh."

It was three in the morning.

He winced. "I'm sorry, I didn't mean to keep you up so late. I must have lost track of time." He looked toward Zander's room, but it remained quiet. He must have fallen asleep. "Well, um, what do you want to do?"

She glanced at the couch just behind them, then gave him a shrug.

"You can sleep in my room if you want. I'll sleep on the couch. I do it often enough anyway."

Smiling, she nodded.

He hunched his shoulders. "Are you sure about this?" She

waved, seemingly unconcerned. "I'm sorry again. I'll set an alarm next time." With another wave, she rose and retreated into Chen's room, leaving her coat draped over the back of the couch. As the door closed behind her, he turned back to the tablet screen and continued working on the antivirus.

He had planned only to work a few minutes longer, but the next time he glanced at the clock, an hour and a half had passed. He sighed, his stomach twisting as he leaned back. Standing, he stretched and walked into the kitchen. The fluorescent light hurt his eyes as it flickered to life and he considered going to bed after all. His stomach grumbled and he reached into the cupboard for bread.

He frowned as he spread mayonnaise on the bread. Even with data never before recorded from a victim, he didn't know how Halcyon infected people so effectively. The virus had never failed to kill someone it infected and yet it had never been found lying dormant in someone's cybernetics. People had gone in to their doctors for a check-up with no abnormality found in their implant software, only to be found dead from Halcyon two days later. Its effectiveness and creativity at using whatever cybernetics a person had to kill them hinted at artificial intelligence far beyond that of any normal computer virus. How it operated remained a mystery.

And where had it come from? A virus so advanced and unstoppable had to have been created by a team of highly skilled programmers. But why? No one had ever claimed responsibility for it, nor had anyone made any demands or attempted blackmail to release an antivirus. It had appeared out of nowhere and had everyone stumped.

Chen took his sandwich back to his computer desk, choking it down as he looked through Elya's status logs again, though his disappointment made the food taste bland and unappealing. Sighing, he returned to the program he had been writing to test a function Dwayne had used that was new to him.

"Chen?"

Chen sat up with a start, not realizing he had fallen asleep until Zander's voice awakened him. The living room glowed from the light of the daylight lamps outside, the directional light newly illuminated. He glanced at his tablet screen, glowing in front of his crossed arms, and didn't recognize the last few lines of code, clearly the last thing he had written before he fell asleep.

"For God's sake, Chen, go to bed."

Chen turned, seeing Zander bathed in the fluorescent light in the kitchen as he pulled a carton of eggs out of the fridge. Elya stood beside him, quietly watching. Zander frowned as he gazed at Chen. Exhaustion weighed heavily on Chen's shoulders, his eyes feeling leaden, and he didn't bother to argue as he stood and stretched.

"Did you get that image file to Tiger?" Chen asked, his voice raspy.

"I transmitted the files to him last night. He said he has to work today, but he'll get on it tomorrow. Now shut up and get some sleep."

Satisfied, Chen stumbled across the living room and collapsed on the couch. Zander spoke to Elya as he prepared breakfast but Chen was too exhausted to pay attention to his words. He dropped his glasses onto the coffee table and settled down on the couch. Relaxing into the cushions, he gratefully let himself drift to sleep.

He felt as if he had barely shut his eyes when his cell phone rang.

He jolted awake, lunging for his glasses as he looked around for the phone. Finding the source of the tone on his desk, he raced over and picked it up. Running a hand over his hair, he put the phone to his ear and answered it. "Hello?"

"Hey Chen. Sorry to wake you."

"Oh, hey Zander. No, it's okay." He stifled a yawn as Elya emerged from down the hall. From the angle of the light coming through the windows, he had been asleep at least an hour. "What's up?"

"I just got a call from Ryn. She's heading over to take Elya out shopping for some extra clothes and stuff."

Chen paused. "Are you sure that's a good idea?"

"Those mercs aren't going to go after her in a shopping mall. And Ryn said she has some hats and stuff Elya could wear. I don't think it's going to be a problem."

Chen frowned as he sat down at his desk, fingering his tablet screen to life. "I don't know…"

"It'll be fine. And you'd better not be working. You need to get more sleep, I just didn't want you to be surprised when Ryn shows up."

"I'm fine. I have to see what I can do with the logs I downloaded from Elya."

"Dude, haven't you heard about those guys overseas who sit in front of video games until they starve to death?"

He felt upset. "I have a lot to do. I don't have any time to waste."

"Yeah, instead you're wasting away. No wonder you only weigh a hundred and thirty. Stop to eat and get some rest sometime today. I have to get back to work. Ryn's on her way."

"Okay. 'Bye."

"Later." With that, the call disconnected and Chen set the phone back on his desk as he looked at the status logs once more.

A shuffling sound nearby drew his attention. Looking up, he saw Elya standing behind the couch. "Oh, that was Zander. He said Ryn's coming by to take you shopping for some clothes and stuff." Her cat ears perked up in interest. He couldn't help but give her a small smile in return.

His attention drifted as he began programming again and it took two knocks on the door before he realized anyone was there. Elya emerged as he hurried to open the door.

"Hi Chen," Ryn greeted. "How's everything going? I was expecting Elya to come back to my place last night."

He stood aside to let her in. "Yeah, sorry, we kind of lost track of time last night. We didn't want to wake you up."

"It's no problem with me." She turned to Elya. "I just hope you were comfortable here." Elya smiled and shrugged in response and Ryn turned back to Chen. "Anyway, I guess Zander told you I was going to take her out?"

"Yeah," he answered, trying to hide his trepidations about Elya going out in public where she could be discovered.

Apparently, he failed. Ryn laid a hand on his shoulder. "Don't worry, we'll be careful. You wouldn't even recognize her."

I don't now, he thought, but he simply said, "Okay. Good luck." Elya flashed him a last smile before following Ryn out the door. He watched them retreat down the hall with a sense of foreboding. He tried to convince himself it was nothing. Zander always told him he worried too much.

Finally, he closed and locked the door and returned to his work.

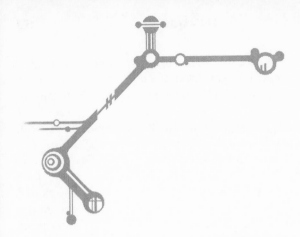

chapter.EIGHT

Nine months ago

"YOU READY TO see it?" Elya smiled slyly as she stood in front of the desk, hands in the pockets of her overcoat.

Dwayne suppressed a chuckle. "Yes." She had told him that she was having another cosmetic implant added and promised him that it would be both interesting and defining, yet she wouldn't tell him what it was. As she stood on the other side of his desk in the army lab, covered in the coat, a pair of khaki slacks over high-heeled leather boots, and a narrow-brimmed hat, he could only imagine what she was about to show him.

"Are you sure?" she teased. "You're not too distracted by your work?"

"You have my undivided attention." He slid his chair away from his computer for emphasis, maddeningly curious about her new cybernetics.

She smiled, satisfied. Then, with a dramatic sweep of her arm, she threw off the hat and a pair of light brown cat ears rising through her hair flicked as they were unveiled. Dwayne laughed, rising from his chair as he examined the ears.

Elya turned from side to side, showing him different angles of the cat ears as they shifted minutely, looking remarkably realistic. "You like them?"

"They look great!" he answered. "Can you actually hear with

them?"

She laughed. "No, IPD isn't paying me that well. I can move them around, though, and I had them wired to follow my emotions." The ears twisted back and forth, one at a time. Her eyes followed him as he moved around the desk toward her. "You really like them?"

He stopped just in front of her, aching to hold her, though he didn't want to risk showing such affection in the office. "I love them. They look great on you."

Murmuring pleasantly, Elya leaned forward and wrapped her arms around his waist. "I'm glad to hear it." Relinquishing himself to her touch, he slid his arms around her and leaned down as she reached up toward him.

Suddenly, the door opened, and with a start Dwayne and Elya stepped away from each other. Colonel Adelaide paused as she glanced at them, her stony expression unreadable as Dwayne rubbed the back of his neck awkwardly.

"Dwayne, may I have a word with you?"

A lump formed in Dwayne's throat at the sound of her voice. "Of course." He glanced quickly at Elya, the new cat ears folded flat against her head in embarrassment, then he followed the colonel out of the lab and down the hall to her office. His skin crawled as he stepped inside her office, Colonel Adelaide closing the door behind him.

She gestured at a single chair in front of her desk. "Have a seat." Dwayne sat uneasily as Adelaide rounded the desk and sat down in her own chair.

"What is this about?" he asked, trying to keep his voice steady.

The colonel sighed. "Elya."

Dwayne leaned back, eyes widening suspiciously. "What about her?"

She gazed evenly at him. "Your relationship with her is unprofessional. The board is concerned that you're putting your own interests above those of the project, jeopardizing its security. They want you to partner with someone else to program the antivirus. Someone from inside our department."

Dwayne blinked, taken aback. "Your department is focused on technology, not bioengineering. Your people don't have the kind of expertise she does."

Adelaide shook her head. "They have a lot of experience dealing with Halcyon. You can create your antivirus just as effectively with their help as you can with hers."

Dwayne leaned forward in his chair. "Do they know how much time it takes for a malfunctioning liver to cause permanent damage? Do they know precisely how much insulin should be in a human body? I need biological expertise to program the antivirus. Elya has that. Your people don't."

The colonel gave him a hard look. "And what else does she have?"

His eyes narrowed. "What do you mean?"

"I know you've gotten close to her. You could have told her something beyond the scope of her security clearance, even accidentally. You're walking a fine line with her already, and the board doesn't trust her as much as you do."

Dwayne leaned against Adelaide's desk, his gaze hardening. "Look, I'm sorry about what just happened in the lab, but I have acted completely professionally as long as I've been working with her. I've upheld all my contracts and I'm a lot further along with the antivirus than I would be without her help. You know that. What's this really about?"

Adelaide leaned back in her chair tiredly. "It doesn't concern you."

"You're damn right it concerns me! This is my work we're talking about here, this is all I've been doing for almost a year."

Her voice took on an edge. "It's something the board of directors has to deal with..."

"This is my project," he cut in firmly. "I deserve to know."

Adelaide gazed sharply at him, but he could see her resolve falter. She sighed. "We're having contract disputes with IPD. They're claiming greater ownership over the project than they initially negotiated. They want the antivirus."

Dwayne leaned back, confused. "But I signed the non-disclosure agreement with you when Requiem started, as did Elya. They know that."

"Yes, but their lawyers are picking apart every word of our contract with them, and if they look hard enough they might find a loophole to get past that." She leaned forward, twining her fingers together on the desk. "Sinclair is determined to grasp as much of Requiem as he can. He's the one I'm worried about. He could pressure Elya into giving up the antivirus, or worse."

He shook his head vehemently. "She wouldn't do it. She has no more love for Sinclair than we do and she's loyal to Requiem."

Adelaide was shaking her head before he was done speaking. "The board isn't going to stand for it. We're already in the process of replacing the engineers from IPD working on the software to catch a copy of Halcyon with our own. General LaCostas has asked that you use that to test your antivirus, rather than Elya."

"What?" Dwayne cried. "There's no way any computer program can completely replicate the complexity of a human body. We can't be sure if it works unless we test it on a human being."

"You could use someone else to test it."

He shot her an odd look. "And that's more secure? Bringing another new person into the project? Releasing an untested or inadequately tested antivirus would undermine the whole operation and make it that much harder to perfect. I can't tell what processes need to be improved upon without testing it on a living person and your people can't tell me how to do that better than Elya can. And her implants are already set up to handle the infection."

"I know," Adelaide snapped, silencing him. "I know that. I tried to tell the board this, but they're too concerned about Sinclair's access to her."

Dwayne leaned against the desk, his eyes pleading. "Elya wouldn't let him take anything he's not entitled to. This is the only way Requiem is going to work. You have to let me continue."

Adelaide let out a sigh and leaned back in her chair. "I know. Believe me, Dwayne, no one wants to see Requiem complete more than I do." She stole a quick glance at a framed photograph on her desk, looking aged beyond her years. He had seen the photo before, a portrait of the colonel with her husband and son. Their son had been infected by Halcyon when he was fourteen. Her husband had been unable to cope with the grief and left her. "We just have to be careful or Sinclair will tear apart everything we've done."

"Colonel…" Dwayne attempted.

Adelaide held up a hand, stopping him short. "I'll try to convince the board that we have to let you work your own way. But for now, just… try to be more discreet with Elya. Sinclair greatly worries me." She looked up at him, her composure restored. "And I hope for your sake that she is as trustworthy as you say." Dwayne only frowned in response.

"I'm sorry about this, Dwayne." Turning her chair, Adelaide waved toward the door. "You'd better get back to work." Dwayne hesitated, gazing at the troubled and conflicted look etched into the colonel's face. She stared off to the side, not meeting his eyes.

Without another word, he stood and strode out of the room. The hall outside remained silent as he walked back into the lab.

Elya glanced up at the door opening, the cat ears rising curiously. Dwayne had forgotten entirely about them in the talk with Adelaide. He could find no joy in them as worries swirled in his head. "Is everything okay?"

Her concern was genuine and he wanted some comfort for his own worries, but he didn't want to trouble her with the legal struggles between the army and IPD. "Yeah," he answered as he sat down at his desk again.

At least, he thought, *I hope it will be.*

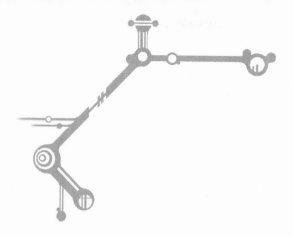

chapter.NINE

ZANDER AWOKE TO the daylight lamps painting stripes of light across his bed as they crept through the blinds. He sat up and stretched with a yawn. The screen on the wall across his room flickered to life with his movement, one of the twenty-four hour city news stations appearing on the monitor. Sliding back the covers, he crawled out of bed, glancing out the window as he pulled his jeans on. The road three stories below swarmed with cars, people crowding the sidewalks and the elevators between city levels.

Grabbing a shirt, he walked around the bed, but paused as he came up beside the screen. Three pundits sat behind a desk in a nest of tickers, weather updates and live traffic cameras. One man in a dark suit with a gaudy tie argued in a raised voice, his flawless female counterpoint responding calmly while a thin man tried to find a middle ground between the two.

"These unaltered are impeding the progress of technology," the man in the gaudy tie argued. "They don't want implants, so they don't think anyone else should have any either. These are the kinds of extremists who try to sabotage life-saving cybernetics and it's hurting all of us."

"That's not being fair," the woman replied. "Less than one percent of unaltered people hold beliefs like the Christian Purity Movement."

"They condone the CPM's actions!"

"No, they don't. I've met dozens of unaltered people and not one of them supported what the CPM does at all. Just because they don't want cybernetics themselves doesn't mean they begrudge others for it."

"Oh, please. Unaltereds hate those of us who have embraced technology. I'm telling you, these people probably created Halcyon to shove their Luddite philosophies…"

With a scowl, Zander reached out and touched the power sensor, shutting off the screen. He shook his head as he stepped out of his room. People had tried to argue for years that anti-cybernetics extremists had created Halcyon, but there had never been any evidence to support that. Zander was cynical enough to doubt that any radical religious group had the resources to create something so powerful, and not so much to think that any group of people would unleash something so deadly just to make a point. He headed into the bathroom, dropping his shirt on the counter as he splashed water over his face. Picking up his razor, he began shaving.

As he was trying to shave off the hairs under his chin, the bathroom door creaked open. Turning, he found Elya giving him an apologetic look as she ducked out of the bathroom.

He blinked. "Oh. I thought you were going to…" He smiled guiltily at her. "Sorry, we don't usually have women around. At least not this early." She flashed him a wry grin, and he cleared his throat. "Here, you can use the bathroom." As he turned to face the mirror again, he saw a curious look on her face.

"Hm?" He glanced at the tile wall surrounding the bathtub, wondering what she was looking at. When he met her eyes again, she pointed at his back. He smiled. "Ah, you saw my wings." He turned, giving her a better view of a tattoo over his shoulder blades. Stylized bird wings glowed in an iridescent, holographic shimmer of red and purple against his skin. "That was the last crazy thing I did before enlisting." Elya tilted her head aside in interest. He grinned. "Yeah, that's me, Corporal Sarkowski of the U.S. army." Facing the mirror again, he continued working at the stubborn hairs under his chin. "I've been on inactive reserve since we pulled out of Somalia. I still haven't figured out what else to do with my life." He rinsed off the razor and toweled himself dry. "Anyway, did you want the bathroom?" Slipping on his shirt, he stepped out into the hall, leaving the light on. "Or would you like some breakfast?" She was about to head into the bathroom, but paused at his words, considering. Turning, she glanced hopefully at him.

He chuckled. "Come on, I'll make you something." She beamed as she followed him out to the kitchen, but he paused before walking onto the tile floor. "Chen?"

Chen sat up with a start from where he sat hunched over his desk in front of his tablet computer. He blinked blearily at the screen, his eyes bloodshot.

Zander opened the fridge and grabbed a carton of eggs. "For God's sake, Chen, go to bed." Chen moaned softly as Zander retrieved a bowl from a cupboard.

"Did you get that image file to Tiger?" Chen asked as he rose and stumbled over to the couch.

Zander rolled his eyes with an amused smile. "I transmitted the files to him last night. He said he has to work today, but he'll get on it tomorrow. Now shut up and get some sleep." Chen said nothing more as he collapsed onto the cushions, pausing only to remove his glasses before he fell still.

Zander shook his head and chuckled as he broke four eggs into the bowl and added a splash of milk. "I swear, if it wasn't involuntary, you'd have to remind him to breathe." He tossed the egg shells down the organic garbage hatch beside the sink. Turning back to the bowl, he met a curious smile from Elya, one eyebrow raised. "What?" She mouthed something. He focused more intently on her lips, and she repeated the movement.

Tiger?

Zander chuckled, grabbing a whisk and beating the eggs. "Trust me, if you saw him, you'd understand." She tapped him on the arm and he met another questioning look. "Oh, you mean the names?" She nodded.

He set the bowl down. "That's for their own safety." Elya tilted her head aside curiously. Zander half frowned. "See, Dwayne told Chen a bit more about Requiem than he should have. I don't know all the details but I know it was classified. We've already had a few close calls when the army caught on that we had copies of Dwayne's research, let alone IPD." He turned on the stove, then crossed the kitchen to put two slices of bread in the toaster. "So we don't use anybody's real name. That way, no matter what happens, if we get caught—by the army, or the police, or whoever —then no matter what they do to us, we can't give them up." She leaned her head back in understanding as he retrieved a pan from underneath the counter.

"These people volunteer their time and put their safety at risk to help us. I don't like asking anyone to do that, but their help has been invaluable. We certainly wouldn't have been able to save you from those mercenaries alone." The eggs sizzled as he poured the contents of the bowl into the pan. He grinned wryly. "Of course, Chen and I are in too deep anyway, so it doesn't really matter who knows our names." He shook his head as he grabbed a spatula and stirred the eggs around. "I figure it's only a matter of time before somebody catches up with me."

Elya frowned softly. He smiled. "I don't mind. It'll be worth it if we can stop Halcyon." His attention returned to the cooking eggs. "Meeting Chen was the first thing to give me purpose after I got back from my last tour of duty. I was actually living back at home with my parents at the time."

He touched the display panel for the stove, shutting off the heat as he smiled away the memories. "So, you ready for breakfast?" He chuckled as the toaster popped up behind him. "Sorry it's not anything fancy. Bachelor cooking, you know." Elya's shoulders trembled with a silent chuckle. He deposited the eggs onto two plates, placing the toast beside them, and handed one plate to her. "Ketchup?" She nodded as she carried her plate over to the table on the other side of the counter. Zander brought a bottle of ketchup as he joined her at the table.

"Just let me know if you need anything. I have to work today, but feel free to call my cell. Are you going back to Ryn's today?" She nodded, though she gave him a questioning look. He smiled as he swallowed a mouthful of eggs. "I work at a hardware store. Not glamorous, I know, but it helps pay the bills and they don't ask many questions." Raising his head, he nodded toward the back of the couch, obscuring Chen from view. "Chen does freelance programming. Of course, he works so fast he spends half the day on Requiem. They don't know what they have with him." He winked. "Just don't tell him I said that." She grinned in response.

Finishing off his toast, Zander stood and took his empty plate back to the kitchen. "Make yourself at home while you're here. The screen in my room has a pretty strong firewall so feel free to browse the net or whatever, though the TV out here tends to have a faster connection." He turned from the sink at a touch. Elya smiled earnestly at him and mouthed, *Thank you.*

He smiled softly. "My pleasure. I'm just sorry we couldn't get you back to Ryn's last night." Glancing over her, he eyed the living room, the coffee table still cluttered and the carpet in desperate need of vacuuming. "I'll have to clean up some more when I get back tonight. Anyway, I'd better start getting ready." Retreating into his room, he combed his hair, pocketed his keys and wallet and slipped on socks and work boots. Grabbing his cell phone and work vest, he walked out. Elya waited at the dining table as he paused in front of the door and shrugged on his vest and jacket.

"I'll only be a couple miles away. If you need anything, just call..." He stopped himself short, gazing at her. He smiled apologetically. "Send me a text. Chen has my number." She nodded, wishing him a silent goodbye as he stepped out the front door. Shoving his hands in his pockets, he climbed the stairs down to the road and left the building, his thoughts on Elya. He hoped she would be alright alone with Chen.

Zander rolled his eyes and chuckled silently. *He can hardly be charming company when he's engrossed in code.* There was enough around the apartment for her to do. Still, he couldn't help but worry about her, especially after having to free her from the grip of the mercenaries from IPD. His smile faded. Sighing, he prayed silently that Chen would be able to finish the antivirus soon and that Elya would remain safe at their apartment.

He shook his head as he strolled down the sidewalk, casting away the dark thoughts. Elya was important to a lot of people and it was natural for him to worry. It didn't mean that there was any active threat to her while he was gone.

By the time he believed it, his phone rang with news otherwise.

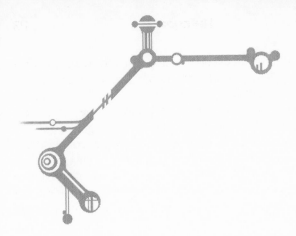

chapter.TEN

ELYA LISTENED AS Zander walked out, locked the door and retreated down the hall. When his steps faded into silence, she turned around.

Zander and Chen's apartment was simple, without many decorations on its walls, but it was homey, the furniture well lived in. It was something that complemented them, a space that was clearly theirs. She wondered where her home was. The news article she had found said little. Morrow Heights had struck her as correct, but she could remember nothing more specific and the borough was large. She might recall something if she went there, but undoubtedly someone would see her there, especially now that she had already been caught. Obscurity seemed a strange defense, but if Zander and Chen weren't part of Project Requiem, she was probably safer here than with someone who was. Although, she thought, Galina and Gerod had clearly met Zander before. Amélie, for her even more distant connection to Requiem, seemed a safer refuge, especially if Zander and Chen didn't even know her real name.

Glancing to the side, she watched Chen breathe softly as he slept on the couch. She still felt uneasy being in someone else's home, though the simple scrambled eggs and toast Zander fixed her for breakfast warmed her throughout and Chen's bed had been extraordinarily comfortable. Both had felt a luxury after weeks spent living in the slums of the first city level, not to mention ground level. Merely having someone to listen to was a welcome change. It would be hard to run away again and she hoped fervently that she would not need to.

Shaking away those dark thoughts, she crossed the living room toward the bathroom.

Inside the bathroom, she locked the door and examined her face in the mirror. Something about it had seemed off when she saw her reflection, but it wasn't until she saw the photograph on Chen's desk that she realized it was because her skin and hair were the wrong color. Looking now, she knew that was it, though she had become used to the way she looked now. It had helped keep her hidden from those who pursued her, though now that the mercenaries knew how she had changed, it would be harder than ever to hide from them. She frowned, wishing she could regain control over the cybernetics that controlled her skin and hair tone, but to repair them would require a trip to a hospital or at least a doctor's office, and one scan of her ID would start an uproar she wasn't prepared to face yet.

Unbuttoning her jeans, she slid them halfway down her legs. She grimaced. An ugly bruise remained on her thigh from falling off Gerod's motorcycle. She prodded gently at the dark purple flesh, wincing as it ached from the touch. It had improved, hurting only a little when she walked, though the jeans were rough on it. A similar wound remained on her upper arm, a scrape stung on her palm, and the side of her head still felt tender, though she supposed she should count herself lucky that she had not been hit by any stray bullets when Zander and the others broke into the mercenaries' base. Zipping up her jeans again, she returned her attention to the mirror.

An empty hallway. A rack of servers popping and sparking. The image was like a fading dream, a memory she wasn't entirely sure was real.

What had happened that night in the lab? She didn't even know the context of that moment but it seemed an essential question. The rest of the world thought her dead, but apparently Sinclair and the army knew otherwise. Did anyone but her know what had really happened?

She shook her head. She couldn't help but think of the other homeless people she had come across in her exile. Now she lived in at least temporary comfort, but only because other people wanted something from her. A bitter part of her mind was glad for her amnesia, that she couldn't give them what they wanted. At least Zander had been compassionate enough to let her leave before.

Sighing, she stepped out of the bathroom. Chen still slept on the couch. She watched him for a moment. Zander was friendly enough but it still felt like she was in a stranger's home. Turning, she retreated into Zander's bedroom and turned on the TV.

She perked up when Amélie phoned and later arrived to take her out shopping. Waving a quick goodbye to Chen, she stepped out of the apartment after the nurse, hiding her annoyance at his obvious reluctance to let her go.

As they strode down the hall toward the elevator, Amélie asked, "So how was it at their place last night?"

Elya shrugged with a smile.

Amélie glanced over her shoulder to ensure the door was closed. "Zander and Chen are nice enough, but honestly, they really don't understand women very well." Elya grinned in agreement, feeling more relaxed already. "Anyway, I figure we should pick up some things you need, a toothbrush, hair brush, your own shampoo. And some more clothes, some that fit better than mine." She gestured at the same sweater and jeans Elya had been wearing since the last night. Frowning, Elya turned out her empty pockets.

Smiling at the gesture, Amélie replied, "Don't worry about it. I can cover it." Elya mouthed a response.

"Oh, here." Reaching into her purse, Amélie handed Elya her cell phone. The cat-eared girl gave her a curious look. "I figure you can talk to me by typing up a text message." Elya brightened. Tapping out a message on the screen, she showed it to Amélie.

This is a great idea. And I'll pay you back.

She waved in dismissal. "Take your time. I'm good for the money, as long as we don't get designer clothes." Elya smiled her assurances.

Amélie led the way out of the apartment building and across the street into a parking garage. "I've got some ideas about where we can go, but let me know if there's anywhere you'd like to stop." Elya simply nodded in response and continued silently to Amélie's car. She leaned back in the passenger seat as the auburn-haired woman drove through the city toward her home. The townhouse was more comforting to her than Zander and Chen's apartment and she felt more at ease as she approached the building.

Miso rose from the sofa as the door opened, but as soon as the calico glimpsed Elya, it leaped off and darted into the kitchen, crouching under the table.

"Miso, you are such a scaredy-cat," Amélie reproached as Elya chuckled silently. The cat had a similar reaction the previous night when they had stopped here. Miso had been friendly enough with the others, a trait that seemed common to the cat, but when it saw Elya's ears its eyes widened and it bolted out of the room.

Amélie rolled her eyes. "Just ignore her. She jumps at her own shadow sometimes. Anyway, let's find a hat for you." Elya followed her upstairs and into her bedroom as she threw open the doors to her walk-in closet.

"Now, let's see what we can do."

For the next half hour, they experimented with looks. Elya tried on numerous hats and countless accessories to go with them before she decided on a dark gray beret and a translucent scarf patterned with butterflies in a shade of green that both complemented the purple sweater she wore and made her sea green eyes stand out less. Then, they moved into the bathroom where Amélie used a hair straightener to tame Elya's stringy locks into smooth, full waves, adding some hair spray that gave her white hair a golden sheen, and applied touches of makeup to make her deathly pale skin less noticeable.

When they were done, Elya felt transformed and she marveled at her appearance in the full-length mirror on the closet doors. Even people who knew her well would have to look twice to recognize her in a passing glance, and with her cat ears hidden under the beret, she would fit in to a crowd with ease.

Amélie clapped her hands together in approval. "That looks great!" Elya smiled as she examined her reflection, looking nothing like it had even a few days earlier. "I could've really laid on the foundation to make your skin look darker, but that blush and lip and eye liner is all you really need." Elya nodded in agreement, then turned to Amélie. She gestured at the auburn-haired woman, but Amélie only gave her a curious look in response. Picking up the cell phone off the bed, Elya typed into it and showed her the message she entered on the screen.

Would you like me to do your hair and makeup?

Amélie smiled and shook her head. "That's okay. Honestly, I don't normally wear much makeup, though right now I'm glad I have it. Well, are you ready to go? I think I owe you a stop at the coffee shop down the street for that double chocolate cheesecake." Elya grinned, her mouth watering at the idea, and with a nod, they walked downstairs and out of Amélie's house.

As they got down to street level and began strolling down the sidewalk of the major road, a few people occupying the walk nodded to them or gazed in interest, but most simply ignored them as they continued on their way. The reactions were welcome to Elya, and for the first time since she could remember, she began to feel comfortable in her own skin. None of them knew what lay inside her, what secrets she kept and what danger she was in. To them, she was a normal city girl, as they were ordinary citizens to her, and outwardly she looked no different than they did. A young man walking down the sidewalk glimmering with cybernetic lights over his face attracted far more attention than she did. It was a welcome confirmation of how commonplace she looked.

"So how are you feeling?" Amélie asked. Turning to her, Elya smiled and nodded, not bothering to use the phone. Amélie halted on the sidewalk, touching her shoulder lightly. "I mean, how do you feel about... all of this?" She waved her hand vaguely, her voice dropping as people strode past them.

Elya glanced away in thought. Surrounded by people leading ordinary lives in the midst of the city, she could easily forget about the deadly danger she had been in so recently and the weeks of living on ground level that had come before then. She felt at ease in the city now that she had less reason to be afraid of being noticed. Things such as the enigmatic Project Requiem seemed too grand to comprehend and too far away to concern her.

Pulling Amélie's phone out of her pocket, she entered a message on the screen.

Well, I'm definitely feeling more like myself again, even if I'm still homeless and surrounded by strangers. She paused as Amélie read the message, then typed into the phone again, flashing another message on screen.

Right now, though, I don't think I even want my life back.

Amélie tilted her head aside in surprise. "Why not? Don't you want to know who you are?"

I know who I am. I just don't remember how I got here.

Laying a hand on Amélie's arm, Elya nodded down the sidewalk and they began walking again. Strengthened by the ability to express herself, something that had been denied to her since she awoke, she continued typing text on the cell phone screen.

All I've learned so far about who I was has been bad news. The man I cared about is dead, people are after me for my involvement in Project Requiem, and everyone who's not thinks I'm dead. Who knows how much work it's going to be to clear that up. That's a lot of stress to deal with and maybe that's why I have amnesia. My mind just decided it couldn't handle all of it and decided to shut it all out.

Amélie nodded, her voice subdued. "That's entirely possible."

At least now I can spend some time feeling normal before I have to deal with it all.

Touching her shoulder, Amélie gave her a sympathetic look. "I don't think anyone can begrudge you that. And if there's anything I can do for you, just ask." Elya nodded gratefully. They both fell silent as Amélie led her inside a coffee shop and they each ordered a latte and a slice of double chocolate cheesecake. They sat in silence for a few bites, Elya relishing the rich dessert and the heat of the coffee sliding down her throat.

Pausing in her cheesecake, Amélie stated, "You know, I've met your parents." Elya glanced up in surprise. "Your mom was really broken up about your disappearance. Well, of course, they think you're dead, though I guess the army told them that no body was found." Elya frowned. "Do you want to see them?"

Elya shook her head. She took another bite of her cheesecake and a sip of her latte before she pulled Amélie's phone out of her pocket once more.

Not yet.

Amélie nodded understandingly. "Would you like me to let them know that you're alright? They don't have to know where you are." Smiling, Elya nodded, and their half spoken, half written conversation switched to more mundane topics.

To her surprise, as they were finishing off their drinks, only crumbs of the cheesecake crust remaining on their plates, Amélie's phone rang. Elya hastily handed over the phone as Amélie glanced at the display. She cringed faintly.

"Sorry, I have to take this." Elya nodded as Amélie answered the call. "Hey baby. How's it going?" Looking at Elya, she mouthed *boyfriend*. "Yeah, I still have the day off, I've just been spending some time with a girlfriend. We were just going to go shopping." A pause, and she laughed. "Oh, don't worry, I don't think we're going to be out that long." Amélie frowned as she gazed at Elya again, but her voice was innocently pleasant as she replied. "Sure, that sounds great. Yeah, I should be back by 2:00 or so. Okay, see you then. Bye." She frowned again as she disconnected the call and faced Elya once more. "I'm sorry, I've really been blowing him off too much recently. Are you okay going back to Zander's for now?" Elya smiled and nodded, though Amélie still seemed remorseful. "Sorry about that. Maybe if I get off early tomorrow, I'll stop by. Anyway, you can hang on to this." She handed Elya the phone as she stood. "Ready to go?" Elya nodded assent and followed her out.

Soon, they immersed themselves in clothes stores, each of them trying on numerous outfits and experimenting with different combinations of clothes and accessories. Amélie put back far more clothes than she continued to hold, though Elya knew she would need to buy enough to last her at least a little while, including a small selection of hats. Still, she relished the act of shopping, making her feel normal again. After picking up various other necessities, Amélie finally drove her back to Zander and Chen's apartment, and a smile remained on Elya's face the entire time.

She flashed Chen a warm smile as he opened the door. Blinking, he straightened his glasses as he focused on Elya, with her straighter and faintly colored hair, makeup and wardrobe toning down the paleness of her skin. "Wow, you look really nice." Grinning, she stepped inside, suddenly feeling comfortable with the realization that his apartment was familiar. It was the familiarity of a cheap motel in a city where one's lost, but in some way, like Amélie's house, it seemed hers. She set her shopping bags down beside the door while Chen continued staring.

"I'd better head back," Amélie said from just outside. "My boyfriend's waiting for me. See you later, guys."

"See you, Ryn," Chen replied, giving her only a brief glance before looking back to Elya. Still smiling, she gave him a pointed look. Clearing his throat awkwardly, he closed and locked the door. "You look really good." She nodded in thanks. "No problems while you were out?" She shook her head. "That's good." Her eyebrows raised, and he looked away. "Well, um, I'd better get back to work. Let me know if you need anything." Nodding, she strode into Zander's room again, preparing to spend a quiet afternoon watching TV.

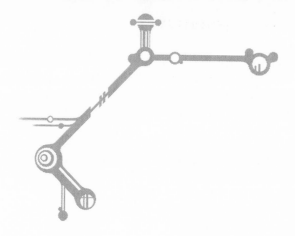

chapter.ELEVEN

Eight weeks ago

CHEN FIDDLED UNEASILY with his ponytail as he stepped off the train and climbed the stairs back up to the road. From the outside, it looked like a decent neighborhood. The daylight lamps shone strongly down on the street and the apartments boasted elegant facades with wrought-iron balconies. But he knew it was a low-income neighborhood and the closer he looked the more apparent it became. The buildings were old and worn, graffiti marked alley walls and the people on the street wore older and simpler clothes and looked more worn and isolated than in other parts of town. Litter danced in the streets as beat-up old cars passed back and forth, some rattling with pounding music that boomed through the neighborhood. The rows of steel girders supporting the higher level buildings and roads rose in regular formation like sentinels, providing a constant reminder that these buildings were only on the first city level above ground. Though the air was clearer here than in other parts of town, there remained a haze that obscured distant buildings. Chen smiled and nodded to a plump woman with tanned, leathery skin that clashed with her overly blonde hair. She ignored him as she passed by him on the sidewalk, complaining on a cell phone earpiece. At least, Chen hoped she was speaking with someone.

He frowned, gazing off to the side as he shoved his hands in his pockets. He passed by a man with scraggly reddish brown hair and a few days' scruff shadowing his jaw. He turned his head faintly as Chen walked by, though Chen couldn't make out the man's eyes beneath the messy locks of hair hanging over his forehead. Swallowing, Chen averted his eyes and faced forward as he continued down the sidewalk.

He had reached the next entrance and stepped onto the first stair before he noticed the teenager leaning against the railing a few stairs up. He gasped and pulled his foot back as the young man turned to face him, pinpricks of glowing lights shining around his temples below spiky, cobalt blue hair. Chen stepped back as the teenager descended the stairs, a smirk on his face. His black leather clothes creaked as his heavy boots fell down onto each step.

"Watch it, uppie."

"S-sorry," Chen stuttered. "I didn't see you. I didn't mean to…"

"Oh, you didn't see him, huh?" cut in another voice. Chen turned to find another teenager approaching from behind him, his clothes as tattered as the blue-haired teenager. Patches of bare skin showed above his ears, where circuitry was visible and a small visor and microphone stuck up over his head, a cheap but intense gaming interface. "Typical topper. Everybody's beneath you."

Chen began to say that he didn't come from sky level but stopped himself. It probably didn't matter to them. He did come from a higher city level than these first level inhabitants. "I was just trying to go inside." He uneasily edged toward the entrance to the building, the blue-haired youth approaching from the stairs.

"You don't belong down here, topper," came a third voice as another teenager approached from the other side of the stairs, coal black hair falling almost entirely over his face, darker than the layers of black clothes he wore that jingled with chains. Chen backed up against the railing of the road, the gap between street and building opening up down to ground level behind him.

"I… I just…" Chen's heart pounded as the teenagers gathered around him, malice gleaming in their eyes.

He yelped as the gamer grabbed the shoulder of his shirt and yanked him roughly over. "This is our territory, uppie." Chen winced as the gamer raised a fist.

"Hey."

Everyone turned at the new voice. The auburn-haired man Chen had passed earlier stood a few paces away, hands in his pockets.

"The hell's your problem? He hasn't done anything to you."

The blue-haired youth sneered. "Who are you, his lawyer? Toppers don't belong down here."

"Doesn't mean you get to pick on them for no reason. Dicks like you are the reason uppies hate firsts."

The gamer shoved Chen toward the railing, eyes widening in fury at the stranger. "What did you call us?" Chen's own eyes widened as the teenagers approached the stranger. He couldn't help but notice that no one else made to intervene or even seemed to notice them. The other people on the sidewalk quietly turned around or cut through the traffic to cross on the other side of the street.

The stranger made no reaction. "You heard me. You're a bunch of firsts."

"Just who—"

The gamer reached out to shove with his words, but with blinding speed the stranger pulled his hand out of his pocket, grabbed the gamer's wrist and twisted it hard. Before anyone else could react, he threw his free hand forward while still holding the gamer, slamming a flat palm against the black-clad teen's chest so hard he tumbled backward to the sidewalk. The blue-haired teen lunged as the stranger wrenched his arm back around, throwing the gamer to the ground. He ducked beneath the blue-haired youth's swing and drove a fist up into his stomach with such force his feet left the ground briefly.

The stranger loomed over the three teenagers, glaring down at them. "Get lost. You don't own anything except your own sorry asses."

The blue-haired teen and his companions looked like they were about to attack again, and Chen tensed. Then, without moving any other muscles, the stranger curled his hands into fists. Giving him dirty looks, the teenagers rose and stumbled off down the sidewalk, shoving aside the first person they came across as they escaped.

The stranger looked at Chen. "You alright?"

Chen shakily pulled himself to his feet, still pressed against the railing. "Y-yeah. Thank you."

The stranger glanced at the teenagers, now receding through

the crowd. "They'll be back at it tomorrow. So what is an uppie like you doing down here?"

Chen had turned toward the building entrance where the boys had been waiting, but paused at the stranger's words. "I'm... looking for something."

"You won't find much around here unless you can pick locks. That place has been closed up since the army came through here a couple weeks ago."

Chen had reached the base of the stairs, but stopped before climbing them. "Oh." He lowered his hand from the railing with a frown. Dwayne had told Chen he hid his notes, but if the army had been through the building already, what chance did he have that the data drive was still there? He turned to leave and found himself face-to-face with the stranger, who gave him a chiding look.

"Come on, don't tell me all that was for nothing."

Chen bit his lip, hesitating.

The stranger shook his head, looking exasperated. He walked past Chen up the stairs to the entrance. Chen watched curiously. Casually, the stranger strode up to the building entrance, leaned back and kicked the door open. Chen jumped at the sudden crash.

He gazed at Chen. "You coming or what? I don't like picking fights with kids for no reason."

Chen glanced in either direction down the street but most people pointedly ignored him. Cautiously, he climbed the stairs and followed the stranger inside the building.

The foyer was dark beyond the daylight lamps illuminating the entrance. Chen paused in the doorway, waiting for his eyes to adjust, but he could see little else. The stranger stood a few paces into the darkness. Reaching into his pocket, he pulled out a key ring and activated a flashlight, revealing the old hallway before them.

Blinking, Chen realized the stranger was looking at him. He cleared his throat. "Er, thanks for helping me."

The stranger shrugged, though he held the light steady. "What are you looking for?"

"It's in apartment 413."

The stranger glanced down the hall. "Don't think the elevators are still working. We'd be better off taking the stairs." Chen nodded faintly and followed the stranger down the hall.

They climbed the stairs in silence, the stranger's flashlight lighting their way as the wood creaked under their feet. Chen glanced around the empty staircase, once grand. Long ago, this part of town had been one of the first areas where a city level meant as a complete neighborhood was built above ground, and only the wealthy could afford to live closer to the sky. That was before a few more city levels were built on top of it, leaving the remains of these condos to people like those teenagers. Now, the wood stairs sagged and the railing had grown dark and stained from the touch of thousands of hands. Spider webs hung in the corners.

As uncertain as he felt about trusting a stranger, especially one in this part of town, he felt immensely relieved to have a confident escort through the building. He wondered about the stranger, still surprised by his agile and coordinated moves against the teenagers that had harassed him.

"Did you know someone who lived here?"

Chen looked up with a start at the stranger's sudden words. He wrung his hands. "Yeah."

"Didn't come by here often, huh?"

"It's just a little far for me to come. It was a starter place. He liked that he could get a much bigger apartment here for the same price as somewhere half the size on a higher level." The stranger said nothing in response.

Finally, they reached the fourth floor of the building and stepped out into the hall. The stranger shone the flashlight over the walls and ceiling. Flakes of drywall lined the floor beneath cracked dents in the wall and stark pale squares remained in the wall where there had once hung signs or pictures. He stepped forward slowly, Chen walking alongside him.

"Keep a sharp eye out," the stranger said softly. "You never know when the army's set up surveillance even after they've ransacked the place." Chen wondered again about the stranger, but remained silent as he followed.

They stopped in front of a door labeled 413. The stranger tried turning the doorknob, but it rattled under his grip and didn't open.

"Deadbolt's locked. I don't suppose you have a key."

Chen shook his head. "Sorry."

"Don't need to apologize to me." The stranger crouched in front of the door, shining his light over the doorknob as he examined the lock. "Stand back." Chen stepped back as the stranger stood. Lifting his leg, he drove his foot down against the doorknob. The door thumped against its lock, but didn't budge. He kicked at the knob again and a shard of wood flaked off, falling down to the floor.

The stranger paused, glimpsing the wood chip. He shone his flashlight over the doorknob again. Chen then noticed the cracked wood in front of the lock, as well as a circular dent in the door at about waist height. The stranger turned an intense gaze to him.

"This is the apartment they were searching."

Chen opened his mouth a few times, trying to come up with an excuse. The stranger stood, his expression placid.

"Do you really think they would've left anything behind?"

Chen swallowed. Knowing he was caught, he uttered, "He swore he hid it somewhere they wouldn't find it."

The frown the stranger flashed him was brief, washed away with a shrug. "Well, I suppose the only way to find out is to look." Chen let out a relieved breath as the stranger crouched to examine the lock again. He wondered how he could have expected to get into Dwayne's old apartment and find the data drive so easily alone. It occurred to him that he hadn't really planned out his trip there.

Fiddling with his key ring, the stranger pulled the flashlight off it and held it up. "Hold this." Chen obediently grabbed the flashlight and shone it against the doorknob as the stranger flipped open a pocketknife. He began prying out flakes of wood from around the lock. Chen glanced around while the stranger worked, wishing he knew enough to help.

Several minutes passed as the stranger whittled away the wood, trying to expose the lock underneath. Chen's gaze frequently wandered back and forth down the hallway, his back hurting from bending over to hold the stranger's light steady.

At last, a click sounded. "Got it!"

Chen drew in an excited breath and returned his attention to the door to Dwayne's apartment. The stranger pushed the door open a crack, the hinges creaking. Taking the flashlight from Chen, he shone it through.

Chen leaned forward anxiously. "Can you see anything?"

The stranger paused, his eyes scanning what he could see. "No, but it doesn't mean nothing's there. Keep your eyes open." He pushed the door open all the way and walked inside.

Chen stepped in after him and immediately his stomach dropped. The damage to the walls and dirt and scuffs on the floor made it clear that the army had ransacked the place. Nothing remained, no furniture, no decorations and no screens. For a moment, Chen hung his head, upset, ashamed and hopeless to see Dwayne's apartment reduced to an empty, condemned unit in an abandoned building, and the pain of his death burned anew.

Inhaling deeply, Chen raised his head. Dwayne had poured his life into Project Requiem and there was nothing Chen could do for the looting of his apartment. He could at least continue Dwayne's work.

Provided the data file was still there.

The floor creaked under his feet as he stepped into the apartment and glanced around. He tried to imagine the spacious rooms as they had originally been built, with fancy wainscoting and furnishings and expensive oriental rugs. That corner might once have held a grand piano, or the entire wall might have been covered by a huge screen. It was difficult to picture. Then, he tried to imagine what it had looked like when Dwayne lived here, with old, mismatched furniture, numerous computers lying around and possibly as messy as Chen's own apartment.

I know I'm not supposed to, but I've hidden a copy of my notes in my apartment.

In the days leading up to Dwayne's death, he had been paranoid about the reach of the army and IPD and didn't dare to tell Chen specifically where he'd hidden the data file in case the phone line was tapped. From the look of the cracks between the wood floor, the soldiers that searched the apartment had even pulled up some of the floorboards searching for the data drive. Where could Dwayne have stashed the drive? Had it truly remained safe?

The creaks of the stranger's steps sounded behind him as he walked up beside Chen, glancing around. He clicked off the flashlight, the room illuminated sufficiently by the daylight bulbs streaming in through the windows. "Any idea where this thing might be?" Chen only shook his head, not wanting to relate Dwayne's story to the stranger. "Do you at least know what you're looking for?"

Chen hesitated. The stranger had undoubtedly already discerned that what Chen sought was valuable, and if he found it first the stranger might decide to keep it for himself or attack Chen for it, even not knowing what the data drive contained. However, Chen had already proven his inexperience in his efforts, and he figured that even if he asked the stranger to leave, he couldn't guarantee he would be able to hold on to the data drive. Hopelessness threatened to wash over him again.

"A data drive."

The stranger nodded, a focused look in his eyes. He moved over to a wall and began feeling along it, prodding and searching. Chen stepped slowly through the living room, looking around for hiding spots the army might have missed. He frowned.

They made their way around the apartment, moving from room to room as they inspected the walls and corners and any items that remained. Chen began to wonder if the drive had been hidden in some furniture that had been looted when the army came through. He continued searching out of habit, gradually accepting that the data drive was probably gone. The only thing he did find was a framed photo of Dwayne and Elya, standing together and smiling on a beach. The glass was broken and the frame was cheap, but tears came to his eyes as he looked at the friend he would never see or talk to again. Pulling the photo out of the frame, he slid it into his pocket.

While he inspected the gaping hole where a toilet had once been in the bathroom, the stranger stated, "Hey." Chen's heart leaped and he quickly returned to the kitchen, where the stranger examined a wall over the counter. A magnetic knife rack had once hung beneath the cupboard, where the stranger's attention was focused. Only a few crumbling screw holes remained. The stranger scraped at the drywall with his knife.

"This looks like it was looted after the army came through. I don't think they would've looked behind here." As he pried away the drywall, a metal plate came into view. Chen's spirit rose as the stranger picked at the wall.

Then, the plate shifted, and the stranger wedged a tiny safe out of the wall. "Bingo." He handed the safe to Chen. It was hardly larger than a box for cufflinks. An old-fashioned combination lock kept it closed with no digital components to be seen. Chen's smile dropped away as he gazed at the thirty-digit lock.

"I guess you don't know the code."

Chen shook his head. "He never told me about any combination lock."

The stranger shrugged. "He never said anything unusual you dismissed at the time? Didn't suggest anything about a series of numbers? A year or date or address or something?" Chen only shook his head, at a loss.

Dwayne couldn't have predicted what would happen but he had wanted Chen to find the data drive if anything went wrong. He wouldn't have made the combination anything obvious, in case someone else found the box before Chen could. It had to be something only Chen would associate with Dwayne. Yet, it had to be something he assumed Chen would guess. What three-digit value would he give the combination?

Then, Chen's eyes widened. Three digits. Three characters. Something close to Dwayne. Counting in his head, he spun the dial as he entered a combination.

Five—nineteen—eighteen.

E-S-R.

Elya Selise Renard.

The lock clicked open.

Chen's face lit up as he lifted the lid of the box. There, resting in the velvet lining inside the safe, was the data drive.

The stranger's eyebrows rose as Chen picked up the drive. "I guess you were meant to get this." Chen simply gazed at the drive in his hand, overwhelmed by the magnitude of what he held. Although Dwayne had been unable to take any copies of his actual work on the antivirus away from the lab even if he had wanted, all his detailed notes on how he had planned to program it, along with things he had learned along the way, were on this drive.

Suddenly, the sound of footsteps tromping up the stairs rang through the apartment. Chen looked up with a gasp. The stranger snapped his head around, then swore. Following his eyes, Chen saw the blinking red light on a tiny sensor hooked up to the far wall of the living room.

Chen froze, trembling as he gazed at the sensor. "They... they've been monitoring us!"

The stranger grabbed his arm and pulled him toward a bedroom. "Probably because they never found that thing. Come on!" Chen stumbled as he struggled to stay with the stranger. He led Chen across the room to the gaping window, broken glass still scattered on the floor underneath it. Chen slipped the data drive into his pocket, glancing back through the apartment to the front door. The footfalls had reached the hallway outside the apartment.

At the sound of a creak, Chen spun. He gasped to find the stranger gone. A metallic clatter rang outside. Darting to the window, he looked out.

The stranger struggled to pull himself up the railing onto a fire escape on the next building over. Chen's throat went dry. It was ten feet over to the fire escape, and even though the stranger had landed a story down, Chen though it was much too far to jump. On the road in front of the building, Chen could see a truck parked on the sidewalk, emblazoned with the logo of Firefly Security, a private firm owned by IPD. Some uniformed officers waiting by the truck pointed up at them and shouted to others.

The stranger climbed over the railing onto the fire escape and turned, holding out his hand. "Come on!" Chen couldn't move, terrified of jumping out the window. There was an alley below on street level, but it was still four stories down.

The stranger reached his hand out farther. "Hurry!"

Security guards charged into the apartment. "There he is!"

The idea that he would be failing Dwayne if he was caught came over Chen, and stepping through the window, he jumped. His heart leaped up into his throat as he sailed through the air and panic washed over him. He screamed as he began to fall, desperately reaching out for the stranger's outstretched hand.

When it came within reach, Chen grabbed the stranger's wrist with both hands. He coughed as he fell, his face smashing against the railing and chest slamming into the floor of the fire escape landing. He kicked his legs out, desperate for footing, but he couldn't reach the wall on the far side of the fire escape. The stranger kept a tight grip on him.

"Hang on," he grunted, his voice strained as he tried to pull Chen up over the railing. "I've got you." Ribs aching, Chen reached his feet up and climbed over the railing. His entire body shook as he collapsed on the landing.

"Come on!" Grabbing his arm, the stranger hauled him to his feet and pulled him along the landing to the stairs leading up to the next floor. Chen could barely stay on his feet, he was so rattled from jumping through the window. He didn't say anything as they continued climbing up the fire escape. No conscious thoughts came to his mind, he simply followed after the stranger out of a primal fear of being caught.

Finally, they reached a landing on the next city level and ran down a bridge from the fire escape to the road. The stranger turned to continue running down the sidewalk, pulling Chen along with him as they fled the building and the security guards.

Here, people stared at them and car horns blared as traffic slowed to watch them.

The stranger turned down the next road, leading Chen farther away as a Firefly truck roared down the street behind them. Chen's chest burned from running and each panting breath made his ribs throb. All his focus went into keeping his feet moving as quickly as possible.

The Firefly truck turned the corner behind them, approaching fast. Chen began to tremble again, only the stranger's tight grip on his arm keeping him moving. His legs ached and he began to feel lightheaded, but the stranger didn't seem affected at all by their flight.

Suddenly, a black car screeched around the corner ahead of them, drifting into a tight turn nearly as fast as its pursuit down the street. Revving up, it tore down the road straight toward them. Chen yelped, terror stealing over him as he thought that they were pursued by someone else as well.

The car slammed on its brakes as it drew within twenty feet of them, spinning around so that the rear passenger door stopped a few paces in front of them. Throwing the door open, the stranger lunged inside, pulling Chen after him. Then, two army trucks drove in, cutting off access to the rest of the street as the Firefly truck roared up behind them.

"Hang on," the driver warned as he shifted into reverse. Chen was thrown against the front seat as the car shot backward, and no sooner had it stopped moving than it lurched forward, flinging him against the back seat. The passenger door slammed shut from the momentum, the frenzy outside muffled by the walls of the car. Reaching up, Chen grabbed the seat belt and buckled it as the car swerved around the approaching trucks. The car careened toward a gap between the army vehicles less than a car length across. Chen yelped, but the black car maneuvered smoothly between the trucks and sped down the street, sliding around the next corner. Chen breathed fast, grasping the door and the edge of the seat tightly as he watched the military trucks pursue them.

"Can you get us away from them?" the stranger asked over the roar of the engine.

"We'll disappear like a mirage," the driver answered calmly. Chen leaned harder against the back seat as the car increased speed, swerving around corners at a breakneck but remarkably controlled speed. He sank down in his seat, the city spinning past out the windows. Breathing deeply in and out, he tried to keep his stomach settled, too terrified and overwhelmed to consider the army and security trucks chasing them.

Eventually, the car's path began to smooth out and it decelerated a little.

"So where're you guys headed?"

The stranger tapped the back of his hand against Chen's arm. "Where you going?" Dazed, Chen rattled off his home address. The driver simply nodded and turned down the next major road, this time at a sedate pace.

The stranger twisted around to gaze out the back window. "Man, that was amazing. I've never seen driving like that."

The driver grinned. "Only the best for the Black Cab."

Chen blinked, faintly registering the conversation. He recalled the stories he had heard about the Black Cab, the secretive, discreet taxi service that had never been officially recognized, either by potential clients or by police. "The Black Cab is real?"

The driver grinned into the rear-view mirror. "You're riding in one. We're here when needed."

Turning his head, Chen glanced up at the stranger. "You called him?"

The stranger nodded. "While we were on the fire escape."

Chen let out a breath. "Thanks."

The stranger smiled as he leaned back in his seat. "No problem. I hope it was worth it." Chen touched the data drive in his pocket, the photograph crumpling beneath it.

I hope so, too.

He remained quiet and hunched down in his seat as the black car drove through the city, his ribs aching and throat burning. Finally, they pulled to a stop in front of Chen's apartment building. He glanced out the window, stunned at everything that had transpired since he left here that morning.

The stranger swore. Turning, Chen found him pulling a card away from the payment console in the center of the front seat. The screen above it read, "Declined." He frowned at the driver. "Any chance I can pay back in installments?"

Before the driver could answer, Chen said, "Here." Pulling out his wallet, he tapped a credit card against the screen. He winced at the charge, more than triple the cost of a normal taxi and nearly as much as a monthly transit pass for train and elevator. And he knew he still had to leave a tip. The driver had saved their lives, however, and Chen felt no regret as he entered a twenty percent tip. He did worry how he was going to afford the next month, though.

The driver smiled as he handed a business card over his shoulder. "Pleasure doing business with you, gents." The stranger stepped out of the car as Chen took the card. It had nothing more than a phone number and the word *Squirrel*.

"Thank you," Chen wheezed as he rolled out of the car. The driver nodded and smiled once more as Chen closed the door and the car drove away.

The stranger avoided his eyes. "I'm sorry. I didn't mean to do that to you. I've... been out of work for a while." Chen nodded. It was a common problem among the lower city levels. "I'll pay you back. I swear."

Chen shook his head. "Don't worry about it." He pulled the data drive out of his pocket and gazed at it. "I never would have been able to recover this if it wasn't for your help."

The stranger frowned. "I hope it was worth it."

"It was," Chen answered without hesitation. The stranger looked curious, but he clearly wasn't going to pry. Chen looked up. "Thank you again." He held out his hand. "My name is Chen."

The stranger shook his hand with a nod. "Zander."

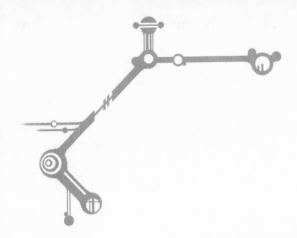

chapter.TWELVE

GEROD SWORE A blue streak as he flopped heavily into the old dentist's chair.

"Oh, quit whining." Galina began searching the drawers and cabinets lining the small room. The thuds of distant music rumbled against the walls.

"Did you see what that bitch did to me?" he snapped, clutching his bleeding face. "Jesus, I think she got my eye."

"She sure did a number on you, Jer," remarked a dark-skinned woman who leaned against the doorway with arms folded. Clothed in a red leather dress that concealed little of her curvaceous body, her straight coppery hair hung down past her shoulders and her full lips glistened with sparkly pink lipstick. Glowing orange tattoos in tribal patterns snaked down smooth arms ending in large but slender hands glittering with rings and long fingernails painted with iridescent polish. "Who'd've thought big, tough Gerod Glass would be beaten by a girl?" Gerod let loose a string of profanities in response, though the woman only chuckled at his vitriol.

Galina shut a cabinet door and stood, a tube of antibiotic cream in hand. "Thanks for taking us in, Solace." Her eyes narrowed. "I must admit they took us a bit by surprise."

"Surprise?" Gerod snapped. "She tore my damn face off!"

Grinning at his suffering, Solace replied, "No problem, Galina. You know I'm always here for you. This is a hell of a mess you've gotten yourselves into, though."

"You're telling me." Galina uncapped the tube. "It's going to be a hassle getting the rest of our equipment out of storage. I really thought that place was secure."

Solace ignored Gerod's curses as Galina rubbed some cream over the wound on his face. "So what's your plan now?"

After wiping off the excess cream, Galina spread liquid bandage over Gerod's face. "You did put the tracer on her when you tied her up, right?"

"Of course," he growled. "But I can't get a signal on her this far away. I need my radio equipment and an amplifier to pin down what sector she's in."

Galina stepped back, replacing the cap on the tube of liquid bandage. "Then clearly I need to go back to the base and get that."

Solace straightened, her ample chest swaying as her shimmering arms dropped. "You crazy, Galina? Even I heard about the cops swarming around your place. They've probably already confiscated everything you had back there."

Gerod sat up in the chair. "I hate to admit it, but she's right. That was a big-ass raid."

"You better come up with a better idea than that."

Galina frowned. She turned to Gerod. "What about the backup unit you have in storage? Can you use that to track her?"

He gingerly touched at the sealed wound on his face, inspecting it in a mirror attached to the chair. "It'll take some reprogramming, but if I can identify the signal I think I should be able to link up the radio to it."

"Alright, then I'll go get it out of storage." Galina shrugged on her jacket. "You stay here."

Gerod shrugged. "Fine by me." He leaned back in the chair, lacing his fingers together behind his head. He grinned at Solace. "You staying too, firecracker?"

Solace scoffed, though she swayed her hips provocatively. "You wouldn't be able to handle me, big man."

Galina edged past her out of the room, eager to leave the conversation behind. Gerod's voice trailed after her into the hall. "Hey, I just got whipped across the face. I'm open to new experiences."

Solace shook her head as she strode after Galina. "I'm surprised he ain't never put the moves on you, girl."

Galina didn't turn as she strode toward the exit, the pounding music from the club within growing louder. "He's kept his distance since I broke his arm in three places when we first met."

Solace barked out a laugh. "Always the ice queen." She stopped in the doorway as Galina stepped out into the neon night and into her car. "See ya, Galina."

"I'll be back soon." Without another word, Galina started the ignition and sped into the street.

She had only traveled a handful of blocks when her cell phone buzzed in her pocket. Glancing at the call display on the car's dashboard, she cringed as she recognized Sinclair's number. Assuming a composed expression, she answered, "Mollis."

Sinclair's voice was barely restrained and she could almost hear his teeth grinding. "Where are you? Why aren't you here?"

"We had an incident," she stated calmly. She had learned throughout her career never to apologize. Always be in command or clients would walk all over her. It was all Sinclair wanted to do and it had rubbed her the wrong way from day one of the assignment. "We're tracking the girl now and should have her ready to deliver very soon."

Sinclair's restraint broke and Galina winced as his screaming rang through the car. "You said you already had her! I've been waiting here for an hour! I do not have time to waste on your incompetence!"

"We have the girl's location," she lied, speaking over his rant. They would have it soon enough and she wanted to show no uncertainty to Sinclair. She had also learned through her career not to give the client specific timelines for work but she attempted a conservative estimate in an attempt to placate Sinclair. "We will retrieve her within a week." She cursed fox-hair's interference even as she admired his skills and daring. Few people she had ever met had shown such determination, let alone the physical endurance, coordination and leadership he had exhibited to pull Renard out from beneath her.

Sinclair barely paused for breath as he continued shouting through the phone. "When I hired you, you told me you would have Elya back within a month!"

"I made no such promise." She struggled to keep her voice even. She remembered that conversation clearly. Sinclair had demanded they find Elya within thirty days, as though they had contacted him for work and not the other way around, and she had repeatedly stressed that she would not make any such guarantees. Sinclair continued to yell over the phone, but she simply said, "I have work to do. I will contact you soon. Good night." Without waiting for a response, she ended the call, ignoring her phone as it began ringing again almost instantly. A car honked as she sped through a red light, trying to release her aggression with speed.

What resources Sinclair must have used to be able to track her phone number, something she kept meticulously blocked and shrouded from the people she called, she couldn't imagine. From the day he hired them he had shown her no respect and it had been an intense struggle for her not to respond to Sinclair's abuse in kind. Ten years ago she had faced similar treatment and had accepted it out of a desperate desire for work when she left organized crime behind. After a decade of hard work, however, she had built up a reputation for efficiency and dedication and she wasn't about to let a self-absorbed CEO tear her down. She was going to do the best work she had ever done and then she was going to cut Sinclair out of her life permanently.

Gunning the motor, she hurried on down the street.

The door creaked open, the noise echoing throughout the spacious living room. Gerod strode inside as Galina examined the walls and corners, searching for potential weaknesses. The hardwood floor reflected the light from the floor-to-ceiling windows stretching across the opposite wall, the towering buildings and elevated roads of the third city level spread out before them. Afternoon sunlight streamed through the gaps between buildings and road, enhancing the daylight bulbs connected to the underside of the road. Galina ignored the tiled kitchenette with its mini-bar, the lavish furnishings and carpets, and the equally elaborate bedroom. The primary amenities of this five-star hotel were unimportant to her. It was space and it was private. That suited her purposes. Gerod whistled as he approached the huge windows.

"What do you think?" Galina asked. "Can you work here?"

He stood in front of the windows gazing out at the city, sunlight glinting off the half-healed wound on his face. "That's a hell of a view."

"Gerod," she growled.

He shot her an annoyed look over his shoulder. "Jeez, what's your problem?"

"This assignment." She strode forward, staring out the windows. She felt too exposed in front of them, but she had to admit that the view from the twelfth-story windows was remarkable. "Sinclair phoned me twice today." His insistence had almost been enough for her to decide to continue tracking Renard from her apartment, or Gerod's. Almost. Though she had little of a life outside her work, she still kept the two meticulously separated and she wasn't going to let Sinclair jeopardize that.

Gerod snorted. "He is one smooth bastard. Didn't even lie about any of the info he gave us, but nothing's been as he said."

"I just want to put this damned assignment behind us." She turned to him. "So? Can you adjust your radio equipment here?"

Gerod nodded, still staring forward. "Should be able to." He pointed out the windows. "This much open space will help the reception."

"Fine." She spun on her heel. "Let's get the equipment up here."

"Sure thing, honey."

Galina halted in place, glaring over her shoulder at Gerod. He grinned at her, though he held his hands up in surrender. She knew the joke was related to the fact that they had checked in at the honeymoon suite of the hotel under the pretense of its intended purpose, though she thought he was taking far too much enjoyment in the ruse.

Narrowing her eyes, she turned and strode out of the suite, Gerod following her down the hall and into the double-deck elevator down to street level. She also knew that she would have ignored the comment entirely if she wasn't so frustrated with Sinclair. They soon brought up the crates of equipment Solace had refused to allow them to assemble in her club. Galina couldn't blame Solace for it, as the frequency it used was notoriously easy to detect, and she had enough concerns about the police raiding her club without Galina and Gerod's advanced military technology added to the mix. However, it had still been an unwelcome setback and they had to wait all night and day to check in to a hotel that could serve their purpose while one of her contacts sought out a new base for them. The useless day spent waiting at Solace's club had been maddening.

Galina helped Gerod assemble his radio equipment but could only stare out the windows or pace restlessly as he configured it to the signal in the tracer he had attached to Renard.

"Are you certain you can find her?" she asked for the third time.

"Don't get your panties in a knot." She shot him a dark look, but he didn't look at her as he continued connecting wires. "She may have ditched the coat, but as long as she still has it, I'll find her. I attached the tracer under her collar. She won't find it." Galina frowned but said nothing more. She could only continue her circuits around the suite and wait for Gerod to finish.

Reconfiguring the radio and amplifying its range took longer than he expected and they ended up making use of the room. She would have preferred to return to her own apartment, but she realized Gerod's suggestion that they remain in the room they had reserved to minimize suspicion was sound. Instead she went to retrieve Indian take-out and ended up going to sleep in the bedroom, leaving Gerod the sofa in the suite's living room.

He assured her he had made progress when she rose the next morning, though he spent further hours working on the equipment, to the point that she had to phone the front desk and reserve the room for another night. Still restless from the wait, she spent most of the day reading, wishing she was out searching for Renard herself but wanting to be near Gerod when he finally tracked down her signal.

Finally, in the middle of the afternoon, he suddenly sat back. "Got it."

Galina rose from where she sat on the floor beside the windows, trying not to sound too excited. "You found her signal?"

He nodded. "Found her. Syncing it up to my maps now." He connected a thin wire from the radio to the panel over his ear. He tapped out a few buttons on the radio unit, then unplugged the wire. "There, now I can access the output remotely. It's a stopgap solution, but it'll do for now."

Galina stepped forward. "Show me where she is." Turning to his notebook computer, Gerod entered the coordinates into a mapping program, pulling up the address, floor plan and photos of the third-story apartment. Cross-referencing information showed that the address was registered to one "Yu, Chen." Galina looked over Gerod's shoulder as she examined the maps.

He leaned back, satisfied. "So what's the plan?"

She straightened and grabbed her jacket. "Let's stake out the place. I want to know as much about it as possible before we hit it." Nodding, he stood and followed her out of the suite and down into her car. Galina had to force herself not to grab extra weapons. Eager as she was to recover Renard, she had to plan her attack carefully. Fox had proven himself cunning twice now and she had to be prepared if they were to pull off the recovery successfully.

Gerod's cybernetic eye flashed with a square display as he continued studying the location they had found. Aside from the directions he called out to guide her, he remained silent.

"Holy shit," he exclaimed abruptly, several miles away. "They must've been on the lookout for the signal."

"What? What's going on?"

He shook his head. "I couldn't encrypt the signal without a lot more work. It's already being tracked."

Galina tensed. "Someone else has picked up on her location?"

"Yep." The square display against Gerod's eye flicked off as he leaned back in his seat. "Well, this is going to complicate things a little."

"What is it?"

He glanced at her. "The army's already on its way there."

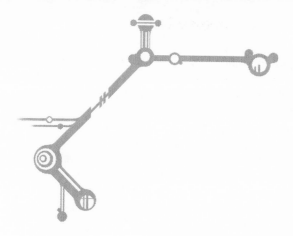

chapter.THIRTEEN

NUMEROUS PEOPLE BROWSED through the store, some wheeling shopping carts or flat-bed hand trucks, but the wide aisles remained largely clear as they often did in the middle of a weekday afternoon. Near the end of an aisle dominated by tubs of putty and shelves of painting accessories, Zander spoke with a middle-aged woman.

"The type of adhesive you need depends on what you plan to use it for," he explained, gesturing at the various types of glue arrayed on the board before them. "If your clock is heavy, then wood glue probably wouldn't hold it together. I'd recommend using an epoxy, though the drying time…"

He trailed off as his phone rang. A chill shot through his heart as he heard the distinctive tone that signified an emergency, the only reason the phone would respond. Smiling at the customer, he tried not to show his uneasiness. "Can you excuse me for just a moment?" She began to protest, but he walked swiftly around the corner into the next aisle before she could stop him. He snatched his phone out of its holster and answered without even glancing at the display. His voice was soft in the wide aisles of the store. "What is it?"

"Zan, we've got big trouble." It was Shad's voice and it was rushed, a panicked edge to his words. "A red flag just went up all over the military channels. They're heading over to your place right now."

Zander swore and turned to stride quickly down the aisle toward the entrance of the store, the customer forgotten. "Have you told Chen yet?"

"I don't have his number. I just have yours."

Zander swore again.

"Do you want me over there? You need help?"

"No, stay away from the apartment. I'll be back there in a few minutes. And shouldn't you be in school anyway?" Before giving him a chance to respond, Zander continued, "I have to call Chen." He hung up and immediately dialed Chen. While the phone rang, Zander called out to an employee at a register, "Cover me! I've got to run home." He broke into a run as he left the building, tearing down the sidewalk as the phone continued ringing.

Finally, a click sounded on the other end, followed by Chen's voice. "Hey Zander. What's up?"

"Chen, you've got to get out of there now. The army's on its way."

Zander heard a stuttering breath drawn in over the line. "W-what?"

"Pack up and get out now! Oh hell." He could hear sirens in the distance. "I'll be there in a few minutes."

"I, ah, alright." Chen's voice was barely controlled.

"Just stay calm, but hurry!" Disconnecting, Zander replaced the phone in its holster. He flipped open a pair of polarized sunglasses and slid them on. Turning his attention inward, he accessed his internal hardware and altered his appearance matrix. When he opened his eyes again, his hair was platinum blonde.

Rounding a corner, he darted across an intersection, his apartment building coming into view a few blocks ahead. He could see the reflection of flashing blue and red lights against buildings growing brighter down another street. He pushed himself faster, swerving around the people crowding the sidewalks. His heart pumped strength through his body as the implants that were installed for his enlistment in the army fed him endorphins.

As he came within a block of the building, three police cars screeched to a stop in front of the entrance, lights flaring. Zander halted, heart pounding. Turning, he ran toward an elevator closing nearby.

He waved his arm at the people inside. "Hold the elevator!" One of the passengers at the front of the elevator hit a button inside and the closing doors swung open again. Pulling his transit pass out of his pocket, Zander swiped it across the sensor and squeezed in. The doors shut behind him and the elevator lurched upward. Panting, blood surging through his arteries, he gazed out the glass walls of the elevator at the scene unfolding down the block.

The police officers had stepped out of their cars and talked through their wrist-mounted communicators as more squad cars pulled to a stop at the other entrances to the building. Zander listened to his own rapid breathing as the road dropped farther away. He always found the silence inside an elevator unsettling, marked only with the murmurs and shuffling of passengers without the drone of traffic and people ever present outside. The lack of background noise made him feel somewhat claustrophobic. A pang of uneasiness grew in his stomach as he saw a military truck covered in dark gray-green canvas pull up to his apartment building.

Finally, the cement wall of the next level's road obscured his view as the elevator slowed to a stop. The doors slid open with a chime, admitting the sounds of the city as Zander edged out. Turning, he immediately continued running down the block toward his apartment building, the façade more glamorous on the higher level.

At the edge of the road in front of the building, Zander paused and glanced over the railing through the gap between the building and the road at the level below. Police cars swarmed around every entrance to the building that he could see. A growing number of camouflaged soldiers gathered at the entrances with the police officers, and some building residents who had evacuated stood beyond the squad cars, gazing on in fear and wonder. Zander frowned as he looked at the crowds. The apartments on the different city levels were owned by different companies and there was no direct access to his building from above. There was no way he would be able to get into the building without being seen. He ruffled his blonde hair, changing the way it fell around his face as he moved around to the side of the building. Soon he found a fire escape climbing down the wall a story below the road where he stood.

Ignoring the potential witnesses around him, he climbed up on the railing of the road and jumped. The road and the upper level sailed over his head as he fell, hoping he would hit the landing outside the emergency exit door rather than the stairs climbing down.

Before he could catch his breath, he hit the fire escape, stumbling as his feet slammed into the metal grate. He collapsed to the floor of the fire escape, sliding down three stairs before he stopped himself with his hands. Shouts and cries rang up from the road both above and below as he threw himself to his feet and raced down the stairs, a brief sting from the impact biting through his knees and hands. He glanced down, finding the distant street crowded with police officers struggling to hold back the stunned onlookers. Soldiers began charging into the building. Zander hurried his pace down the stairs, hoping he could get to Chen before they could.

Locked from the inside, the emergency exit doors would be no help. As he reached the landing the next story down, he ran to the edge of the connecting platform. A few feet away, a window was set in the wall.

Climbing over the railing, he braced one foot against the metal bars and kicked out with the other, the window shattering as his boot drove through the glass. He scraped the sole of his shoe along the bottom of the window as he pulled his foot back, clearing away the shards of glass protruding from the frame. Balancing himself against the railing, he reached out and slipped his arms through the window, grabbing the inside wall. With a grunt, he let his legs fall away from the railing, kicking himself up the wall and climbing inside.

A TV was on in the room he entered, the floor cluttered with children's toys and full laundry baskets, but no one was in the apartment. Glancing toward the bedrooms, he saw the nearest one filled with a set of bunk beds and guilt overcame him for breaking the window. Quickly, he reached into his wallet, pulled out a fifty dollar bill and dropped it on the coffee table. He hurried through the living room to the front door and stepped out into the hall.

Pounding footsteps echoed up the stairs at the far end of the hall. Zander raced down the hall toward a different staircase closer to his and Chen's apartment. He leaped down three stairs, then swung over the railing to fall directly onto the landing of the floor below. Ignoring the stinging in his feet from the hard landings, he continued jumping down the stairs until he reached the third floor and threw open the door into the hallway outside.

Out in the hall, the thumps of feet ringing through the building grew louder. Abandoning caution, Zander yelled out, "Chen!"

Soft footfalls behind him drew his attention. He spun into a crouch to find Elya doing the same, Chen's tablet computer clutched in her arms. She blinked as she looked at his hair, nearly as pale as her own, but as she met his eyes she nodded. He glanced hastily around but saw no sign of Chen. The drumming of boots up the stairs drew closer.

"Where's Chen?" Down the hall, a cry answered him. "Chen!" Zander leaned forward, preparing to run toward his apartment, though Elya grabbed his arm, holding him back.

Then, the helmeted faces of soldiers crept around the corner at the end of the hall.

Zander leaned back, adrenaline flooding his veins. Sighting him, the soldiers darted around the corner. "Hold it right there!"

Spinning around, he bolted down the hall, taking Elya's free hand. Rubber bullets ricocheted off the walls and carpeted floor as they darted around the corner toward the stairs.

Before they reached the door leading into the stairwell, however, it flung open, more soldiers pouring through into the hall ahead of them. Elya inhaled sharply as she pulled to a stop. Zander paused, eyes darting around as the soldiers pounded toward them from ahead and behind. They had stopped beside a corridor leading to an emergency exit door.

He flew down the short hall and kicked the door open, leading Elya out onto the fire escape. The soldiers followed close behind as Zander and Elya ran around the swinging door. Looking down, Zander cringed. More soldiers had entered the fire escape from the first floor and began climbing up after them.

In his hesitation, the emergency exit they had left swung open again as soldiers reached the door. Zander kicked out, slamming the door against the protruding arm. A yelp rang from inside and in the confusion Zander ran up the stairs, Elya close on his heels. His additional distraction only bought them half a story of time and the fire escape soon rocked from the pounding of feet up the stairs after them.

On the next landing he let Elya pass in front of him. The soldiers came within a few stairs of him. Grabbing the railing, Zander swung himself around, slamming both feet against the nearest soldier. The soldier went flying backward, several others behind him tumbling down the stairs like tipped dominoes before those at the bottom could stop their fall. Not waiting to watch the reaction, Zander ran after Elya as soon as his feet hit the metal grate.

Before long they made it to the top of the fire escape, the landing outside the highest emergency exit standing alone against the brick wall. The soldiers reached the landing below. Zander glanced around, desperately looking for a way out, but the fire escape wasn't meant to evacuate people up. The upper level was too far away to jump and the lower level loomed many stories down. The depths of space plummeting below them between the layers of road and building descended into a dizzying haze. He couldn't make out the ground somewhere far below. There was another window leading into an apartment close enough to reach, but he knew they wouldn't be able to escape once they were inside. The only thing in reach was an old telephone cable running along the wall above them.

"Freeze!" a voice barked out from below. "Surrender quietly and you won't be harmed."

Elya pressed herself up against the wall, an uneasy look on her face. Zander sucked in a breath, knowing they were trapped. He turned an uncertain smile to her. "Plan B?" She gave him a brief, measuring look, then turned back to the soldiers, beginning to climb the stairs below. With a helpless grin, she shrugged.

"Then hang on tight." He turned to face the railing as Elya wrapped one arm around Chen's computer and the other around Zander's neck, pressing up against his back. He lifted her up, letting her weight fall on his shoulders, and climbed up on the railing of the fire escape. He reached up for the telephone cable.

"Stop right there!" one of the soldiers ordered.

The soldiers pounded up onto the landing and reached for him, but Zander swung his legs off the railing, suspended by the telephone cable. He balanced himself against the wall with his feet as he moved hand over hand down the cable.

"Sir! Take my hand!"

Zander ignored the reaching hand even as the cable sagged down, dropping him lower. Elya's arm trembled as she clutched him tightly. He clenched his teeth and tightened his fingers around the cable.

Then, one of the metal clips holding the cable to the wall snapped off. Zander yelped as he dropped another few inches abruptly and Elya gasped over his shoulder. He felt the tablet slip out from between them. Elya's arm flailed after it but it plummeted down the side of the building.

"Don't worry about it, just hang on." He struggled to continue down the wall along the cable, the brick face scraping his knuckles. She wrapped her free arm around his shoulders. On the emergency exit landing, soldiers tried reaching out objects for him to hold to climb back onto the fire escape. Several stories below, one reached out and caught Chen's falling computer.

A breeze tousled Zander's hair. Fifteen stories of open air hung below him to the road and almost fifty dropped away beneath his feet between the building and the layers of road. His heart pounded in his chest. He hadn't even made it halfway to the corner of the building and his arms ached already. The idea that he had done something monumentally stupid rang through his mind.

Suddenly, their weight snapped the cable at the wall over the fire escape landing, and as they dropped down from the lack of support, every other clip holding the cable to the wall snapped off. Zander yelped as he fell, his voice echoed by startled shrieks from the road while Elya remained disturbingly silent behind him, clutching his shoulders tightly.

For long seconds he was in free fall, forgetting to breathe. As he continued gripping the cable tightly, however, he reached the end of its slack and began swinging toward the corner of the building, where the cable continued along the wall on the other side. He struggled to kick away from the wall every time the cable pulled him near it, trying to avoid scraping along the brick or slamming Elya against it. The street whirled toward him as he fell toward the corner.

Finally, they swung out over the road from the momentum of their fall, people on the street shrieking and shuffling backward as he flew over their heads. The cable supports on the other side of the wall held and they swung back toward the building.

Clenching his teeth, Zander loosened his grip to slide down the cable, dropping them closer to street level. His hands seared from the friction as he grasped the torn end of the cable tightly. They swung down to within three stories of the road.

As they reached the building again, Zander stretched his legs out and kicked along the wall to swing higher on the cable again. The effort brought him close to the fire escape still lined with soldiers. As he neared the railing, his momentum slowing, he grinned and winked at them.

Turning around, he let their weight carry them along the wall, swinging them like a pendulum back toward the road. When they swung past the corner of the building, Zander kicked out with all his strength, pushing them beyond the gap beside the building and over the railing of the road. Then, he let go.

Bracing himself, he spread his body out like a cat as they fell toward the street, reaching his hands and feet out. He faintly registered squealing tires around the corner before he landed.

Not willing to risk Elya, he allowed all his weight to fall on his hands and feet. The hard asphalt tore at his burning palms while his knees banged against the road. He forced himself not to roll to soften the landing. As Elya's weight fell on his back, the pain in his hands caused his arms to give out and he slammed into the street. He wheezed as the air was squeezed out of his lungs, the world spinning before him. Startled exclamations sounded around him as the crowd that had parted for him gathered close again, though he could hear police officers and camouflage-clad soldiers approach from the front entrance of the building.

Wooden boards crashed aside as a van hurtled through the police barricade that had left the road empty. The crowd yelped, backing away from the vehicle. Zander felt Elya's weight lift off him. Trying to ignore the pain wracking his body, he stood with her help. He wobbled in place, his legs pounding. He could feel that his jeans had torn at the knees and warmth ran down his shins. There was no pain that he could sense, however, and he dared not drop his head to look. His vision swam before him and it was all he could do to remain on his feet. Elya grabbed his arm as the crowd parted. A blue van screeched to a halt not five feet from them and the cargo door was thrown open, Ryn and Deadeye visible inside.

Zander stumbled into the van after Elya. He had barely reached the interior of the vehicle before it sped out into the street. Losing his balance from the momentum, he fell over, Deadeye and Ryn just catching him before he crashed onto the van floor. From the sounds and the bumps under his aching body, the van crashed through another police barrier before it tore off into the street.

"Holy shit, man, that was hardcore!" Deadeye's voice was suitably impressed.

"Are you out of your mind?" Ryn exclaimed. She lifted one of his arms to inspect his hands.

Despite everything, Zander chuckled. He rolled his head back and forth as the van lurched to the side. Lightheaded, he felt warmth seep down his chin. He hadn't even realized his head hit the pavement. His voice came out somewhat strained.

"I ain't doing that again."

He felt a cool cloth press against his face. He moaned as aches sprouted all over his body, the endorphins beginning to wear off. His vision grew fuzzy as he gazed up at the blue metal roof of the van.

"Damn," he said suddenly.

Ryn leaned over him anxiously. "What? What is it?"

Zander tried to glance around, but everything began growing dark. "I think I lost my shades." Deadeye chuckled as Ryn fumed. They were the last things Zander heard.

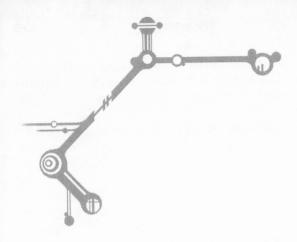

chapter.FOURTEEN

Seven weeks ago

IT WAS THE kind of place that many, if not most people his age spent their free time. However, Chen preferred to be alone, and even with entertainments ranging from karaoke to bowling, he couldn't get comfortable in the club. Even as he took a seat in a quiet booth surrounded on all sides by heavy curtains in a secluded corner, music thrummed through the walls and floor, a constant reminder of the crowds of people swarming close by.

A bouncer hovered outside the curtains at the exit to the booth, quietly keeping people away from the table. Chen couldn't help but worry that the bouncer would listen in on their conversation, despite his promises of discreetness. Desperation and fear had driven him to this meeting, however, and neither of those had faded as he spoke. He looked across the table at the stranger who had helped him recover Dwayne's data drive. His hair was now blood red with two locks of black hanging over his forehead. It had startled Chen at first, but not as much as his statement now startled Zander.

He lowered his drink, staring back at Chen. "An antivirus for Halcyon? Does it work?"

"It's gone. I only have his notes." Chen took a sip of his water. This club was supposedly renowned for its food, but the cover charge for the club had eaten away at enough of his grocery budget for the week that he had ignored the menu, despite his grumbling stomach. "But it was supposed to. The army hired my friend to develop it."

"So where's your friend?"

Chen hunched his shoulders. "He's dead."

"Oh."

He shifted in his seat, consciously aware of the bouncer hovering just outside their table. "All he wanted to do was finish the antivirus, but the army will never finish it now."

"Why not?"

"Contract disputes with the company that provided the technology for the project."

Zander let out a scoffing noise as he took another sip of his drink. "Politics."

"He must have wanted me to finish his work if anything happened to him. I don't know why he'd tell me he made a copy of his notes otherwise. I just want to finish it."

Sensing something in his voice, Zander gave him a quiet look. "You've lost someone, haven't you?"

Chen frowned, staring at the table top beneath his sweating drink. "My mother's best friend since elementary school died from Halcyon a few years ago. She hasn't been the same since."

Zander bowed his head. "I'm sorry." Raising his eyes, Zander faced him again. "What do you need from me, though? I'm not a programmer."

"I just… can't do this alone. I don't have the same knowledge my friend did, I don't have any way to know if what I do write works, and the only person who might still have a copy of the antivirus is missing… or also dead."

Zander considered that. "So what did you want from me?"

Chen hunched his shoulders. "I don't know. I just need help to finish the antivirus, but I'm afraid to go to anyone I know because the army and IPD are still looking for the data drive I have. Especially after what happened when we went to my friend's apartment. I just didn't know where else to go."

Zander looked nearly as taken aback by that as he had by learning what was on the data drive recovered from Dwayne's apartment. He gave an uncomfortable frown. "Well, I could try to help, but I don't really have much privacy right now."

"Oh." Chen tried to hide his anxiety, though he apparently failed, as Zander gave him a half-grin.

"It's nothing so dramatic. I'm just still living with my folks. I haven't been able to afford to move out."

"Oh. Well, actually, I've been looking for a new roommate."

Zander blinked. "What?"

Chen squirmed, realizing belatedly what he had just said to this person he didn't even know. "I mean, my old roommate moved away. I've been trying to make it work on my own, but I don't think I can manage it with what I'm making." He shrugged. "I don't know, maybe I could keep that place if, you know, you could pitch in." It was no different from putting out an ad for a roommate, he told himself. He didn't know Zander much, but Chen already believed he could trust him. Besides, if he lost the apartment and had to move back home himself, that would only endanger his own family.

Zander shook his head slowly. "Why don't you tell me about this antivirus project first?"

Chen hesitated. "Here? But what about…" He nodded toward the closed curtain, outside which the bouncer stood.

Zander grinned, gesturing over his shoulder. "What, him? He's a professional. We can trust him not to spill." He parted the curtain and glanced out at the bouncer. "Right, deadeye?"

Chen's eyes widened nervously, but the bouncer simply chuckled at Zander. "Whatever, man."

"See? Don't worry about him. Guy like that is handy to have around." He took another sip of his drink.

"So tell me about this Project Requiem."

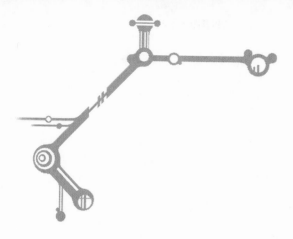

chapter.FIFTEEN

Amélie shuffled sideways through her front door as she supported Zander's weight, Elya holding him up with his other arm. Startled by the commotion, Miso leaped off the sofa and fled into the kitchen. Amélie ignored the cat.

"Ryn, I'm fine," Zander said, trying to pull his arm out of her grip.

"Don't put weight on that leg," she ordered.

"You're fussier than my mother."

Ignoring the comment, she led Zander over to the couch and gently lowered him onto it. He winced as he settled into the cushions, rolling his shoulder into a more comfortable position. Amélie leaned over him and began examining his various wounds. Elya hovered nearby, largely unharmed due to Zander's care that all her weight fell on him.

"Get me a glass of water," Amélie told her. "And there's some ibuprofen over the sink." Elya nodded and scurried into the kitchen. Retrieving a flashlight from the end table next to the sofa, Amélie shined the light into Zander's face. He squinted and she saw that his pupils, no longer dilated by endorphins as they had been in the van, now seemed almost too constricted. Elya returned with a glass of water and held out a bottle of ibuprofen to him.

"It's just a few scrapes," he said as Amélie rubbed her thumb over the dried blood on his chin. Despite his assurances, he seemed glad to take the medicine Elya offered. "It's not a big deal."

Amélie put her hands on her hips and glared at him. "You jumped off a building."

He paused. "Okay, that was kind of a big deal."

Moving down, Amélie touched the shoulder he had favored, feeling for broken bones. Her voice dropped as she asked the question she dreaded. "What happened to Chen?"

Zander sighed and lowered his head onto the back of the couch. "They got him. They took him and all the work he's done on the antivirus." Amélie and Elya exchanged a frown. Elya's cat ears sank despondently.

"We have to get him back."

Amélie shook her head. "First we need to get you patched up." Crouching down, she looked at one bloodied knee. She had staunched the wound in the van, and though it bled less now, she still could see little through his torn jeans.

"Will you wet a cloth for me?" she asked Elya. "A dish towel is fine. They're in the third drawer next to the fridge. And bring me the medi-kit under the sink." Elya scampered out of the room once more as Amélie picked at a frayed string of his jeans around the wound. "I don't think this is as bad as it looks, but you'll have to take off your pants so I can dress the wound." She bit her tongue as she expected him to crack a lewd joke, but to her surprise, none came. He simply murmured in response as he unbuttoned his jeans. She wondered if he was hurt worse than she thought.

Elya returned with a damp dish towel and the medi-kit and Amélie swiftly cleaned and dressed the wounds on his knees, the room silent as she worked. Once finished, she stepped back as he pulled his jeans back on. "Where else does it hurt?"

He flopped back onto the couch, cringing with the sudden motion. He grinned wryly. "Maybe I should give you the list where it doesn't. That one's shorter." Amélie frowned down at him and he chuckled. Unhelpful as the response was, she was relieved he felt well enough to joke.

He turned his palms over. "My hands still sting a bit." Amélie lifted one hand and examined the dried blood covering his palm.

"Well, those have already closed up but this should take the edge off." Reaching into the medi-kit, she spread a soothing lotion onto his hands. "Rub that in." He rubbed his hands together as she replaced the bottle of lotion. "Where else?"

He tapped at his solar plexus. "Right here." Amélie frowned, but simply gestured for him to remove his shirt. Obediently, he shrugged off the work vest he still wore and pulled his shirt over his head. The muscles of his arms, chest and stomach were sharply defined, showing that he maintained his army conditioning. He still sported several bruises from his flight from the police and the fight with the IPD mercenaries and now the center of his chest was badly scraped.

Amélie shook her head, exasperated. "Zander, you're falling apart."

He grinned. "It's been a busy week." Sighing, she leaned forward and touched his chest, feeling his ribs.

She frowned as he winced from the attention. "You may have cracked a rib. You really should go to the hospital to be sure."

"Hell no."

She lowered a level gaze at him but before she could say anything more, there was a knock on her front door. Frowning at Zander, she rose to answer it. Through the peephole, she saw Deadeye and Shad waiting on her door step. She opened the door wide to let them in.

"Hey guys. That was fast."

"Your directions were bang on," Shad remarked as he strode inside.

"We got to the train station just as he was arriving," Deadeye added. Amélie nodded at Squirrel following them inside, a brief pang of uneasiness creeping over her stomach. She hoped Jason wouldn't decide to drop by unannounced.

"Hey, Zan, I was able to..." Shad began, but cut himself off as he stood just inside the living room, trying to hide a smirk.

Zander gave Shad an odd look. "What?"

Amélie couldn't help but grin as she followed Shad's eyes. "You're still blonde."

"Oh." Zander cracked a smile. "What, it's not a good color on me?" Shad snickered as Deadeye rounded the sofa. Zander's gaze unfocused and his hair returned to its usual blood red with locks of black in front.

"You okay, Zander?" Deadeye asked, gazing down at him on the sofa.

"I'll live."

Deadeye turned to Elya. "How 'bout you?" Elya nodded with a

smile.

Zander looked at Shad. "Did you find out where they went?"

"Glen Speck Air Force Base. The trucks were blocking traces but I was able to use traffic cams through the city to track their progress." Zander sucked in a sharp breath as Amélie rubbed lotion onto his chest.

"Sorry." Leaving the skin moist from the lotion, she applied some antibiotic ointment to the scrape under his chin.

"You're sure?" Zander asked Shad intensely, leaning his head back from the attention.

Shad gave him a curious look. "Yeah. Why?"

Zander leaned over his knees as Amélie finally finished her ministrations and stepped back, his tattoo glowing against the couch. "Because the air force wasn't involved with Requiem. They'll have to take him somewhere the people in charge have jurisdiction." A few eyes widened as he stood and replaced his shirt. "And we'll have to get him back on their way."

"Whoa, wait a minute," Amélie cut in.

Deadeye spoke over her. "Hitting an army convoy? You really think we can do that?"

"Army drivers can be tricky business," Squirrel piped in, though his voice was more matter-of-fact than concerned like the others.

Zander shook his head, dismissing their arguments. "This is our only chance to get Chen back. We can't break into a base, our only hope is to get them on the road."

Amélie stepped forward, gazing sharply at him. "Zander, you're in no condition to go chasing after a military convoy driving down the highway!"

He returned her determined look. "You said it's not that serious, right?"

She folded her arms. "You probably didn't break any bones, but I can't be sure you didn't crack a rib and exerting yourself could seriously aggravate your other wounds. I can't allow you to go."

"Let us take care of it," Shad offered placatingly.

Zander shook his head. "I can relax and recover when Chen's safe. You guys are going to need me."

"But…" Amélie attempted.

"Shad, keep a close eye on the security feeds," Zander continued over her, ignoring her protests. "If you find out anything about them leaving, I want to know immediately." Shad nodded and as he turned his head aside, the light of a cybernetic display flashed against his eye. "I don't think it's likely we'll be able to get any updates before they're ready to move Chen, so we should leave now and stake out the base."

Amélie's voice hardened. "Zander, this is a really bad idea. If anything goes wrong…"

"Then it won't make much of a difference anyway," he cut in. "Because we're screwed as it is." He glanced around at everyone. "They've got Chen, his computer and all that's left of Dwayne's work. I'm not abandoning Chen to them and if we don't get at least one of the other things back, then finishing Requiem is hopeless." The room fell silent for a moment as they all contemplated what remained unsaid. If they didn't recover Chen and his work, all their efforts over the past weeks rebuilding Requiem would be for naught and Halcyon might never be stopped.

Finally breaking the silence, Deadeye raised his head. "How soon d'ya think they're gonna move Chen?"

Zander frowned. "From what he's told me about Requiem and how the army handled it, they'll want everything they've got as soon as possible, as secure as possible, and they'll want to keep it under wraps. I doubt they'll take a big convoy, especially considering you don't need much to overpower Chen." He smiled wryly, but there was little humor in it.

"Zander…" Amélie attempted.

"I know," he said softly. "Believe me, I'd sooner not go charging into a raid feeling like this." He didn't look at her, but she could see the weariness he tried to keep hidden. "But we have no idea when they're going to move Chen out and we need to be prepared to catch them before we lose our chance." Amélie frowned but said nothing more. He turned to Elya. "Elya, you should stay behind." Folding her arms, she raised one eyebrow at him in challenge. "Please. This is going to be really dangerous and I'd hate for anything to happen to you." Her gaze darkened and he frowned. "These are the same people who just tried to grab you back at our place. If anything goes wrong…"

She snatched up the phone Amélie offered and typed out a message.

Okay, I'm getting tired of the whole delicate bird treatment. I was living in the slums for weeks, remember? You want me to be a part of this, you ASK me.

Amélie smiled in approval, though Deadeye and Shad looked uncomfortable. Zander shifted. "I didn't mean to undermine your judgment. I just want you to stay safe." Elya typed out another message on the phone.

I'll stay. Just don't decide for me.

He nodded and smiled. "I won't do that again." She looked satisfied and Zander turned. "Shad, can you stay behind too? I want you to keep tabs on the base and make certain no one else finds Elya."

Shad continued gazing unfocused at the wall across the room, fingers working in midair as the display flickered against one eye. "No problem."

Zander turned to Deadeye. "Any chance they can hide out in your club?"

"No need to go that far," Amélie replied first. "There's a library a few blocks away. I don't think anyone would go after her there."

Zander nodded. "That should be fine." He faced Amélie and Deadeye. "We should get moving, try to find somewhere close to the base where we can wait." He laid a hand on Elya's shoulder. "Stay safe. Shad can keep you updated on our status." She nodded.

Turning, Zander led the way out of Amélie's house. "Let's go." Amélie frowned as she watched everyone pass out of her house once more, Elya's cat ears twitching uncertainly before she covered them with a hat. With a sigh, Amélie followed behind Zander, Deadeye and Squirrel, afraid of what they were about to do.

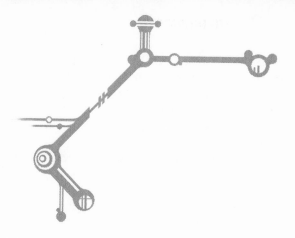

chapter.SIXTEEN

GEROD SHIFTED AS he lied on his stomach at the edge of the roof, his false eye working as he gazed at the complex across the road.

"I'm not saying it's impossible. I just don't see why it's worth the risk."

Galina crouched nearby. She glanced across at the inconspicuous roof-level building, trying not to focus on the enormously empty sky hanging above. She said nothing in response.

He grunted. "Why're we going after this, anyway? They didn't get the girl."

She shifted. "Because Yu's computer has the data he recovered from Gillespie's apartment on it. And right now it's the only lead we have."

As soon as she said it, she regretted it. A grin crawled across Gerod's face, though his focus remained across the road. "Still sore about losing fox-boy in the raid?"

"He managed to lose the army," she snapped in defense. "He's put together a hell of a team."

"He's military," Gerod stated offhandedly.

Galina shot her gaze over to him, wondering how long he had been withholding this observation. "How do you know?"

He made a movement that could have been a shrug. "The way he moves. It gets drilled into you enough times it leaves a hole in your brain the size of a dump truck."

She didn't doubt his assertion. Gerod had boasted of his extensive military record when they first met and the digging she had done afterward had confirmed it, dishonorable discharge notwithstanding. She frowned. It explained a lot. Fox had escaped them before and was the only one to best her as thoroughly as he had to pull Renard out from under her nose.

Turning, she nodded at the military base across the expanse of open air before them. "Can we do it?"

"Well, see, the problem with attacking a military convoy is that they tend to put a lot of soldiers on them." Galina glared at him but before she could spit out a retort he continued, "But it's doable."

"And how do you suppose we can do it?"

Finally turning from the complex, he grinned at her. "We'll just have to be part of the escort."

She avoided looking at anyone straight on, but her eyes focused on Yu as soon as he was brought out. Flanked by two guards, he walked subdued down the row of soldiers leading to the armored truck, shoulders hunched and eyes on the ground in front of his feet. Galina was concerned that Yu would remember her, but the only time she had encountered him before had been weeks ago and their glimpses of each other were brief. Dressed in army fatigues with her hair tucked up under her hat and dark sunglasses covering her eyes, even Gerod had claimed not to recognize her. As Yu was led past her and into the truck, he didn't look at anyone.

Clutching her assault rifle, Galina turned on her heel with the other soldiers and marched into the truck after Yu. Gerod's hasty work on her false military identification was quality and she had encountered few questions as she infiltrated the base. She sat across from Yu inside the truck, his thin wrists handcuffed and eyes on the floor in front of his feet. Out of the corner of her eye, she saw one last soldier climb into the truck, holding a closed black briefcase. Yu's computer was inside.

More orders barked outside the truck as the rear doors slammed shut. Soon, two soldiers climbed into the driver and passenger seats in the cab and the truck roared to life. She braced herself, shifting slightly as the truck rolled forward after a second truck leading the way. The vehicle bounced along the road as it picked up speed, the soldiers inside swaying in time to its movements. She could hear the whine of a helicopter as it lifted off the ground, rising over the truck.

Soon, the ride smoothed out as the truck pulled onto a highway. Light flooded the inside of the truck through the windshield and the small windows embedded into the back doors, real sunlight as they drove along the top level of the city. The drive passed in silence, the dozen soldiers inside the truck like statues in their stillness. Every now and again, Galina heard the helicopter as it drew closer. She sat perfectly still, waiting for her opportunity.

Suddenly, the soldier in the passenger seat turned his head slightly, holding a hand to an earpiece he wore. After a pause, he turned toward the back of the truck. "Sergeant, do you see a blue van behind us?"

A few of the soldiers, having heard the announcement, turned their heads and craned their necks in an attempt to look out the rear windows as one stood to peer outside. Yu looked up, baffled and worried. "What is it? What's going on?"

"Quiet," hissed one of the soldiers sitting next to him.

The headset clipped to Galina's ear came alive with Gerod's voice through an encrypted signal. "It's him, fox-boy." Galina's eyebrow twitched, but she suppressed any other reaction. The tone of Gerod's words was faintly inquisitive, waiting for instruction, but the soldiers in the truck weren't distracted enough to risk talking to him. She could hardly believe Fox's daring.

She realized she hadn't heard the passenger's reply through his own earpiece. Yu gazed around, clearly desperate for answers. As a few more soldiers rose to peer out the windows, she realized that Fox's appearance could be beneficial to her.

Carefully, she reached down, acting as though she was scratching an itch but slipping her hand inside a pocket. As they shifted from a bump on the road, she dropped a vial on the floor, the cap popping off as it hit the bed of the truck and gas silently escaping. She ran her tongue over the fine-mesh filter placed at the back of her throat, a matching one invisibly covering her nose.

The smaller truck leading them switched lanes, decreasing speed to fall back. Galina remained in her seat, though she could discern the truck's movement from the attention of the soldiers watching out the rear windows. Slowly, the truck fell back, moving toward the van.

Gerod's voice came over Galina's headset again. "We're

halfway there. I'm going for it." She tensed. As her attention turned to Yu, she saw his eyes glazed. He swayed in his place, moaning softly.

The passenger turned to glance around the seat at the soldiers gathered around the rear windows. "Sergeant! What's going on back there?"

One of the soldiers answered, "He's trying to direct the van off our tail, sir, but they're not responding." The passenger faced forward again and spoke through his radio, but Galina missed his words as Yu tipped over and collapsed unmoving on the floor.

A soldier sitting beside him leaped to her feet, gazing down at Yu. "Hey!" As soon as she spoke, a soldier looking through the back window tumbled to the floor, his knees buckling beneath him. Galina's eyes began to water and she felt lightheaded from the gas that escaped through the air filters, but she blinked and focused her full attention on staying awake. She stood, donning a stunned expression as more soldiers crumpled to the floor of the van.

"Sir!" she barked, gazing around at the bodies littering the floor. "Something's wrong…" The rest of her words were drowned out by the cracks of artillery shells ripping into the road not a car length in front of the truck. Galina swayed and nearly lost her balance as the driver swore and turned the truck sharply in compensation. The lurch caused one of the soldiers at the back of the truck to lean against the door handle, throwing the back door open. He screamed as he flew out the back of the truck, his voice echoing the squeal of tires from the escort truck spinning off to the side in an attempt to avoid the fallen soldier. More tires shrieked as cars braked abruptly behind the out of control military truck and the second vehicle was soon left far behind. The blue van tailing them swerved from the truck's erratic movements but remained on course ten feet behind them.

"The escort's firing at us!" the driver snapped. Galina struggled to regain her balance. Most of the soldiers in the back of the truck lied unconscious on the floor, a few of them piled on top of each other.

"Sir, orders!" Galina exclaimed, though the passenger was busy trying to communicate with the helicopter flying overhead. At the sound of an engine revving up, she turned.

The blue van sped toward the truck, engine roaring. She took a step backward, eyes wide at the reckless driving. At the last moment, it careened into a sharp turn. As the open cargo door came into view, Fox and the same large, dark-skinned man that had invaded her base leaped through it into the truck. In the confusion, they knocked down two of the remaining five soldiers standing. Before they could advance further, the black man was shot in the leg and a charge from another soldier sent him flying out of the truck. The van's tires squealed as it turned sharply, the black man falling against the corner of the open cargo door. He struggled to maintain his grip on the floor of the van, legs dragging against the asphalt.

Galina tried to move toward Fox, but the remaining soldiers crowded between her and him. The passenger ran up beside her and raised his pistol, waiting for an opening. She hesitated, realizing that only the driver remained in the cab.

Grabbing the passenger's extended wrist, she thrust her palm up against the underside of his elbow. Bone snapped and he yelped from surprise and pain. Before he could recover, she slammed her elbow against his chest, then threw the back of her curled fist up into his face. As he turned away from the blow, she lifted her rifle, thrusting the butt of the gun against the base of his neck.

A soldier in front of her turned in surprise as the passenger crumpled beside her. "Hey!" Not pausing, Galina leaned back and kicked out, knocking the soldier out the back of the truck. The van's tires squealed again as the soldier tumbled along the hard road, cars screeching as they struggled to avoid him.

The last two soldiers were momentarily distracted. Fox punched one hard to the floor and kicked the legs out from under the other. Galina raised her rifle, but Fox snatched the barrel away. She tried to pull it back and found no resistance. The rifle came back to her too easily as he thrust the butt up into her face, snapping her sunglasses in half as they cracked against her forehead. Still gripping the rifle tightly, she was thrown to the floor of the truck from Fox attempting to yank it out of her hands. The broken pieces of the sunglasses fell away and the sunlight pouring through the back door blinded her.

Blinking, she found Fox's eyes enlarged as he glimpsed her. "You!"

His pause allowed the last soldier still standing to drive a fist into Fox's stomach. He coughed and doubled over from the blow, though he still held onto the barrel of Galina's rifle. Swinging her leg around, she kicked him, her boot reaching around his back and pushing him out the door of the truck. He yanked on the barrel of her rifle, but his grip soon released as he fell out.

Galina turned over onto her stomach to find him hanging on to the handle of the open door, his legs swaying in the open air over the road screaming past inches beneath him. His face contorted from pain and she noticed he favored an arm. He tried to swing his legs around, using his body weight to pull the door closed and reach for the opening with his foot, but the speed of the truck was too much to counter and he couldn't get close. The blue van followed at an uncertain distance behind them, Fox already too low to the road for the vehicle to rescue him. Galina rose casually and raised her assault rifle.

A gun cocked behind her. "Hold it right there."

Sighing, she lowered the barrel of the rifle, standing straight. Then, she ducked and spun, throwing her foot into the soldier's stomach. Two shots rang out, the bullets pinging off the gaping door Fox still held on to. Swinging her leg back around, she kicked the back of her heel against the side of the soldier's head. The pistol clattered to the floor of the truck beside the unconscious Yu as the soldier collapsed, leaving her alone in the back of the truck. Turning, she raised her assault rifle and pointed it at Fox once more. He still tried to reach for the step into the truck but a look of resignation was in his face as he gazed at her.

She pulled the trigger. She wasn't certain exactly where the shot hit him, but he immediately lost his grip and tumbled into the road. The van shrieked as it swerved to avoid him. He continued rolling over and over again from the momentum as he disappeared into the distance, the van braking hard in front of him. Lowering her rifle, Galina breathed out a relieved sigh.

Suddenly, screams rang out around her, the soldiers on the floor convulsing and arching their backs. She gazed down in bewilderment, every one of the soldiers awake and howling in pain. The truck lurched to the side as the driver's voice echoed them, the movement nearly throwing her off her feet. She grabbed the closed rear door of the truck before she fell through the open side, the road speeding past two feet below the step into the truck.

Struggling for balance, she made her way to the front of the truck, soldiers coughing up blood as she went. "Gerod!" she shouted through her headset. "We're clear. Let's go, now!"

The driver's head rolled back, eyes open as he stared unseeing at the ceiling. Galina threw the dead man out of the seat and grabbed the wheel as it began swerving toward the concrete barrier. Slipping into the seat, she pressed on the gas pedal, the truck picking up speed again. Once the vehicle was under control, she touched the headset again. "Gerod! Did you hear me? I said…"

She stopped herself short as she looked up through the windshield. Rotors still spinning at maximum speed, the helicopter plummeted toward the road just ahead of the truck. Through the window she could see Gerod sprawled limply over the controls.

Slamming on the brakes, she steered hard around the falling helicopter. The main rotor churned up the asphalt as the helicopter crashed into the road with a jolt heavy enough to shake the van. Pieces of the propeller ricocheted off the side of the truck with a shriek like nails on chalkboard. The cockpit crumpled, windows shattered, and propeller blades snapped and sprayed debris twenty feet into the air. Moments later, it exploded, flames filling up the rear-view mirrors on the truck. As she glanced back through the still gaping door of the truck at the fireball blooming from the wreckage of the helicopter, she saw all the soldiers splayed over the floor of the truck. Of all the bodies covering the floor, only Yu still breathed.

Facing forward again, she shifted gears and pressed the gas pedal harder, speeding off down the highway.

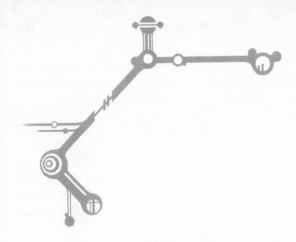

chapter.SEVENTEEN

Five months ago

DWAYNE RAN A hand through his hair as he descended the stairs below street level to the loading platform for the suspension train connected to the underside of the road. The night lamps flared, throwing his shadow down the concrete stairs, and the murmurs of other passengers and traffic on the road above droned.

Suddenly, as he reached the platform at the base of the stairs a voice hissed, "Psst."

He spun, tensing at first and then relaxing as he saw Elya waiting beneath the staircase. "Hey." Reaching out his arms, he pulled her close as she approached. He breathed in the scent of her hair, soft against his cheek, before pulling back to kiss her. "I thought you'd already gone home."

She smiled softly. "They can't keep me away from you that easily."

He sighed as they separated, lacing their fingers together as they waited for the train. "It's really getting bad. Colonel Adelaide is being pressured to cut you out of Requiem completely."

She frowned. "Sinclair has been saying the same thing. He keeps asking me about the project, things he knows are classified. He won't say it, but I think he wants me to spy on you."

He squeezed her hand. "The servers are operational. If we could just capture Halcyon we could finish the antivirus, but it's getting harder and harder to just do my work."

"We can't let Sinclair get his hands on the antivirus. He'll copyright everything about it and sell it for thousands a copy and leave people like us in the dust."

Pulling her closer, Dwayne reached an arm around her. "Well, I agree with Colonel Adelaide there, but Sinclair still controls the engineers who set up the servers and the board is about to lock them out. If we don't get some help soon, I think they're going to shut down the project."

"But you're so close! They wouldn't really kill Project Requiem this close to finishing it, would they?"

"I think so." He ran a hand through his hair uneasily. "The longer we keep working while the contract disputes are going on, the closer we get to something going seriously wrong. Sinclair keeps threatening to file a lawsuit and Adelaide thinks he's already looking for lawyers."

She sighed as the train slid smoothly up to the platform and the doors opened. "We shouldn't have to be part of this. God, we're trying to stop Halcyon. Are they really so self-centered that they'd sabotage that?"

They stepped onto the train, the pale fluorescent lights illuminating advertisements lining the walls. Dwayne shook his head tiredly. "Politics run the world. That's why it took so long for my professor in college to accept my master's thesis."

Elya squeezed his hand as they took seats and the train slid forward. "How much longer would it take for you to finish the antivirus? Without testing it, I mean."

"Depends how hard I work." He gazed distractedly at the floor, leaning against his knees. "If they'd let me put in overtime, I could have it done in a couple months. But at this rate I don't think I have that much time left to work on it."

She paused, glancing out the windows at the darkened buildings rushing past. When she finally spoke, her voice was quiet. "What if we just finished it ourselves?"

Straightening, he blinked at her. "What?"

She gazed seriously at him. "We don't need anyone else to finish programming the antivirus. The servers are already set up to catch Halcyon. We could just finish our work and release it ourselves."

His voice dropped. "Elya, we can't. The contracts, the NDA…"

"Dwayne, you've played by the rules your entire life. Take matters into your own hands for once. For all the work we've put into this project and for everyone who's died from Halcyon."

He glanced away, licking his lips. "It's not that easy. Entry into the lab is restricted now. They wouldn't even let you in the door."

"We could find a way inside. You know how to get in there. Besides, I'd only need to get in there once so you can test the antivirus."

"That's not true. I can't take any piece of the antivirus out of the lab. I can't connect a data drive to the computers, I can't transmit it. The only way to get it onto your software is to bring you in and then we'd have to go back later to test it." He was making excuses and he knew it.

The look in her eyes made it clear that she knew it as well. "If we released the antivirus, then other people could fix any issues it has. We don't have to test it first."

The conversation was making him increasingly uneasy. Not just from the idea of betraying Adelaide and the board, but because he knew Elya was right. "Sinclair and the army could ruin our lives if we go behind their backs. There's no way we'd be able to do it without being caught."

She laid a hand on his arm. "Think about all the lives we'd save if we did it, though. Isn't that worth any repercussions?"

Dwayne glanced up as the train pulled to a stop at the station nearest his apartment. He didn't rise, and a moment later the doors slid shut and the train continued on its way. He let out a sigh.

"I'll think about it."

She smiled. "Do." Leaning her head against his shoulder, she stared out the windows of the train once more. "I love the way downtown looks at night. All the lights combine together, so it seems like the whole city is helping you find your way home." Dwayne followed her eyes outside to the spread of glowing windows, headlights from cars and transit vehicles, street lamps, neon signs and pot lights on elevators illuminating the darkness. Near his own home, nighttime bred danger, but here on the third city level, the various lights did exude a warmer atmosphere.

Elya rolled her eyes back to look up at him. "So you want to come back to my place?"

He couldn't help but smile at the thought. "You don't think

Kara will mind?"

She grinned. "She can sit on the balcony and plug her ears. I have to listen to her and her boyfriend of the week often enough."

Wrapping his arm around Elya, Dwayne smiled wider, but it soon faded as he continued looking out the train windows. It was said that no one in the city had not been touched by Halcyon. He had been fortunate so far, but some of his friends had lost people close to them and he had attended a few funerals in his time. He also thought of Colonel Adelaide, who had lost both her son and her husband because of the virus. The thought of what could happen to him and Elya if they completed and released the antivirus themselves, defying both the army and IPD, sent a shiver down his spine.

But isn't it worth it if we can stop people from losing loved ones?

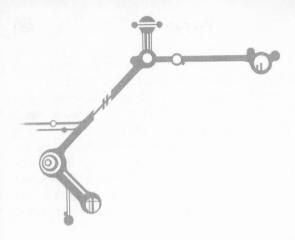

chapter.EIGHTEEN

"THIS IS IT?" Sinclair slapped the back of his hand against the briefcase. "You lose Elya, you report success and all you bring me is this?" His eyes were narrowed and his face flushed with anger.

Galina stood in the middle of the rich office on a Persian rug over a hardwood floor, unmoved with her hands folded behind her back. "That computer contains all of the research for Project Requiem, including more information about the antivirus than—"

"I don't care about the antivirus!" He slammed his hands on his huge mahogany desk. "I wanted Elya! That little stunt of yours was all over the six o'clock news. How many people saw you, and if they trace you back to me..."

"Everyone who saw me is dead." Her eyes narrowed. "As well as my partner."

Sinclair leaned back with a sarcastic frown. "What do you want, a sympathy card? You took on this job, you promised me you would find Elya and all you bring me is a tablet and some loser kid?"

Galina's voice took on an edge. "Chen Yu—"

"Is not Dwayne Gillespie!" Sinclair cut in. "And a computer is not Elya Renard! How damn hard is it to find one stupid girl? I have hired private detectives, corporate spies and you, and all of you have been too incompetent to do what I paid you to."

She clenched her teeth, biting back a retort about how so many unsuccessful attempts must be due to Renard's skill, rather than their lack of it. "With all due respect, Mr. Sinclair, you could finish the antivirus yourself and make millions selling it."

"Hundreds of millions, more likely." He leaned over the desk, glowering at her. "If it wasn't violating a slew of intellectual property laws. The government owns it and any revenue from it unless I can successfully sue for the rights, but I don't have a strong enough case without Elya. My company poured millions of dollars in technology into Project Requiem. I have worked tirelessly to make this company successful and I will not let the army walk away with my property." Throwing the tablet computer back into the briefcase, he slammed the leather cover shut.

Galina raised her chin. "I need only a little more time to recover the girl. A week at most. They're on the run now and I—"

"No," Sinclair snapped, cutting her off. He huffed, his jowls quivering as he stared her down. "I put a lot of money out for you and you've consistently failed me. I'm tired of your mistakes. You're off the job."

She stepped forward. "We had an agreement."

He tapped at a display on his desk, the symbol he touched glowing red. "Don't come any closer." She stopped. The coldness in his eyes was implacable. "Our deal was for you to bring me Elya. I already gave you your advance and it's more than you deserve for your failures. I suppose that money is gone now, but you won't be costing my company anything more."

Galina stood still as footfalls entered the room. Guns cocked and stun guns powered up behind her. She narrowed her eyes at Sinclair.

His expression never changed. "Make sure she's never found." Footsteps approached across the room.

Lunging to the side, Galina drew her pistol and fired, two bullets shattering the lights above her. The room went dark as sparks flew out of the light fixture, only a few indicator lights breaking through the black. Scrambling sounds rang out as Galina ducked behind a wide bookcase, the guards stumbling over the carpet where she had just been.

"Find her!" Sinclair snapped. "Do not let her escape!"

Galina darted around the bookcase toward the door as one of the guards ordered the others into silence. A light flared out from the palm of one of the guards, but as soon as it illuminated her she grabbed his extended arm and yanked him down, driving her knee into his gut. The light faded as the guard coughed and she threw him against the guards beside her. Spinning, she kicked up, her boot smashing against a guard approaching from her other side. Before they could recover, she bolted for the door, glad for Sinclair's extravagance as the Persian rug muffled her footsteps.

Light poured into the room as she threw open the door into the hallway. Sinclair's voice rang over a radio attached to the belt of a guard down the hall.

"Stop her! Don't let her get away!"

The guard began to raise his gun, but Galina was upon him before he could fire. She threw a flat hand against his sternum, then slammed her other hand against his forehead, smashing the back of his head against the wall behind him. Leaving him as he crumpled to the ground, she continued fleeing down the hall, pounding footsteps following behind her. She turned a corner, then swung her gun back and fired multiple shots as the guards from Sinclair's office chased after her. Yelps sounded as they struggled to retreat behind the wall. They didn't emerge before she turned the next corner.

Ahead, she found a heavy metal door opening onto the roof. She flung the door open, the deep night sky looming large overhead and lights from offices, clubs and elaborate rooftop condos glimmering in every direction. Gravel crunched under her feet as she darted over to the edge of the roof and looked down. She could see the visitor's parking lot on street level twenty stories down. Several armed guards hovered around her car.

The door into the building was thrown open and she glanced over her shoulder to find several security guards piling onto the roof. She raced to the far edge of the rooftop as gunshots ripped through the air in her wake. Reaching the edge of the roof, she leaped.

She aimed her gun down as she fell toward a sky bridge connecting the building to the second IPD tower two stories down. The first bullet pinged off the hardened glass canopy. The second ricocheted as well, and the third. She fell to within ten feet of the sky bridge before two bullets broke through. Quickly, she tensed her legs and crossed her arms over her face.

The canopy shattered as she fell through, shards of glass bouncing off her skin as she hit the floor. She threw herself forward into a roll, the bridge trembling from the force of her impact. Ignoring the bullets that pinged against the canopy overhead or broke off more fragments from the hole she had cut through the glass, she lunged forward and raced into the connecting building.

Her escape from the IPD office towers passed in a daze, gunshots and shouted warnings blaring through silent halls and dark offices. A few janitors or late workers yelped as she darted past them, sporting more bruises and blood stains the closer she got to the exit.

She arrived at the only place she could go forty-five minutes later, bleeding, panting and lightheaded to find the club owner pointing a shotgun at her face.

"Solace," she snarled.

The dark-skinned woman gazed unwaveringly at her, her smooth curtain of coppery hair swaying as she shook her head. "Sorry Galina, but Sinclair's got a hit out on you. Anyone finds out I let you stay here it'll be my life on the line, and my club."

"He betrayed me." Frustration burned in her to find the ferocity in her voice lacking. She was exhausted and alone and her vision began growing hazy from a bullet wound in her shoulder. Spots flared in front of her eyes.

A faint apologetic look glinted in Solace's eyes but she didn't relent. "I'm sure you're right, Galina, but he's a lot more powerful than you are. I can't help you this time. I'm sorry. Now just go."

Trying to hide her weariness, Galina turned and walked away, rage building. It didn't take long to find that Sinclair's goons had overrun the hotel room she and Gerod had rented so recently and even her own apartment was no longer safe. She staggered in desperation through the lower tiers of the city for most of an hour, struggling to remain conscious and on her feet, before she found a clinic where she could pay in cash without giving her name. The whole time she moved through the city and while the surgeon removed the bullet and glass shards and stitched her skin back together, her thoughts focused on revenge, and she thought to the one person who had brought her down, who had consistently bested her and kept her from fulfilling her mission.

As she stepped out of the clinic where she had been patched up, her thoughts focused single-mindedly on Fox. Strolling down the street, she accessed information about recent arrivals in city emergency rooms.

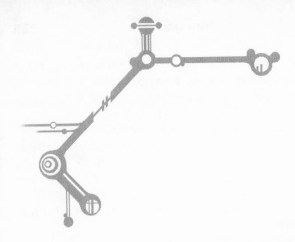

chapter.NINETEEN

Amélie SIGHED AS she stepped through the swinging doors into the hallway, the sterilized walls quiet. Behind her, she heard two other nurses wheel the gurney out, though she didn't turn to watch its progress. She tugged off her blood-stained rubber gloves and tossed them in a biohazard chute as she strolled toward the hospital cafeteria. Reaching into a pocket of her scrubs, she checked the time on her phone. The display indicated that she had a message. She tapped out the keys to watch the message as she stepped into the cafeteria and an image of Deadeye appeared on the screen, a wall in the club where he worked visible behind him.

A notification that she checked the message was sent out and no sooner had the message begun to play than the image changed to a live view of him.

"Ryn, thank God, I've been trying to reach you for an hour."

Amélie retreated into a reclusive corner of the cafeteria and sat down. "I told you I'd call you when I got off work. The hospital monitors every transmission sent through its walls." Her voice was tired and lacked the reprimanding tone she wished she could convey.

"I don't care, I had to know. How is he?"

She sighed, uncomfortable with the memory of Zander lying prone, unconscious and severely injured on the hospital bed. He had been a rock to their ragtag group, always in control and undaunted by anything he faced. She had never seen him looking so frail, so vulnerable. "He's suffered a lot of trauma. The bullet didn't pierce any vital organs and the doctors were able to get all the debris from the road out of him, but it's really touch and go right now. What about you? How are you feeling?"

"Leg still hurts, but nothing some good vodka won't fix."

Amélie found her scolding voice. "You're not supposed to mix alcohol with your painkillers."

"Look, we've got bigger problems right now. Have you watched the news yet?"

She shook her head tiredly. "I've been in the O.R. for the past two hours."

"The number of deaths from Halcyon have spiked. It's getting stronger."

Amélie blinked, weariness melting away under the weight of Deadeye's words. "What?"

"If Zander pulls through, it may be just as well he fell off that truck. The soldiers and the truck were found some miles up the road. Every one of 'em was infected with Halcyon at the same time."

Her eyes widened and her voice fell to a whisper. "What?"

"Shad scanned the transmissions leading up to the crash. He said the server logs were altered so it couldn't be traced, but somethin' locked on to that truck, and the helicopter, too. It specifically searched for a military ID in the cybernetics on board. Halcyon targeted that truck."

A chill stole through Amélie's heart. "What... what should we do?"

"I don' know." For once, Deadeye's voice sounded lost. "I've been tryin' to get a hold of Tiger, but he left me a message sayin' he doesn't have enough of Chen's work to do anything. We've still got Elya here, but without Chen or even Zander..." His voice trailed off.

Amélie laid a hand over her eyes. "I don't know what to do. Everything's falling apart so fast."

She could hear Deadeye shifting over the phone. "Well, d'ya mind if we drop Elya back at your place?"

"Go ahead," she answered, glad to be able to help at least that much. "I told my boyfriend I'd be working late, so nobody should be stopping by."

"Thanks. I'll talk to Shad and see what we can figure out. We'll let you know when we come up with somethin'."

Her exhaustion was clear in her voice. "Thanks. I'll call you when I have any news on Zander." She ended the call and slid the phone away in her pocket. Sighing, she buried her face in her hands.

After a long moment, she pulled her hands away and stood. She began to walk over to the cafeteria counter, but paused as she glimpsed a screen displaying a city news station. The headline flashed underneath the newscaster and her heart skipped a beat.

Eighty-three people had been reported dead from Halcyon that afternoon. Fewer people had fallen in the twenty-four-hour period prior to it.

Amélie shivered. Enough corpses had come through the hospital doors with formatted cybernetics to keep her constantly afraid of being infected, or worse, losing someone close to her. It had taken two years for her to overcome the grief from the death of her last boyfriend and get together with Jason. Even though her relationship with her ex-boyfriend had been far from ideal, she still loved him when he was infected. Knowing that Halcyon was suddenly attacking more people than before left her with a chill she could not shake. And how could it have known to target the army convoy? If the virus knew that Chen's tablet contained the best chance of stopping it, then there was no hope for any of them.

Shuddering, she turned away and ordered a meal from the cafeteria without making eye contact with anyone. She had just grabbed a handful of napkins from a dispenser when she caught a glimpse of the hospital security cameras and froze in her place.

She was inside the hospital, the blonde woman with the blue LED lines on her arm, exactly as Zander and Chen had described. The mercenary for IPD. And in the low resolution security footage, Amélie could see that she strolled out of the ICU.

Dropping her tray, Amélie broke into a run, calling for security as she raced through the halls back toward the intensive care unit. The updates on the search for the mercenary rang through her headset, but all she understood was that the woman was not found. Amélie's mind was too focused on Zander to pay close attention to the security bulletins. Her pace sped as she entered the ICU, terrified at what she might find. Finally, she skidded to a stop in front of Zander's bed and threw open the curtains.

He slept on the bed, partitioned off in the large ICU. Wires from various machines hooked up to connectors on his chest beneath the hospital gown he wore, an IV was taped to the back of his hand where it inserted into a vein, and a nasal cannula hooked over his ears pumped air into his body from an oxygen tank. A number of bandages and stitches were visible on his head and arms and he sported some additional bruises in various shades of black and purple, and a few older wounds that had faded to green.

Amélie darted over to him and checked his life signs. His pulse and breathing were normal. There were no signs that anything had been injected into him or slipped into his mouth and he showed no other wounds. The monitors displayed nothing out of the ordinary. She ran a quick diagnostic on the machines, but nothing had been tampered with. She checked for anything put on the bed or under it, scanned for anything that had been added to the room and looked for anything that had been placed beneath the sheet or beneath Zander. She could find nothing out of place.

Two security guards appeared in the ward. "Ma'am, did she do anything to him?"

Amélie stepped back, baffled. "No. Thank you." Nodding, they walked away, announcing reports on their wrist-mounted radios. She frowned as she glanced around the partition once more, but everything looked normal.

She touched Zander's hand, feeling the fresh bandage against his palm, and walked out, closing the curtains behind her and wondering why the mercenary had come.

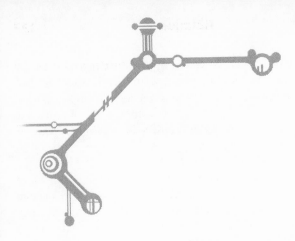

chapter.TWENTY

Six weeks ago

AN OBSCURE MESSAGE board for hackers had brought them to Shadow Morl and Shadow Morl had brought them here. Chen wrung his hands as he stared at the building. With a modern, glass-fronted facade and surrounded by clean and welcoming, if largely commercial buildings, it was a far cry from Dwayne's old neighborhood, though Chen felt no less uncomfortable with his approach.

"Stop doing that," Zander said beside him. "You look suspicious. Just put your hands in your pockets and act like you live here."

"Sorry." He shoved his hands into his pockets, trying to look as though he belonged.

Zander chuckled. "Just relax. That Shadow Mole guy from the message board seemed like he knew his stuff. We shouldn't have any problem getting in here."

"I thought it was Shadow Morl."

He grinned. "Whatever."

Chen fell silent as they approached the entrance to the building. Coming here had seemed like a good idea at the time, since he could find something of use that Zander might dismiss as irrelevant, but now that he actually stood outside what had been Elya's home he felt like he was invading her privacy.

"We'll just tell her roommate the truth," Zander said. "You're Dwayne's friend and you just wanted to see if she still had anything of his. She shouldn't have a problem with that."

What if she does? Chen wondered as they walked inside the glass doors at the front of the building. *Should we have called her first to arrange a meeting?*

He gave the security guard sitting just inside the locked entryway his best casual nod, though Zander didn't even look at her. He simply strode over to the building directory and punched in a code on the keypad, the one Shadow Morl had given them. The doors leading into the lobby clicked. Chen followed as Zander opened the doors, crossed the lobby to the elevators and pressed the elevator call button.

"Which floor was it again?" he asked softly.

Chen watched the digital display over one set of elevator doors count down. "Fourteenth." The elevator chimed and the doors opened. They stepped inside, Zander pressing the button for the fourteenth floor. They rode up in silence as Chen tried to calm himself for their introduction with Elya's roommate.

"Hopefully her stuff hasn't all been cleared out by now," Zander remarked quietly. Chen frowned. He hadn't considered that.

Finally, the elevator chimed again and they stepped out into the hall. Following the signs, they turned to the right and walked down the hall, looking for Elya's apartment number. They turned a corner and saw it ahead down the next hall.

Zander laid a hand on Chen's shoulder. "You're a lousy liar, so just remember, you're telling her the truth." Chen nodded guiltily and Zander laughed. "Relax, man, you'll do fine." He nodded down the hall. Swallowing uneasily, Chen continued alone. It made sense that Zander stay behind since his story was far less persuasive, but Chen still felt uncomfortable approaching Elya's former roommate alone. At the door he raised his hand to knock. Then he paused.

Voices spoke inside.

He hesitated, listening. There were definitely two people within speaking, perhaps three, and he could hear distant shuffling, likely in a room far from the entrance. Leaning close to the door, he could just make out the conversation inside.

"No, she didn't tell me anything. She just said she was going out with her boyfriend." A young woman, sounding distraught.

"She didn't say anything strange to you before then that you dismissed at first?" Another woman, older and with a firmer voice.

"No. We didn't talk much about work."

"This stuff's been moved around." A man's voice, gruff and scratchy.

"That was when the police came through for their investigation."

"Did you get any messages for her?" the other woman asked.

"If people wanted to talk to her, they'd call her cell. I didn't get anything."

There was more shuffling and Chen leaned back, baffled. Other people were here looking for information on Elya? And it wasn't the police? What did that mean?

A hiss down the hall drew his attention. Turning, he found Zander leaning around the corner. He gave Chen a questioning shrug.

Chen tried to answer quietly, though loud enough for Zander to hear. "Someone's here." Zander gave him a curious look, but before he could say anything else, the apartment inside went abruptly quiet. Chen held his breath, not daring to move. Then, footsteps inside approached the door.

Heart pounding, Chen darted back down the hall toward Zander. "They heard me!" he whispered, terrified. Grabbing his arm, Zander led him back down the hall toward the elevators as the door to Elya's old apartment opened.

They stood in front of the elevators by the time the footfalls rounded the corner into the main hall on the fourteenth floor. Zander pulled out his cell phone and checked the time with an impatient look as though nothing was going on, but Chen couldn't help but look. A woman his height strode down the hall. Blonde hair hanging down to her chin in the front and the base of her skull in the back swayed with her purposeful stride. She stared intensely at him as he watched her, a tied-off plastic bag in her hand. He hurriedly turned his gaze to the elevators as she passed behind him, heading for a garbage chute farther down the hall. He listened to her open the chute, toss the bag down and walk back down the hall, turning the corner toward Elya's apartment.

Once the door shut in the distance, Zander said softly, "I guess IPD's looking for her too."

Chen looked to him in surprise, his unease with the woman

momentarily forgotten. "How do you know?"

"Logo on her jacket."

Chen hadn't noticed a logo on her jacket and didn't know when Zander had even looked at her. Her gaze had grabbed his attention so firmly that he couldn't even say what color her jacket was.

The elevator chimed and the doors slid silently open. "Come on. If there's anything left to be found here, they'll find it first." Zander's eyes narrowed as the doors shut again. "And I didn't like the looks of that one bit." Chen frowned, as distraught that they wouldn't even get to look in Elya's apartment as he was worried by the people from IPD who were already there.

This time, Zander favored the security guard in the lobby with a nod, though Chen's eyes remained on the floor in front of his feet. They quietly left the building and began walking down the street back toward the suspension train station.

At the next corner, however, Zander nodded across the road at a convenience store on the other side. "Let's cross here, I want to get something to drink."

Chen blinked. "Oh. Okay."

As they stood waiting for the light to change, Zander spoke softly without looking at him. "We're being followed."

Chen drew in a sharp breath. "What?"

Still Zander didn't look at him. "Don't freak out, and don't look back. It's one of the people from Elya's place. We're just going to find out how serious he is about us." The crosswalk light turned white as the lights changed. "Come on." Chen strode after him, unable to believe Zander could be so calm with those people from IPD following them.

He tried not to look around for the person following them as Zander bought a bottled soda from the convenience store, though now it felt as though everyone stared at them. He was afraid to turn his back on anyone.

"We'll go to that mall around the corner and then split up."

Chen shot him a terrified glance.

Zander grinned wryly at him. "Will you quit looking like a tortured puppy? Everything'll be fine." He took a sip of his drink as they walked out of the convenience store and approached a shopping mall a few doors down. "It'll look less suspicious if we split up and he'll have to pick one of us to follow." He grinned again at Chen. "Although you're hardly acting inconspicuous, I'm clearly the bigger threat. Just take your time, exit out a different door, and head to the train. Take a circuitous route back home if you think you're still being followed. Okay?"

"Ah, okay."

Zander clapped him on the shoulder. "Just relax. You'll be fine."

Despite Zander's assurances, Chen couldn't help but feel nervous as he turned a different direction inside the mall. He tried to surreptitiously study the people around him, looking for the one that had followed them from Elya's apartment, but he had no idea who it was. Zander had not dared to look at their pursuer straight on, so his description was vague.

He wandered the mall, browsing through a few stores that would normally interest him, but he didn't even see any of the merchandise he looked at. He simply counted down the minutes, waiting until an unsuspecting amount of time passed before leaving. It seemed to take forever.

At last, he left the mall, not hurrying as he walked down the street toward the nearest train station. He began to relax since he hadn't noticed anyone who specifically seemed to be following him. His thoughts shifted to his latest freelance programming job and how he would set up the database requested by the client as he passed by an alley leading to a loading dock for one of the buildings beside him.

Suddenly, someone grabbed his shoulder and yanked him into the alley. He had barely inhaled before he found a large knife pressed up against his throat, a muscular arm holding him around the shoulders with a grip like steel. Chen twisted his head to gaze up at his attacker.

Big guy, light hair, some implant over his ear. Jeans and a leather jacket with the Firefly Security logo. It was undoubtedly the other person who had been in Elya's apartment. His swarthy and lined face broke in a grin as Chen met his eyes.

"Hey there, sport. Let's have us a little chat." He pressed the knife harder against Chen's neck. "Quiet-like." Chen screwed his eyes shut, not daring to make a sound. The large man half dragged him deeper into the darkness of the alley, none of the lights on the sides of the buildings surrounding it turned on. "So you're looking for Renard, are you?"

Chen struggled to keep pace with the man's long stride, wishing someone would notice him. "I-I don't know."

The big man laughed harshly. "You were trying to snoop

around her apartment and you don't know? Come on, buddy, you can do better than that. You show up at her apartment and now I know you're the guy who broke into what's-his-name's place and made off with something. There's no denying either of those facts, so let's try this again. Who are you and what's your angle?"

Chen swallowed, the man pulling him farther away from the safety of the street and into the premature twilight cast by the buildings to either side. *Should I lie?* He knew he was a bad liar, but it would only make things worse to tell the truth. As he tried and failed to come up with an explanation that would suit his appearances at both Elya's and Dwayne's apartments, he began to understand how far he was in over his head.

The knife pressed against his throat again. "What, are your ears as bad as your eyes? I said…"

Chen had barely registered the rattle of the broken lamp post overhead when someone slammed into his attacker, throwing both of them to the ground. Spinning onto his side, he found Zander crouched just in front of him.

"Run!"

He needed no further urging. Chen threw himself to his feet to race out of the alley. Before he had moved two paces, however, his attacker grabbed him by the ankle, wrenching his foot out from under him. He yelped as his foot twisted awkwardly and the loss of balance made him tumble back to the ground. The large man reached for him, but Zander stepped between them, kicking at his arm. The large man blocked the blow and flipped onto his feet to retaliate. Chen scooted back, his ankle throbbing, as Zander engaged the large man once more.

"I said go!"

Leaving them, Chen stumbled to his feet and scrambled back toward the street as fast as he could manage. When he tried to put weight on the twisted ankle, pain lanced up his leg and made his eyes water. He limped down the alley, supporting himself along the wall with one hand, as the sounds of fighting rang out behind him.

The moment he turned the corner out of the alley, he ran into someone and fell back to the pavement with a yelp. He moaned in pain as his injured ankle hit the ground beneath him.

"Oh my gosh!" said the person he had struck. It was a woman with auburn hair that just reached the base of her neck. She crouched before him. "I'm so sorry! Are you okay?"

He could still hear the punches and kicks down the darkened alley, too close for comfort. He winced as he tried to rise on his good leg. "I have to get out of here."

"Don't get up, let me see your ankle." She reached down for his hurt leg.

"I have to get out of here!"

"It's okay, I'm a nurse." She pushed him back to the ground, then began examining his ankle. The fight down the alley still terrified him, but he allowed her to gently prod his foot, testing the injury. "Well, I don't think it's broken, but you should get it X-rayed before you do anything else."

He looked up to thank her and then blanched. Over her shoulder, he could see the blonde woman from Elya's apartment approaching down the sidewalk.

"Oh God, oh God." The woman from IPD was already increasing her pace as he tried to scramble to his feet.

"Wait!" said the nurse, grabbing his arm to help him up. "You should get to a hospital."

"I have to run! They're after me!" His heart pounded as he realized there was no escape. The nurse continued holding onto him as he limped across the alley, approaching the train station once more.

"What? What do you…"

A truck engine drowned out the rest of her words. They both looked over their shoulders and found a semi-trailer turning carefully into the alley, blocking the blonde woman from view. Chen's eyes widened as he realized he finally had a chance to escape.

"I have to go," he said quickly to the nurse, turning and hobbling on as fast as he could. "Thanks for your help."

"Wait! Let me help you." She kept her grip on his arm and matched his pace as he continued down the sidewalk, though a curious expression remained on her face.

There was no train in sight as he neared the station and instead he continued to a city elevator that lowered to its platform half a block farther on. The nurse continued helping him into the elevator and over to a seat along its edge. He stared out the window as the doors closed. Down the block, he could see the truck just pulling into the alley, but the elevator sank beneath the street before he saw any sign of the blonde woman. He let out a breath.

"What was that all about?" the nurse asked quietly.

Chen shivered with the memory of the blonde woman's fierce gaze in the apartment building and the feeling of being grabbed by the large man. He knew Dwayne told him more about Project Requiem than he should have and that both the army and IPD had been very protective about it, but he had never imagined that trying to finish the antivirus would bring him into so much danger. It would likely mean the same for anyone else involved with him.

"I can't say."

She frowned, but didn't press the issue. "Well, you should still get that ankle looked at."

"I... by who?"

"Your family doctor?"

"Oh." He looked away. "I don't have one."

She sighed, glancing out the window before meeting his eyes again. "I can get a lab requisition for you and have one of my doctors look at it."

He glanced up at her hopefully. "You'd do that?"

A tired look crossed her face. "Most family doctors have a pretty big waiting list for new patients and the walk-in clinics don't follow up so well. I'd hate for you to do any permanent damage before it could even be looked at."

The elevator glided to a stop on the second city level. With the nurse's help, he rose to his good foot, keeping the other off the ground as he limped out. The nurse continued supporting him as he made his way toward the nearest train station on this level. There, she gave him her name and phone number.

"If you need anything else, give me a call," Amélie said as she turned to leave him at the train station.

Chen nodded. "Thanks for your help."

She smiled wearily. "Well, that's why I became a nurse in the first place. Take it easy and remember to put that foot up when you get home."

"I will. Thanks."

Zander returned home soon after Chen arrived, sporting a few bruises but little the worse for wear. "You're a disaster," he said with a grin when he saw Chen's swollen ankle, propped up on the couch as he worked on his tablet computer. "What happened?" He listened intently as Chen related the events after they split up to him.

"I got her number," he said of the nurse as he showed the entry on his phone to Zander. "I don't want to bother her again, though. Do you think it looks bad?"

As Zander focused on Chen's cell phone, his eyes turned suddenly dark. "Change the name."

Chen blinked. "What?"

"Change the name on your phone. Use an alias. And we should hide the number somehow. Maybe Shadow Money or that friend of his can write a program to scramble it in the phone logs."

Chen shook his head. "Why?"

Zander straightened with a sigh. "I learned two things today. First, that you're not fit to go on any raids." He shot a pointed look at Chen's ankle. "We're going to need some more muscle.

"And second, that the army and IPD both mean business. Anyone who gets connected to what we're doing is in danger and I can guarantee they'll go after them if they can. So from now on, no more real names. We use aliases and we cover all tracks that can lead to anyone else."

Chen swallowed uncomfortably. "What about us?"

Zander shrugged. "We can use aliases too if you want, but I figure once they pin either of us they've got us both. At least we can keep anyone else from being dragged down with us."

Chen nodded, the weight of Project Requiem suddenly feeling very heavy indeed.

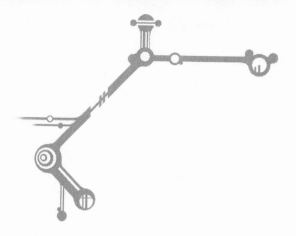

chapter.TWENTYONE

ZANDER AWOKE TO a rhythmic beeping. He blinked blearily, his head pounding and aches rising all over his body. Slowly, he opened his eyes, pale light blinding him. As the world around him came into focus, he found himself in a sterilized room, surrounded by curtains, with machines set up on every side of his bed. He frowned, recognizing it as a hospital immediately. He tried to move but pain surged through his body at his efforts and he lied back down with a hissing breath. He could feel bandages and stitches all over his body and his left side seared with pain.

It was much like how he had lost consciousness in the first place, he reflected. Adrenaline pumping, reflexes highly tuned, his entire being focused on the fight. Chen lying on the floor of the truck. He had not even been afraid when he flew out the back of the truck and knew he had the strength to pull himself back in, until the rifle was pointed at him. In that moment, he knew with complete certainty that he had failed, that he was about to die. Then, nothing but pain and darkness.

And yet, here he was. Still alive and still in pain. And in a hospital. He wasn't certain which was worse.

Twitching his fingers, he found a strange lump in the bandage against his right palm. Wincing, he lifted his left arm and worked the small item out of the top layer of bandage. It was a data drive. He glanced at it curiously for a moment, then connected it to a screen attached to his bed. The diagnostic graphs the screen had displayed disappeared and a map showed instead, with a glowing beacon at an intersection. Next to it was an image of a woman. He narrowed his eyes, recognizing the mercenary that had been aboard the truck, and who had shot him off it. Below the map and the image of the woman was a place to input a date and time.

She wanted to meet with him.

Hearing footsteps approach through the ward, he unplugged the data drive and laid his hand down on the bed, hiding the drive under his palm. The curtains parted and Ryn appeared, dressed in scrubs. She smiled as she glimpsed him and stepped within the partition.

"Welcome back. How are you feeling?"

He frowned softly. "I shouldn't be here."

Turning, she adjusted some of the knobs on the monitors. "You'd be dead right now if you weren't."

His voice dropped. "I know you don't work in a private hospital, and even if you did, how long do you think it'll take before the army gets hold of my ID?"

Ryn turned to him, her voice mild. "I don't know what you're talking about, Mr. Brown." Zander paused, taken aback. "You're Michael Brown, an investment broker from Chancey Park." She leaned against the bed rails as his eyebrows rose in realization. "It'll be weeks before they figure out the paperwork. Trust me, you're safe."

He leaned his head back with a smile. "Thanks." As his gaze dropped, however, the smile disappeared. Her name tag read "Amélie Rissell, R.N." He frowned softly.

She straightened with a sigh. "Look, I know what you think, but we've been working together too long for you to not know my name."

He stared at the ceiling, his voice quiet. "I know it. I know everyone's names."

She blinked in surprise. "What? I thought…"

He gave her a wry grin. "Come on, with the kind of shit IPD's pulled, you think I'd let anyone in without doing some back checking first?"

She stared suspiciously at him. "You mean you…"

"Have been cyber stalking all of you?" he finished for her. "Yeah. I'm sorry I never told you."

"But then why the aliases?"

"To minimize the danger. Chen doesn't even know anything

aside from what you told him." Closing his eyes, he sighed. "I just feel bad that I'm the one most likely to get caught so it'll probably be me dragging you all down."

She shook her head. "I can't speak for the others, but I'm willing to accept the consequences for my actions. I agreed to be part of this and I don't regret that decision."

"But I would if anything happened to you."

She let out an exasperated grunt. "Stubborn as a mule."

He grinned. "I'd probably be dead otherwise."

Her voice softened. "I can't argue with that." She straightened the blanket lying over him.

"How soon can I get out of here?"

"You really shouldn't be in such a hurry to leave. You suffered a lot of injuries."

"And I don't like hospitals. How soon?"

She sighed. "The doctors repaired the tissue pretty well but the stitches will burst if you try to do too much too fast."

He fixed her with his gaze. "How soon?"

Leaning against the bed, she shot him a stern look. "A week. No sooner." He frowned, but nodded. "Everybody's been really worried about you." She grinned. "Elya wouldn't shut up about seeing you, as it were."

He chuckled. "I hope you didn't cave. I know you're a sucker for a pretty face."

Amélie bumped his good shoulder playfully. "Speak for yourself. But no, she's been kept locked tight at my house. I can shuffle around insurance papers to keep you under the radar, but it's a bit harder to hide her from hospital surveillance." He murmured, thinking about how she had kept herself hidden for two months. "So how are you feeling?"

Zander leaned his head back with a sigh. "Like I fell off a truck speeding down the highway."

She chuckled. "Well, you are one lucky man. You almost died."

He shifted. "Got too much to do for that. Did we get Chen back?"

She looked away uncomfortably. "No. Those mercenaries got away with him. And..." She shook her head. "Never mind. I'll tell you later."

His stomach turned over at the look in her eyes. "What is it?" Frowning, she glanced around distractedly. "Ryn... Amélie, tell me."

She glanced up with a start when he used her real name. She sighed. "Halcyon is getting stronger." Zander's eyes widened. "Tiger has been monitoring the infections and he says that there's some trigger that's building with each case. It's… it's nearing a breaking point. He thinks the virus is going to hit the entire city at once, and soon."

Closing his eyes, Zander leaned his head back against the pillow. "And we don't have Chen or his work."

She rubbed her arm uncomfortably. "It's worse than that."

His eyebrows rose. "Worse?"

Her gaze traveled everywhere but at him. "After you fell off the truck, the soldiers on it were infected with Halcyon. All of them." Zander's eyes enlarged. "It knew to attack that truck. Zander… Halcyon is *aware*."

He swallowed uncomfortably, thinking that he was fortunate to end up in a hospital after all. "So if it finds out we're trying to stop it, we're all dead." Amélie only frowned in response. He supposed it was a good sign that they had not all been infected yet if the virus knew about Requiem, but how could they stop it if it had a self-preservation instinct when it had already stayed a step ahead of them, and the rest of the city, for this long? Did it even matter, now that all they had worked for was gone?

"What are we going to do?"

It took him a moment to notice the reluctance in her voice. She didn't want to trouble him with this but she was lost. She was looking to him to make things right, she needed him to know what to do. They all did. Somehow, the thought gave him strength.

"I'll figure something out." She gave him a hopeful look. Shaking his head, he tried to focus on something else. "Is Deadeye alright?"

"He'll be okay." She seemed glad to steer the conversation in a different direction. "I patched him up in the van."

"That's good." Silence fell as Zander considered his options.

Amélie cleared her throat. "Well, you need to get some more rest. Do you need anything else?" She tried to speak authoritatively but Zander could discern the worry and uncertainty in her voice. He shook his head in response, though he immediately regretted it as the world swam before his eyes. "Well, if you need anything, just press the call button. I won't be far. And if the pain gets too intense, this button is your morphine drip." He followed her eyes, thinking that he was going to become intimately familiar with that button. Amélie hesitated, then stepped out into the rest of the ward, sliding the curtains closed behind her.

Once she was gone, Zander opened his eyes and turned his hand up to gaze at the data drive. The mercenaries had stolen all their work and now they wanted to meet with him.

He plugged the data drive back into the screen over his bed. Glancing at the time on one of the monitors, he entered a time and date and touched the "send" button. He leaned his head back on the pillow with a sinking feeling that he had just signed his life away.

He closed his eyes and fell asleep thinking about Chen.

He wasn't used to feeling the wind, aside from the gusts that chased cars down the street. Zander rarely ventured up to sky level, having little to do with those who could afford a view of open air. Many of the buildings surrounding the park still rose above it, but the city had designed it so that no roads crossed overhead. The park seemed feral, the untamed and asymmetrical trees and grass lost in shadow beyond the lamps along the paved path. Lights from the surrounding buildings glowed, but they seemed as far away as the stars hanging above. They were faint and difficult to make out, drowned out as they were by the city lights, but it was an unsettling reminder of his time overseas. Although he could see much farther down in the highlands there than he could here on sky level, the park was reminiscent of the stillness, darkness and wildness of the natural land in Somalia. It was, however, under less surveillance than most other places in the city.

Pain shot up his side as he put his weight on his left leg, the side of his body that had hit the road first. He suppressed all reaction to the discomfort, the ache providing a regular counterpoint to his pace. He knew he was supposed to be using his cane, but he didn't like showing such vulnerability and he was eager to return to normal. It had been a very long and dull week in the hospital and despite the pain surging through his body as he walked, he was relieved that he had been able to bargain an early release from the hospital staff. The open air made him feel alive again.

As he crested a hill along the path, he saw a lone bench thrown into sharp relief from the light of a street lamp mounted on a pole. There the blonde woman stood. The LED lines on her arm were covered by a leather jacket that looked new and the edge of a bandage was visible beneath the strap of her tank top. As soon as she came into view, he wondered what he was doing. Yet, the nagging question of what she wanted remained. She could have killed him in seconds when she sneaked into the hospital while he was recovering from surgery, but instead she offered him amnesty. It would make no sense for her to invite him here only to kill him, and she couldn't have asked him to come so she could demand that he hand over Elya.

Besides, even after a week with little to do but think, he still had no ideas what to do next. Curiosity had won out over common sense and his uncertainty heightened when he noticed that she wore no visible weapon.

Zander scanned the surrounding area, but he couldn't see any other people nearby. He paused halfway down the hill, just close enough so he wouldn't have to yell. "Where's your partner?"

The woman stood still, hands in her pockets. Poised, but not ready to attack. "He's dead."

Zander remained as impassive as her. "Can't say I'm disappointed."

With only the distant drone of traffic murmuring through the air, her voice was stark against the silence in the park. "He wasn't a good man, but he was a good partner."

Zander narrowed his eyes. "You didn't call me out here for my condolences, or my apologies. What do you want?"

She shifted, raising her chin. "I want to make you an offer. Not many people have defeated me as well as you have."

He shot her a hard look. "I seem to recall you got Chen and his computer."

Her expression didn't change. "But not the girl. Despite my best efforts, you took her away from me and you kept her hidden. My employer wasn't happy about that."

"Rough luck for you. You're not seeing her again."

She shook her head. "She's not my concern anymore. I'm no longer on that job."

"So what do you want?"

She gazed him in the eye, sharp even at her distance. "I want you to be my new partner."

He leaned his head back and raised an eyebrow, perplexed. "Are you serious? You shot me off a moving truck and you've been hounding us for over a month. How do you expect me to trust you?"

She remained unmoved. "I was doing my job. I never held anything against you. In fact, I respect that you were able to evade me as long as you did."

Zander shook his head. "Even supposing I was willing to work with you, I'm not a criminal."

"Your current endeavors seem to suggest otherwise."

"We're trying to save lives, not destroy them."

"Your skills are worth a hundred times what you make at a hardware store."

Zander's voice hardened. "Forget it. Maybe you're telling the truth but there's no way I can believe you right now." Turning, he began walking back out the park the way he came.

Her voice rang behind him. "Then let me offer you my services."

He stopped in his tracks, nearly at the top of the hill, and turned. "What?"

"I can help you get your friend, and your data, back."

He blinked, astounded. "You stole our work from us and now you're offering to steal it back?"

She stepped forward a pace, sliding her hands out of her pockets. "Work with me and we can recover it. I already know the layout and security system in the IPD offices."

"So now you're turning on the guy who hired you." Zander shook his head. "Why?"

"Sinclair betrayed me. He held back on my pay and then he tried to kill me, and now he's put a hit out on me. I don't take kindly to that. I'd be glad to help you recover what you lost if it means I can ruin him."

He scowled at her. "And how can I be sure you won't ruin me, too?"

She stepped closer, stopping at the base of the hill. "Gerod was the second partner I've lost to Halcyon. I have nothing to gain by stopping the only people with a real chance at curing it."

He folded his arms. A jolt of pain speared up his arm with the effort and he struggled to steady his voice. "You're still missing the big issue."

She put her hands on her hips as she looked up at him. "Which is?"

"You haven't given me any good reason to trust you."

She tilted her head back. "You need to trust me."

"And why would that be?"

"Because I'm your only chance to get your friend and your data back."

Zander's eyes narrowed as he gazed at her. He knew she spoke the truth and she knew it too.

"I'm offering you a chance for help," she continued. "I'm going to take my revenge on Sinclair whether you choose to accept it or not. But I still need a new partner and I admire your skills."

He looked away, frustrated and conflicted. After a long moment, he stated, "Be here tomorrow night at midnight."

"Are you accepting, then?"

Turning, he began walking away. "You'll know if I show up."

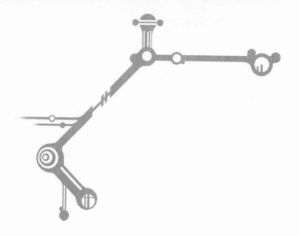

chapter.TWENTYTWO

"Infiltrate IPD's head office?" Shad asked, eyebrows raising incredulously. "That place has enough goons to make the mafia think twice." Elya gave Zander a look that showed she agreed with Shad. All of them stood together in Amélie's living room.

"I have access to layout maps and the security grid," Zander replied.

"IPD does some of the most advanced cybernetics on the market, including police and military," Deadeye said. "You can bet at least some of their own security guards are going to be just as high-tech. And the towers are massive. We don't stand a chance of getting in."

"Besides, you're not in any condition to be doing this at all," Amélie added, clearly looking like she wanted to offer more strongly worded arguments. She shot a pointed look at his cane, leaning abandoned against the wall.

"We can't wait any longer," Zander answered, fixing his gaze on each of them in turn. "The police have no idea where Chen is and they'll never get enough evidence for a search warrant just based on a tip-off from one of us. And the army's not doing a damn thing. We're the only ones who can help him and the only ones who can recover his work on the antivirus. While we've been sitting out here hoping someone else will solve our problems, Chen's been held hostage. I don't care how dangerous it is, I am not going to leave him there one minute longer. He's never done anything to anyone and he doesn't deserve this. I'm sick of the army and IPD thinking they can do whatever they want. I'm going to show them that they picked the wrong guy to mess with. None of you have to come along if you're not comfortable with it, I won't hold it against you, but I'm going in."

Silence fell over the gathered group, everyone stunned at Zander's vehemence. After a long moment, Shad stepped forward, the fiber optic strands in his hair shifting colors steadily. "You're right. We can't let these assholes win. I'm in."

"Me too," said Deadeye.

Amélie sighed, a grim look on her face. "Well, I still don't think you should be pushing yourself this hard, but I agree, Chen needs our help. I'll go too, just as long as you take it easy." Elya nodded in agreement.

"You can count on me, boss," Squirrel said, nonchalant as ever.

Zander inclined his head. "Thanks. I know this is going to be dangerous, probably more so than anything else we've done." He turned. "Elya…" She took a step closer, holding her chin up. He frowned softly. "You know you're just what IPD's looking for."

She narrowed her eyes at him, cat ears folding flat against her head, and all the men in the room squirmed.

"Hell hath no fury," Squirrel remarked wryly.

Zander held up his hands defensively. "I'm not trying to tell you what to do. I just don't know what's going to happen. They've been holding Chen hostage this long and he wasn't even involved with Requiem. If they catch you, you can bet they're not going to let you go."

Amélie offered Elya her phone. Nodding in thanks, Elya took it and typed out a message for Zander.

You're forgetting that you guys are all I have right now. I'm not just going to sit here twiddling my thumbs and worrying. I'm going.

"You're sure about this? A rescue op is hardly your field of expertise."

She raised an eyebrow at him and gestured at the others in the room. A bouncer, a nurse and a computer geek who barely looked old enough to grow facial hair. Zander grinned humorlessly.

"Point taken."

Taking the phone back, Elya tapped out another message.

If you try to leave me behind, I'll just go there on my own.

Zander smiled faintly. "Then I won't stop you. Just as long as you know the risks." Elya nodded.

"So what's the plan?" Deadeye asked.

"We'll meet up outside the IPD offices tonight at twelve thirty," Zander said. "There's bound to be an alley or something around there where we can stake out the place."

"I'm on it," Shad said, a square display winking to life against one eye. "I'll see what else I can find out about the place too, maybe I can get the layout."

Zander nodded at him. "Good. Let us know what you come up with. I have a few things to take care of. I'll meet you guys there tonight."

"Wait, you mean that's it?" Amélie asked. "The biggest raid we've pulled and you're not going to give us a plan?"

Zander hesitated very briefly, though long enough to make Elya suspicious. "We won't have a better idea of how to handle this until we know the layout and security system better. Don't worry, I'll figure something out." He sighed. "In the meantime, I have to find myself a weapon. Shad, keep me posted."

The others nodded as Zander turned to walk out. Elya could only watch as Deadeye, Shad and Squirrel followed him, leaving her and Amélie alone.

Amélie glanced at her. "Well, I guess we should try to get some sleep if we're going to be up at all hours of the night." Turning away from the closed door, Elya nodded. "You can take my bed if you'd like. I'll sleep on the couch. I'm sure Miso would appreciate it, anyway." Elya smiled toward the kitchen, where she could just see the calico's yellow eyes peering out from a chair slid up beneath the table. With a nod, she retreated upstairs.

A neon night and a star field of glowing apartment windows shone against the dark outside the parking garage. Within, the layers of concrete were deserted. Squirrel's blue van sat alone in a parking spot against the outer wall, the front windshield facing the twin towers of the IPD offices down the block. The mood in the van was somber and Elya wasn't the only quiet one inside. Amélie frowned as she sat against the wall of the van, arms folded. In the front passenger seat, Deadeye peered through a pair of binoculars. Shad's fingers twitched in midair, his eyes unfocused as a square display gleamed against his eye again, though Elya began to suspect he was playing a video game rather than researching or hacking anything. Only Squirrel seemed at ease, leaning back in the driver's seat with one arm dangling out the window.

Elya watched the others, anxiety mixing with determination as they prepared to infiltrate the IPD head office. With a layer of makeup darkening her skin, hair spray giving her plaited hair a light tan sheen and her cybernetic cat ears hidden beneath a hat, she was not easily recognizable at first glance, but strolling into the IPD offices would give her no chance to hide. And they all knew that if any of them were caught, IPD would not contact the police to resolve the matter. Chen's continued imprisonment in the offices down the street was proof of that. If they were caught attempting to free him, they were on their own.

Which was why Zander's disappearance had them all on edge.

He had called them on the group connection earlier to confirm the meeting place and time Shad recommended, but half an hour had now passed since their scheduled rendezvous and he had failed to arrive, phone or even answer any calls. At first, they had brushed off concern that anything had happened, but after so long without any word from him, the tension in the van was palpable.

Finally breaking the silence, Shad asked, "Anything yet?"

Deadeye lowered the binoculars and shook his head. "Nobody's there."

Elya leaned forward and gazed out the front windshield of the van. The opening between the railing and the higher floor of the parking garage looked out onto a city street on sky level. Down the street, they could see the imposing IPD office towers. She forced herself to sit back. After waiting for so long, she was anxious to go inside. She narrowed her eyes, annoyed that Zander would put them through this.

"Something must have gone wrong," Amélie said. "He's never late checking in."

Deadeye snorted. "Except when he was being chased by the cops a few weeks ago."

Amélie's frown deepened. "That's exactly my point! Something's happened."

Before Deadeye could respond, Shad's phone chimed with a familiar tune. They all started in surprise. Shad fumbled as he pulled out the phone and answered it. Zander's voice could be heard throughout the van.

"Shad, maps coming your way."

Reaching over, Amélie grabbed Shad's phone and pulled it toward her. "Zander, where the hell are you?"

Zander continued as though she hadn't spoken, his voice ringing through the phone's external speaker. "I'm going to sneak into the security room and try to disable the alarm. You guys go in through the southwest emergency exit on the western tower." Amélie tried to object, but Zander left no lull in his words with which to cut in. "They're holding Chen in a storage room on the sixth floor, sector 7-G."

Shad, still holding onto his phone, tried to pull it closer to reply, but Amélie continued holding it near her. "You can't possibly get through security alone. Let one of us come with you!"

"We need all of you to get Chen out of there," Zander replied, the conviction in his voice dismissing Amélie's objections. "Security's tighter than a duck's ass in there. We'll give you a hole to get in."

Shad snickered uncontrollably, though Amélie yanked the phone over again. "Wait, we? Who's with you?"

"None of you are going to follow me, is that clear?" Zander replied, once again ignoring her objection, though Elya noticed an uncertain note to his voice. "I do not want us falling as a team. If I don't make it back, you leave me behind. Your job is to get Chen out."

Deadeye and Amélie each began to rebuke, but before they could speak, Zander continued, "I'm about to go into the building. Stand by at the southwest street level emergency exit. Squirrel, you stay in the van. Next update will be confirmation that you're clear to enter." Deadeye, Amélie and Shad all shouted warnings but the phone hung up, leaving their voices arguing only with those in the van already. They all fell silent simultaneously. Amélie hissed out a frustrated sigh.

"Well, I guess we better get movin'," Deadeye stated after a moment. Elya exchanged a frown with Amélie and Shad, then they all stood and climbed out of the van.

Quietly, they strode out of the parking garage and down the street to the IPD offices. The wealth of the company was obvious by the land surrounding the building reserved for parking spaces, with even some patches of grass outlining the parking lot. Nearly all of the spaces were empty at this time of night, streetlights shining down on bare asphalt suspended a hundred and fifty stories off the ground. Moving quickly, they veered around to the side of one of the two towers as they entered the grounds of the building. Elya glanced up at the towering glass building they approached. It didn't look familiar.

Soon, they reached the emergency exit door Zander had referred to and sat in wait nearby. Keeping themselves outside of the light of a lamp over the door, they tried to stay unnoticed by the surveillance camera fixed on the exit.

"This is crazy," Amélie said softly. "He should have let one of us go with him." Elya frowned.

Deadeye shifted. "Let's just worry about gettin' Chen outta there. Zander's givin' us a window, we should use it." They all fell quiet again, waiting and wondering.

At last, a click sounded from the emergency exit door and Shad's phone chimed once. Without bothering to answer it, Amélie, Shad, Deadeye and Elya made for the door and sneaked inside.

Amélie glanced down the hall before turning to Shad. "Which way?"

The glowing display flashed against Shad's eye. "Looks like Chen's being held in a storage area for custom implants, sixth floor." He strode forward, the display flickering as the information shifted.

"Good place for 'im," Deadeye remarked dryly as they hurried down the hall toward a flight of stairs. "Those things don't come cheap." Amélie and Elya fell into step behind them, the building uncannily quiet around them. No security could be seen as they strode down the hall.

"This isn't right," Amélie said quietly. "Zander must be completely outnumbered. We have to do something."

Deadeye shook his head. "We need to get Chen first. If we get caught tryin' to save Zander, then we're all up shit creek."

"We can't just abandon him!" She gazed imploringly at Shad. "Shad?"

The younger man held his hands up, looking uncomfortable. "I don't know…"

Deadeye's voice hardened. "Look, if we don't take the opportunity Zander's given us, then all he's doin' is for nothing. I don't wanna leave 'im either, but we may not even get out safely. We get Chen first, then we decide what to do next." Amélie let out a short sigh but said nothing more.

Elya turned as they strode past a short hall. One wall was taken up with a pair of elevator doors and a brass-plated directory listing. She halted, gazing at the directory, and one label caught her eye.

"14th Floor – Research and Development."

Her eyes narrowed as a plan formed in her mind.

"Elya?"

She turned back to the others, a few paces ahead and looking back at her. Shaking her head, she jogged to catch up with them. Silently, they all filed into a stairwell and climbed the stairs to the sixth floor. At the door into the adjoining hall, Deadeye paused, peering through the window.

"Let me take care o' this. We don't wanna start shooting anyone unless it's absolutely necessary." He flattened himself against the wall beside the door. "Stand back." Elya retreated a few stairs down while Amélie and Shad backed away from Deadeye on the landing. Deadeye flung the door open, quickly pulling his arm back as it swung wide and shut again. Silence followed, and after a moment he opened the door again. Listening carefully, Elya could just make out footsteps approaching down the hall inside.

As the stairwell door opened, Deadeye swung his arm around, his forearm slamming into a security guard's neck. Before the guard had time to recover, Deadeye spun around the door and grabbed the side of the guard's head, slamming it into the wall. He gestured to the others as the guard collapsed inside the hall. "Come on! Which way, Shad?"

Elya hesitated as Amélie and Shad crept into the hall after Deadeye, the three of them peering ahead for signs of other security. As the door clicked shut, she hurried up the stairs to the next floor. Seeing no security through the window, she slipped into the hall and made for the nearest elevator. Soon, the door slid open with a chime and she stepped inside and pressed a button. The wood-paneled elevator with dark, reflective glass covering each wall from the waist up stirred her memory. She gazed into her reflection for a long moment, various half-formed faces appearing beside her, and she thought back to the photograph on Chen's desk. In the deep glass of the elevator, her skin looked darker and the image from the photograph began to feel familiar. She recalled the image of Dwayne, the lead engineer for Project

Requiem, the man who had been her boyfriend. She still could not remember him.

Closing her eyes, she shook her head and set the uncertainty aside. The elevator chimed as it rolled to a stop on the fourteenth story. She set her shoulders back as the doors slid open.

An empty hall greeted her, much like the one she had just left behind. She listened carefully, holding the elevator door open, but heard no sign of anyone else nearby.

She stepped into the hall and glanced to either side. Something more had drawn her here besides causing a distraction to allow the others to escape, yet nothing looked familiar. She frowned, annoyed that she effortlessly remembered the layout of the city and complex bioengineering principles, but places that had been so important to her were beyond her grasp. Quietly, she wandered through the halls, gazing at each door she passed by. None had any label more descriptive than a room number and each was flanked by a security card scanner.

Suddenly, a voice crackled out of a radio near the elevators. She darted down the nearest adjoining hall, pressing herself against the wall and falling still. To her relief, the elevator doors opened and a pair of footsteps retreated into it, and as the elevator doors whooshed shut, silence once more fell over the hall. As she glanced around at her surroundings, she found herself in a corridor that ended in pair of heavy doors painted with stenciled letters "Level 5." Her eyes widened as she gazed at the doors.

She recognized them.

Slowly, she approached the doors, half-formed faces appearing in her mind again. She had been here before. As she drew near to the doors, however, she frowned again. Beside the door lay a glowing handprint scanner panel along with another security card reader and a keypad for password entry. Unauthorized access to this room would be sure to alert security, but even if she stole a security card she had no chance to get inside.

No harm in raising a few flags for the security team, anyway.

She laid her hand flat against the handprint scanner and turned to leave. To her surprise, however, a line of text reading "Renard, E" flashed above the scanner and the doors slid open. She blinked, then her eyes narrowed.

So they were expecting me, were they? Well, I'd hate to disappoint.

She stepped inside, glancing all around. The room within was large, encompassing much of the floor space on the fourteenth story. Dozens of screens, desks, work tables, electrical monitors, robotic manipulator arms, sterilized cybernetics tools, surgical equipment and other unrecognizable machinery crowded the room. To her left, a set of double doors opened into a small disinfecting chamber leading into a clean room, visible through a large window set in the wall next to the doors.

As her eyes fell on an inclining table surrounded by machinery and illuminated by bright lights directly overhead like an operating table, an image flitted through her mind, as faint as it was brief. She had lied on that table before, watching as her implants were altered to prepare her for something. Something to do with Project Requiem. A roundish face appeared at the edge of her memory, but she could recall nothing more than a silhouette as he stood out of the blinding glare of the lamps.

She shook her head, the image fading away. A blinking red light caught her eye. Turning, she found the light indicating that a large terminal in the corner was on, though the screen was dark. She approached the terminal, fingering the monitor to bring it out of power-saving mode.

As the screen brightened, a password prompt appeared. The screen looked familiar and she had already entered a sequence of letters and numbers before she realized she had done it. As the screen focused, her eyes widened.

A program icon in the corner was labeled "Requiem."

She opened the program. Computer language appeared on the screen, though the comments at the beginning of the file drew her attention. Her eyes enlarged.

> // Project Requiem: antivirus for Halcyon
> // Written by Dwayne Gillespie
> // Last updated July 13

Scrolling down, she found the code intact, not garbled like what remained on her implants. Stunned, she accessed the program options and scanned it, wondering how Sinclair had been able to obtain a copy of the antivirus that everyone else had lost.

The program was fully operational. Despite the unaltered comments at the beginning of the file, the last modified date had been less than a week ago. Yet it sat here, unused on a restricted terminal, while outside, thousands of people died from Halcyon's increased attacks.

A silent moment passed as she gazed at the antivirus. Hastily, she placed her hand on a spherical implant synchronizer attached to the console and downloaded the antivirus to her own implants. Disconnecting the synchronizer, she logged out and approached the doors, touching a control panel to open them.

A line of security guards stood outside the door, holding stun guns toward her.

She inhaled sharply, then slowly raised her hands, palms out. The guards charged into the room, surrounding her inside of two seconds, and roughly grabbed her arms, twisting them behind her back as they handcuffed her wrists together.

One of the guards holding her arms nodded to another. "Call him."

The second guard pulled out a company cell phone, and Elya could see him enter a password before selecting a number to dial. Two rings sounded through the speaker phone before the call was answered.

"What is it?" The voice on the other end sounded groggy and more than a little annoyed.

The guard holding the phone answered, "I'm sorry to bother you this late, Mr. Sinclair, but we got her. We caught Renard."

Sinclair's voice immediately sounded more alert and very pleased. "Excellent. Take her to my office. I'll be there in fifteen minutes." With that, the connection severed.

A dark look crossed Elya's face as the group of security guards escorted her out of Level Five and back toward the elevators, a few still holding active stun guns in her direction.

Time to see who's been pulling the strings.

As the guards all piled into the elevator, however, she couldn't help but dread the meeting she was about to have. She hoped that her distraction bought Zander, Amélie and the others enough time to escape, because she knew she wasn't going to get the chance to do so.

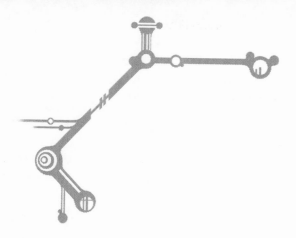

chapter.TWENTYTHREE

PANIC CREPT INTO the city. The people out in the streets and on trains and elevators were restless, distracted and frightened for their lives. All spare emergency personnel had been called in for the endless calls about people falling to Halcyon and tow trucks were in short supply for the increasing number of wrecks littering the roads.

The pain in Zander's side had faded to a dull throb that was easy to ignore as he walked, feeling almost unnoticeable when he stood still, though the recovering bullet wound in his shoulder still ached sorely. Ignoring the pain, he strode into the quiet park, the night sky looming overhead once more.

She had the decency not to gloat. The blonde mercenary stood next to the bench under the street lamp when Zander crested the hill in the park. His eyes narrowed faintly as she turned her head to look at him, her expression stoic.

"Let's go," she stated by way of introduction and turned to walk away.

"Wait." Zander stopped a few paces away from her. "I'm not going in blind. I want all the information you have on the IPD offices."

Turning back, she fixed him with her gaze for a long moment. Finally, she pulled a data drive out of her pocket and tossed it to him. Catching it, he pulled out his phone and hooked the drive up to it. Maps flashed on the small display screen.

"Suspected I'd ask for these?"

"Good partners coordinate their efforts, and knowledge."

Unhooking the drive from his phone, Zander tossed the drive back to her. "I'm not your partner."

Her expression didn't change. "You seem to be tonight."

His eyes narrowed, but he said nothing more. Turning, she began leading the way down the path out of the park. Reluctantly, he fell into step beside her. He examined the maps he had downloaded as they walked.

"I assume you already have a plan."

"My goal is simply to take my revenge on Sinclair. Though I imagine you want a safe way to recover Yu and the data." Her gaze remained focused ahead, never looking at him. "You can take the maps and work on your own if you wish."

Zander turned to shoot her a hard look. "You said you'd help us recover Chen."

She gazed evenly at him. "If you want."

"And what would you do?"

She faced ahead once more. "Keep security busy while your friends try to recover Yu."

He frowned. "You don't seem to have much loyalty for your own proposition. You won't leave me hanging if I ask you to help us get in, will you?"

She stopped in her tracks, staring him down as he turned to face her. "That depends what you want. Are we partners for the night? Are you going to trust my judgment, and I yours, and are you going to help me fulfill my mission, as I'm helping to fulfill yours?" She held out her hand, her eyes sharp, challenging. "I look out for my partners, but I have to know that the person I'm working with is just as dedicated. Tell me you want to work with me and my skills are yours. In return, I expect no less than one hundred percent from you." Gazing fiercely at him, she continued holding out her hand. Zander stared at her for a long moment, considering. Their weeks of history weighed on his mind, not least of which was the bullet wound throbbing in his shoulder. And helping her get back at Sinclair wasn't something he wanted to waste his time or jeopardize his safety on. He thought then of Chen, imprisoned in the IPD offices, alone and helpless while Halcyon tore its way through the city.

Finally, he reached out and shook her hand. She didn't smile, but her eyes seemed to gleam with a satisfied look. Without another word, she turned and continued through the park, Zander striding alongside her.

Out in the deserted parking lot, he recognized the motorcycle her former partner had been driving when he chased Elya on the lowest city level.

"Your partner's really dead, is he?"

She didn't face him. "He was piloting that helicopter." Her voice was even. After falling off the army truck, he had lost all awareness well before the helicopter had crashed, but Amélie told him what happened and Shad had showed him the news footage. The fireball had been a choking cloud of black and red and he hadn't needed the reporter's words to know that no one had survived the crash. After all the trouble the mercenaries had given them, it felt odd to think that the man was dead.

The blonde woman's pants stretched over her legs as she swung over the motorcycle and Zander could see the toned thighs beneath. He remembered seeing her when he and Chen had gone to Elya's apartment. Even from the corner of his eye, her poise, patience and control were clear and he had recognized her as a formidable foe. As she kicked the motorcycle to life, he saw her muscles tremble from the vibration of the engine. Coiled and tensed, ready to strike, like a viper.

Sighing, he climbed onto the back of the motorcycle and gripped the seat underneath him. He wasn't willing to hold on to the mercenary for balance, even though his shoulder flamed from the effort. The machine roared as she gunned the throttle and it sped out of the parking lot. They spoke little on the way to the IPD offices.

Soon, they reached a parking garage adjacent to the IPD office towers and gazed down from the roof at the building. After calling Shad and sending him the layout maps, Zander turned off his phone, cutting off Amélie's objections. Although the mercenary seemed strangely trustworthy, he couldn't be certain of her intentions. If anyone was going to suffer betrayal at her hands, it would be him.

"So how do you propose to get into the building?" he asked, gazing over the concrete railing. "You still have security clearance?"

"Unlikely. I don't think Sinclair is the type to take any chances."

Zander leaned on the railing, giving her a dubious look. "Then what's your plan? Trying to get in through an emergency exit is bound to set off alarms and we could be waiting awhile if we try to sneak in while someone's leaving."

She leaned back, though her gaze remained fixed on the offices before them. "We walk in through the front door." He raised an eyebrow as she turned and opened one of the saddle bags attached to the motorcycle. Reaching in, she pulled out a gray-blue janitor's jumpsuit and held it up to him. "Ever worked a demeaning job?"

He grinned. "Sure. I was a teenager once." He took the jumpsuit from her and shrugged off his jacket.

"I hacked the security system and downloaded profiles of the night workers just before I was locked out."

Zander slipped his arm through one of the jumpsuit's sleeves. "How prudent of you." He caught her cell phone as she tossed it to him.

"Stay in the shadows if you can, Manuel. Your complexion will give you away. I'm assuming you can go fully raven-haired." Zander gazed at the display screen in his hand. A profile and identification photograph was on the screen, showing a man by the name of Manuel de la Garza.

He raised an eyebrow at the screen. "This is the best you've got? I can do black hair but I'd need advance notice for the mustache."

She pulled a second jumpsuit out of the motorcycle's saddle bag. "It's that or you play the old woman." Frowning, Zander accessed his internal hardware and darkened all his hair to jet. He paused as the mercenary shrugged off her jacket. She wore a tank top beneath it, and the LED lines across her upper arm glowed their blue light unhindered.

Zander zipped up his jumpsuit as she stepped into hers. He nodded at the LED lines. "What are those for?"

"They're reminders." She didn't face him. "Each one represents one of the people I've killed throughout my career." He leaned his head back, surprised. Straightening, she slipped her arms through the sleeves. "Yes, I've only killed five people throughout the course of my career. I don't actually like to do it. I avoid it whenever possible."

He frowned. "No new reminder for your partner?"

She zipped up her jumpsuit, her gaze growing dark. "Gerod knew the risks of this line of work from day one." She sobered.

"Though I suppose no one could have expected a mass infection from Halcyon."

He tilted his head aside. "He was military?"

"Career sniper for almost twenty years." She reached into the motorcycle's saddle bag again. "Check the pockets."

He blinked, surprised at the abrupt change of subject. Reaching into the pockets of his jumpsuit, he pulled out a fake mustache wrapped in plastic, thin and dark like the one in the photo of Manuel de la Garza. He raised his gaze to her. "What's your name?"

She turned to him, pausing just briefly with an unreadable expression. "Galina Mollis."

Hesitating, he held a hand out. "I'm Zander Sarkowski." She eyed his hand for a moment, then shook it. "And hey..." He frowned. "Thanks."

Galina looked as if she was about to say something, but she merely tossed him a cap that matched his jumpsuit. "Show's on, Manuel."

"Come on, man!" Zander shouted into the intercom, imitating a Hispanic accent. "It took me an hour to get here on the train, man. I just forgot my pass. Please let me in!"

"Dan," Galina hissed from behind him, hunched over with her face shadowed by curly gray hair pouring out of her hat.

"Come on, Dan," Zander added. "How long you known me?" He hoped he could at least convince the guard to come have a look. No one else stood by the front entrance to the building.

At last, a grumbling came through the intercom before the connection severed and the door clicked. Trying to hide his satisfied smile, Zander opened the door and walked in, Galina following behind him.

The building opened into a large foyer floored in granite. Potted trees stood at each corner and a fountain rose from the center of the room, sculpted of the same granite as the floor, turned off and quiet for the night. A long, polished mahogany desk for reception sat at the far side of the room in front of a suspended staircase and a smaller desk for security lay in the nearest corner to the glass doors leading into the building.

As soon as Zander stepped inside, the security guard seated at the desk stood, flashing Zander and Galina a suspicious look.

"Hey, wait a minute…"

Zander briefly considered charging the guard, but he was far enough away to be able to draw a weapon or alert security before Zander would reach him. He settled for a shrug. "What?"

The guard strode over toward them. "You didn't say Anise was here."

Zander glanced at Galina, trying to keep his fair complexion hidden from the guard. "What about it?"

"You both forgot your passes?" the guard asked skeptically.

Zander tensed as the guard drew close. "Look, what's the big deal?"

The guard drew himself up in front of them. "I don't think…" He cut himself off with a gasp as he looked closely at Zander.

Leaning back, Zander kicked the guard in the stomach. The guard tried to reach for a radio as he doubled over the blow, but Zander stepped forward and slammed his elbow down on the back of the guard's neck. With a grunt, the guard collapsed to the floor, moaning.

"Put him back at the desk," Galina hissed. "If we're lucky, maybe nobody saw that on camera." Grabbing the guard's feet, Zander dragged him back to the security desk and hefted him into the seat, shoulder raging as he did so. "Let's go." She shuffled as she walked toward the elevators. Zander jogged and fell into step beside her.

She straightened as they entered the elevator and punched the button for the eighth floor. "We'll split up when we get there. It'll look less suspicious than if we're together. You take the eastern hall. Just try not to alert too many guards before we get there."

"I'd be more worried about you, Anise," he replied with a smirk. "You don't play a very good hunchbacked old woman."

She shot him a hard look, but after a moment, she grinned faintly. Sobering, she faced the elevator doors. "The main surveillance room is secured. Can you get a badge from one of the guards before we get there?" Zander simply nodded as the elevator rolled to a stop. "Remember," she hissed, "Manuel and Anise don't work this floor normally." He nodded once more as they stepped out of the elevator, letting his dark hair and cap shade his face. Turning right, he strode down the hall without looking back, Galina's shuffling steps sounding behind him.

At the next corner, he began to turn, but stopped himself and veered toward a janitorial closet. He wasn't quick enough to escape detection.

"Hey," came a voice from down the hall. "What are you doing?"

Zander held up his hands, imitating the Hispanic accent again. "Sorry, man. I don't normally work this floor." He glanced up as the security guard began to approach. He was the only visible guard.

"Let me see some ID."

"Oh yeah, it's right here." Zander dug in a pocket, nothing but the wrapper for the fake mustache filling its space. He groaned. "Oh, man, I totally forgot, I left it at home."

The guard's eyes narrowed. "How did you get in the building?"

Zander jabbed a thumb over his shoulder toward the elevators. "Dan let me in." The guard gave him a dubious look. "At the front door."

The guard's skepticism grew. "And he didn't give you a temporary badge?"

Zander shrugged. "I don't know 'bout no temporary badge, man, I just clean the floors."

Grumbling, the guard picked up his radio. "Front desk, did you let a…" He gazed expectantly at Zander.

"Manuel," he offered.

"Did you let a Manuel into the building without issuing a temporary security pass?"

There was a pause.

The guard's voice hardened. "Front desk, respond."

The radio remained silent. The guard glared at Zander.

Zander held up his hands placatingly, suppressing a wince as his shoulder flamed from the movement. "Hey, I don't know, man, he was fine when I saw him."

Grumbling, the guard turned to issue more orders into the radio. Zander's gaze dropped. The guard's security pass dangled off his belt. Reaching forward, he grabbed the badge and slipped it off the guard's belt.

The guard spun as the clip came off his belt. "Hey!"

Zander punched the guard and then swung his elbow back against the guard's face, adrenaline beginning to pump through his body. Moaning, the guard hit the wall and collapsed. Pulling a mop and bucket on wheels out of the janitor's closet, Zander shoved the unconscious guard inside.

Suddenly, sounds of struggle emanated down the hall and

around the corner. Cursing under his breath, Zander grabbed the guard's baton and bolted down the hall, abandoning the mop and bucket. He unzipped his jumpsuit down to his sternum, keeping it over his clothes but providing access to the pistol in his shoulder holster.

Around the corner, he lurched to a sudden stop. Several security guards crowded the hall, teeming as they struggled to get through each other. Zander saw a flash of Galina's blonde hair swinging through the air through some of the uniformed guards, all of them facing away from him.

Stepping forward, he slammed the baton he took down on one standing before him. A guard standing next to him spun as the first crumpled. "Hey!" The second guard barely had time to face Zander before he swung, the baton cracking against the side of the guard's face.

Zander dodged as a recipient of one of Galina's kicks stumbled past him. Seeing Zander, the remaining guards swarmed around them both.

"Whatever happened to stealth?" Zander called out as he struggled to block blows and swing back, keeping his left arm lowered to avoid aggravating his injured shoulder.

"They saw *your* attack on camera," Galina snapped as she kicked the legs out from under a guard.

Zander threw a punch up under the ribs of a guard as he spun to kick another. Endorphins pumped through his body from his implants, masking the growing pain running up the left side of his body. "How did you think I was going to get it?"

Galina recoiled from a punch to the face, but quickly recovered to block the next blow. "Haven't you ever picked pockets?"

Zander slapped a pointing gun out of the way and slammed a flat hand against the wielder's chest. "I told you, crime's not my game."

Galina yanked Zander out of the way of a swing from behind. "Well, it is now." Zander leaped back as two guards converged on him. She tapped his arm. "Throw!" Grabbing her arm with both of his, he swung her around, flinging her toward the remaining guards. His shoulder seared, blinding him with pain from the exertion. Galina kicked out as she swung around to the guards, the force knocking them back several paces. He held on to her as she dropped and regained her balance. "Let's go!" Turning, they raced down the hallway toward the surveillance room. The ruse gone, Galina left her hat with its gray curls behind.

"You're not as strong as you look," she stated, her voice surprised and eyes disbelieving.

"Oh, sorry I failed to impress, someone shot me off a truck speeding down the highway," he snapped back.

"Whine, whine. I was shot too but you don't hear me complaining about it."

Zander shot her a dirty look. The pain in his shoulder faded to a steady throb and his attention returned to the hall they ran through. He swiped his pilfered security badge across the access panel outside the surveillance room. The guards down the hall pulled out their guns as they charged toward them. The doors slid open, another two guards waiting behind it with pistols pointing forward. Zander and Galina dove forward, rolling into the guards' legs and knocking them to the floor. Spinning to his feet, Zander kicked one of them hard in the head as Galina darted toward the interior security panel.

Zander lunged aside as the second guard fired. A bullet seared across his hip. Ignoring the pain, he kicked the gun out of the guard's hands, then brought his foot back against the side of the guard's head, knocking him down.

More bullets ripped across the room. Zander dove behind a console as the doors slid shut and Galina darted beside him. Footsteps rang around the side of the console as Zander pulled his gun out. As soon as the guard appeared, he fired. The guard cried out and stumbled as a bullet hit her leg. Zander prepared to fire again, but as the guard collapsed, her head hit the corner of the console and she fell unmoving to the floor. He cringed at the sight.

"Is that all of them?" Galina hissed. The door rocked from the pounding of the guards outside.

"Almost." Jumping to his feet, he quickly sighted the last guard in the room and fired. Two bullets cracked back toward him, but both missed and the guard crumpled to the floor. Galina stood and moved around the console as Zander pulled his phone out from beneath the jumpsuit. He groaned, feeling warmth seep through his shoulder and the bandage covering it growing moist.

"Damn it, it's bleeding again." Pulling off a loose strip of tape over the bandage, he plastered it tighter against his skin. "You got those exits open?"

"One moment," Galina said calmly as she tapped at the

controls on the console. "There, it's clear."

Zander lifted his phone and pinged Shad. He unzipped and threw off his jumpsuit, tore off the cap and fake mustache, and restored his hair to its usual colors. He cringed as he examined the bullet graze on his leg. It just had to have hit the left side of his body. He felt his heart race as his cybernetics pumped more endorphins through his body.

Looking up, he found Galina had already shed her jumpsuit as well, the blue LED lines on her arm glowing freely. He nodded at the console she faced. "How's everything look?"

"Your friends should have a small window. I've disabled the alarms on the emergency exits, though I need greater clearance to open up secured rooms. I imagine our alert has gone straight to Sinclair, especially if any of those guards recognized me."

Zander strode over to the windows lining the far wall and looked out. "So what now?" Turning, he found her facing him, a focused and very dangerous look on her face.

"Now we find Sinclair."

Zander frowned. Now that he had given Shad, Deadeye, Amélie and Elya an opportunity to get in to the building, he wanted nothing more than to find and help them, but he had promised Galina his assistance. "And do you plan to…" He trailed off as the pounding on the doors suddenly decreased. Through the banging that continued, they could make out thumping footsteps retreating down the hall. "What the…" His eyes were drawn to the console as Galina glanced down at one of the surveillance screens. "What is it?"

She pointed at the screen. "I imagine it has something to do with this." Stepping forward, he glanced at a flashing red icon. It was a special alert that had been triggered on the fourteenth floor.

Zander's eyebrows rose as he gazed at the screen. "R&D?" He knew it wasn't where the others were heading to recover Chen, though he couldn't imagine that anyone else would be breaking into the building at the same time. Had they split up? Why would they go to Research and Development? And why would security decide it was so much more important than Zander and Galina's attack on the security system itself?

Suddenly, a chilling thought stole over him. His eyes widened. "Oh no…"

Elya.

Looking up, he said, "Well, if we have less security to deal with now, then let's get the hell out of here."

Galina pointed to another screen showing the footage from security cameras in the halls outside the surveillance room. A few guards remained at every door, but not as many as there had been a moment earlier. More bodies lay unconscious on the floor than those that tried to fight their way inside. "They must have thought that other alert was very important." She stepped back from the console. "Let's shut this thing off. It won't blind security but it will help keep them occupied."

Glancing around, Zander found an uninterruptible power supply lying on the floor, several power cables connecting it to the machines around them. Pulling his gun out, he shot into the power supply. Sparks flared from every connection as the bullets dented the plastic and all the screens and power indicators in the room went dark. The room became starkly silent as the hum of the consoles faded away and cooling fans winded down to a stop.

Zander checked his clip and stretched out his neck, the doors still rattling from the pounding of guards outside. "Let's go."

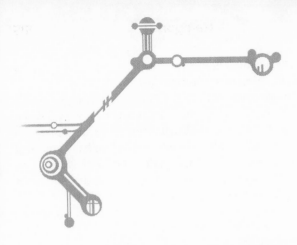

chapter.TWENTYFOUR

AMÉLIE'S HEART RACED as she followed Deadeye and Shad out of the stairwell into a quiet hall. She had rarely gone on raids with the others before and had always stayed on the sidelines, being given tasks out of the main action. Never before had she delved so deep into danger, and never had any of them taken on a mission directly into IPD control. Deadeye seemed quietly focused, but even Shad looked nervous. That didn't surprise her. Still in high school, his role in their group had largely been limited to hacking and surveillance and he had no more experience with this kind of action than she did. Her companions' unease did nothing to allay hers and she wished more of them felt more comfortable with their task.

As she looked back, she jolted to a stop with a surprised noise.

Shad and Deadeye spun quickly from where they stood a few paces ahead. "What is it?" Shad asked.

Amélie stared down the empty hall. "Where's Elya?"

Deadeye cursed.

Amélie began to say something, but then a woman's voice barked out around the corner, "Who's there?" Shad and Deadeye spun and Amélie was torn between staying with them and going back to look for Elya.

A security guard rounded the corner. As she looked at the three of them, her eyes narrowed and she pointed the pistol she held more firmly at them. "Don't move! You're coming with me."

Amélie froze, her heart pounding.

"Look, I don't..." Deadeye attempted.

"Quiet!" the guard said over him. Two more guards approached, also holding guns out. She nodded at one of them. "Get behind them." Deadeye turned to look at Shad and Amélie as the second guard began edging around them. Deadeye pointedly looked down at their feet before his eyes returned to their faces. Amélie gave him a confused look, but before she could do anything more, he turned around and lunged.

Amélie ducked down as Deadeye bodily lifted the guard trying to move around them and threw him against the other two. Two shots rang out, the bullets ricocheting off the ceiling over her head, and she crouched as low to the floor as she could with a yelp. Terror coursed through her as Shad rushed in to join Deadeye, though she couldn't lift her head to look.

Oh God, I'm in so far over my head...

Chen's plight and Zander's determined speech earlier disappeared from her mind as the hall pounded from the fight and she could only wonder what she was doing here. All she wanted to do was stop Halcyon. She wasn't cut out for fighting people or breaking into a high-security building, and the club that Deadeye had given her, hanging from her belt, seemed as useless as a pool noodle in her hands.

"Ryn!"

She raised her head from beneath her arms with a start. Deadeye and Shad stood a few paces ahead, the guards lying unconscious around them. Deadeye waved her toward them. "Come on!" Rising, she loped after them, Elya forgotten as Shad murmured directions and Deadeye took the lead. Closing her eyes for a moment, she inhaled slowly, trying to force calmness through her. Zander was counting on them. Deadeye and Shad needed her support. They were Chen's only hope. Opening her eyes again, she noticed Deadeye favoring the leg that had been shot so recently, and she remembered the sight of Zander in the hospital barely more than a week ago.

They've been through worse, she told herself. *I can do this.*

"He's just up ahead," Shad said.

Deadeye swiped a security pass from one of the guards over the scanner and the doors slid smoothly open. The room that opened before them was large, filled with rows of digitally locked metal and hardened plastic boxes of varying sizes. The air was cool, dry and stale, an environmentally controlled storage room for high-priced cybernetics before they were installed in their buyers. Amélie walked slowly inside, eyes roaming all around as Shad shut and locked the door behind them.

"Jeez," Deadeye stated as he examined the towering piles of crates and cases. "With Halcyon as strong as it is, it's a wonder so many people are still getting custom implants done."

Shad glanced around, though the display screen continued to flash against one of his eyes. "Most of these were probably ordered months in advance. I wonder if less people have been picking 'em up, though."

"Who's there?" barked a voice from the far side of the room. Deadeye hissed something under his breath. He pulled out his gun and gave a quick nod to Shad. Shad retrieved his own gun with an uneasy frown and Amélie slid the club out of her belt. Carefully, they began creeping through the room. They could hear an order being given on the far side of the room, followed by distant footsteps. She followed close behind the others, the rows of crates turning the room into a veritable maze.

Quietly, they made their way toward the back, Shad and Deadeye ready with their guns and Amélie listening carefully for any signs of approach. Her palm began to sweat as she clutched the club tightly. Once, the tone of a radio rang out, but it was soon silenced and they heard little else.

Suddenly, as Deadeye peered around the end of a row at the back of the room, gunshots pierced the air. He lunged back and Amélie jumped, failing to completely swallow a yelp of surprise. Reaching around, Deadeye fired back, then gestured to Shad. Shad took his place at the corner as Deadeye crept down the row to the other side of the room, pausing at the far end. Amélie's gaze flitted between the two, Shad exchanging shots with the security guard while Deadeye waited.

Her attention was on Shad when a cry rang out from the other end of the row, and turning, she found Deadeye taking down another security guard.

"Hamid!" exclaimed the other guard. Shad raced around into the last row of crates at the back of the room and the sounds of punches filled the room. The guard grunted as a pistol clattered to the floor. Amélie ran after Shad to find him struggling to hold off the guard. Rushing forward, she slammed her baton against the guard's head, holding it ready as he collapsed.

"Thanks," Shad breathed, wiping his hands on his jeans, his gun shoved into the waistband. She looked past him down the row of crates. An open space had been cleared along the center of the back wall, and there Chen sat tied to a chair.

"Chen!" she cried, running forward as Deadeye approached from the opposite end of the row.

"Ryn?" Chen's head sprang up, though worry remained etched into his eyes. Deadeye pulled a switchblade knife out of a pocket and began cutting Chen's bonds, Shad trying to untie knots at his ankles.

"Are you okay?" she asked, checking him over.

"My stomach hurts." He winced as he leaned forward.

Amélie's own stomach turned with the look on his face. "Have they been feeding you?"

"Not much." He looked up at her. "Are Zander and Elya okay?"

From the corners of her eyes, she could see Deadeye and Shad exchange a glance. She hesitated, Chen looking hopefully at her.

She had just realized that he didn't know what became of them after the raid on their apartment when the doors on the other side of the room slid open. They all froze as distant voices cut through the air.

"I don't see anything."

"There's no reason the door would've been locked from the inside. Something's going on." The voice rose, his shout ringing off the piles of crates. "Nik! Hamid!"

All four of them looked at each other, and in the distance footsteps began moving through the room.

Deadeye swore under his breath. He pressed the handle of his knife into Amélie's palm. She could barely nod in understanding before he turned and moved silently down the row of crates at a crouch, pulling his pistol out again. Hands trembling, she continued slicing at the ropes. Shad worked at another knot, but his progress was slow as he glanced frequently over his shoulder down the way they had come.

Amélie swallowed as she heard the steps creeping through the piles of crates through the room. More than two pairs of feet approached, though she couldn't tell how many guards converged on them. They had to have seen the others lying in the hall.

Finally, the rope severed, and folding the knife away, she unwound the coils of rope around Chen. Untying the ropes around his legs, Shad helped Chen to his feet. The three of them cringed as the chair creaked and the footsteps approaching them began running. Then, gunshots rang out just around the corner where Deadeye had disappeared.

"Go," Shad uttered, gesturing Amélie and Chen on. He brought up the rear, keeping a careful watch behind them. Taking Chen's arm, Amélie continued as quietly as she could.

"Northwest corner!" one of the guards shouted. "Hurry!" More shots cut through the air and a cry briefly filled the room.

As they reached the end of the row, Deadeye appeared, pistol held at the ready. He jerked his head toward the distant doors before facing forward again. Amélie held Chen's arm to steady him and followed after Deadeye, glancing all around and looking for guards. She felt trapped in the confines of crates and boxes.

A few turns along their path, they encountered another guard. Not close to any connecting rows, Amélie and Chen could only throw themselves to the floor as bullets pinged off crates around them. Deadeye dropped to one knee and fired back. He grunted as a round grazed his arm, but the security guard collapsed.

Glancing over his shoulder, Deadeye started to say, "Y'all…"

Amélie could see another guard appear from a row closer ahead. She opened her mouth to shout a warning, but before she could speak three shots fired off. Deadeye lurched and fell over backward, dreadlocks swaying around his head.

"No!" she cried. Chen only let out a terrified noise.

The guard continued holding his gun out, only a few paces away. "Don't move!" Amélie leaned forward, breathing fast as she stared down at Deadeye. He winced, his dark shirt glistening as wounds in his chest and stomach bloomed blood.

The guard crept forward, one hand pointing his gun and the other holding a radio to his mouth. "Twelve thirty-six to HQ, I've got the intruders in storage room F." He frowned. "HQ, can you hear me?"

Two shots suddenly barked from behind Amélie, but she barely flinched at them. The guard collapsed with a groan. Shad raced up as Amélie crawled over to Deadeye.

Blood dribbled from the corner of Deadeye's mouth. "Fuck, that hurts." His voice was strained.

Tearing a strip off the bottom of her shirt, she pressed it against one of the bullet wounds. "Can you move your feet?" Shad glanced uneasily between the guard he had shot and Deadeye, gun held at the ready.

"Go on," Deadeye coughed out. "We don't want to fall as a team. Remember what Zander said."

"Well, Zander's an idiot," she snapped. "I'm not leaving you."

Footsteps drew near on all sides. "Ryn," Shad uttered, looking uncomfortable.

"Come on." Draping one of Deadeye's arms around her neck, she stood. He clenched his teeth and sucked in a breath.

"Here," he said, holding his gun out to Chen with a trembling hand. "Wouldn't be much help now anyway." Chen reluctantly took it, his hand shaking nearly as much as Deadeye's as he held the gun gingerly. Ahead, Shad fired off a few shots and urged them on. Amélie followed, trying to hurry without jostling Deadeye too much.

She wove through the rows of crates as quickly as she dared, talking softly to Deadeye to try to keep him focused. She knew she shouldn't move him so much, but desperation to get him out of there and to a hospital kept her pushing on. Chen hovered close behind, looking sick and holding Deadeye's gun as he might a live cobra. Shad had taken control effectively, but it was easy to see the fear that drove him. The entire mission seemed to be unraveling around them.

Shots ricocheted off a crate behind them. Amélie pulled Deadeye into the nearest aisle as Chen yelped and followed. "Use it!" Deadeye groaned, growing heavier against Amélie. She glanced over her shoulder in time to see Chen shakily raise the pistol and fire off a few rounds. The shots were erratic and she doubted he could have hit the wall if he had been aiming for it, but it was enough to keep the guard that had approached from drawing closer and gave them time to gain more distance. Straining to haul Deadeye along, Amélie continued in the direction Shad had gone.

Finally, they reached the storage room doors to find Shad waiting for them. To her surprise, the hall outside was empty except for the guards they had encountered on their way in, still lying unconscious on the floor.

"Why aren't there any more?" she asked.

Shad sidestepped down the hall, eyes darting around and gun held out. "I don't want to find out. Come on!" He led the way back to the stairwell they had climbed and held the door as Amélie and Deadeye stumbled through, followed by Chen, who began to sway as he walked. They descended the stairs in silence, Amélie growing increasingly worried about Deadeye and struggling to support his weight. Shad moved nervously, glancing out the window on every floor they passed in search for signs of detection.

A few stories down, Chen stumbled, barely grabbing the railing before he tumbled down the stairs. Deadeye's gun clattered to the stone steps at his feet.

"Chen!" Amélie cried.

His arms trembled as he struggled to pull himself upright. Dark circles accented his eyes and he breathed heavily. She hadn't stopped to consider it, but he was likely malnourished. Clearly he had been let up from the chair occasionally, as he wore unfamiliar clothes and had obviously showered not too long ago, but if he had spent most of his time tied to the chair, the strain of their escape could be too much for him.

She leaned Deadeye forward, speaking to Shad. "Take him back to the van, and hurry. We'll be right behind you." Nodding, he took Deadeye's other arm and half dragged him down the stairs. Amélie's shoulders ached as the pressure was lifted off them. Turning, she helped steady Chen instead.

"Are you okay? Can you walk?"

He nodded, but cringed with the effort. Shad had already carried Deadeye another story down as she draped Chen's arm around her shoulders instead. The weight was much lighter, though it would be enough to take her down if he fell. She took the stairs carefully so he wouldn't lose his footing again.

By the time she reached the second story landing, the door into the first story hall closed and silence filled the stairwell but for their own efforts. Slowly, she made her way down the last flight of stairs, Chen nearly as weak in her arms as Deadeye had been.

At last, they reached the bottom floor. Gratefully stepping off the last of the stairs, she opened the door into the hall back toward the emergency exit where Squirrel waited.

A security guard stood waiting behind the door.

He fired.

She cried out as she fell back, the bullet driving into her side just below her ribs. Chen fell to his knees beside her, shouting her name. The gun continued pointing at them.

"Don't move!"

She pressed her hand over the wound, trying to gather her

strength. It occurred to her belatedly that they had left Deadeye's gun where it had fallen a few stories up, and both of them were too hurt to overpower the guard unarmed.

Then, as her grip shifted, she felt something in her pocket. Deadeye's switchblade.

The gun fixed on Chen. "I said get up!" Chen slowly pulled himself up with his hands on the door handle.

Lunging to her feet, Amélie opened the knife blade and shoved it into the guard's abdomen, deep enough to incapacitate but hopefully not to penetrate the abdominal cavity. He screamed and fell over backward, a shot popping off and hitting the ceiling as he grabbed the protruding handle with his free hand. Abandoning gun, knife and guard, she grabbed Chen's hand and staggered on down the hall, her stomach twisting with every move.

She began to feel lightheaded, her vision fading in and out of focus as she moved down the hall, struggling to support Chen's weight. Another figure appeared around a corner ahead of them. She could only stare hopelessly at the approaching man, unable to make out any other features than the gun in his hand.

As he drew near, however, she found a familiar figure. "Shad?" she uttered.

He raced down the hall, just grabbing her arm before she fell over. Chen swayed beside her.

"It's okay, I've got you," Shad said as he slipped between her and Chen, an arm around her waist.

Pain surged through her as he began leading them toward the emergency exit. Her voice drawled wearily. "Deadeye..."

"He's in the van," he answered. "Take it easy."

The walk out of the hall, across the parking lot, and into the waiting van passed in a haze. She moaned as Shad lowered her to the floor of the van, Deadeye laid out to her side and Chen clutching his stomach as he sat on a bench seat. She faintly heard the engine turning over.

Amélie grabbed Shad's hand before he moved away. "Thanks."

He squeezed her hand in return, attempting to smile. "We are a team, all of us. I couldn't leave you behind."

"Zander," she suddenly stated. "Where's Zander? And Elya?" She caught only a brief glimpse of Shad's uncertain expression before her strength left her.

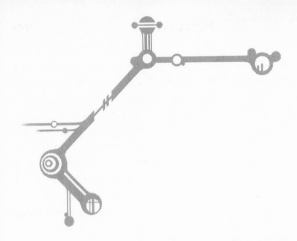

chapter.TWENTYFIVE

IT WAS DEFINITELY an awkward silence. Elya stood in the middle of the large, richly appointed office, not looking at any of the half dozen security guards that loomed around her, shifting where they stood, clearing their throats or just glancing around distractedly. The only one that spoke was the guard who had called Sinclair back to tell him what they knew about the raid on the buildings, and his last conversation ended a few minutes before, leaving an uncomfortable quiet hanging over the group. Elya merely stared out the window encompassing the entire back wall of the office, waiting for Sinclair to arrive. She didn't regret her decision to confront the man who had caused her so much trouble, though this delay didn't make it any easier.

Finally, footsteps approached down the hall and the double doors to the room were thrown open. The guards jumped to attention and Elya turned around. For a moment, the figure was silhouetted by the brighter lights in the hall outside. Then, the half-remembered image in Elya's mind solidified into the real Sinclair, gray-haired, round-faced and smiling darkly as he walked into the room.

And she recognized him. No specific memories came to mind as she looked at him, but anger boiled up at his appearance and she knew it went far deeper than what he had done since she lost her memories. She narrowed her eyes at him.

"Elya," Sinclair said, striding confidently around the guards to stand in front of his large desk. The guards spread out in a line behind her. "I knew you'd come back if I held on to that kid long enough. That's why I reinstated your permissions."

Her hands clenched into fists behind her back at his complete disregard for Chen. All she could think about was the antivirus she found in Level Five, hidden away on their secure systems while so many people died from Halcyon. Had she lost other people close to her in the recent surge of the virus? She could only wonder.

"Did you really think you could just run away after sabotaging everything I put into Requiem?" Sinclair shook his head. Her cybernetic cat ears flattened against her head. "We paid you good money to be a part of that project and you went behind my back to misuse all that equipment. Your little stunt at the lab was a breach of contract and against the law. I don't appreciate being used, Elya."

Her head lowered, glaring at him. *Behind* your *back?* she thought. *You are such a hypocrite.* She could remember little about Project Requiem, but she knew that no remnant of Dwayne's antivirus had survived its dismantling. Yet Sinclair had just that.

"Yes, I know you saw the antivirus in Level Five. It was obvious you and Gillespie were up to something, so the last time your implants were updated here I had a program installed that transmitted any new files you copied onto your implants to the system here." Elya's eyes widened, shocked at the invasion of her privacy. Sinclair leaned back casually, seemingly pleased with her reaction. "Which gave me the antivirus when you two decided to break your contracts. Of course, we can't release it without winning the rights to it from the army, but we need your testimony to make a case against them. So really, the delay is your fault."

She seethed, spitting out words with no voice and infuriated that she couldn't be heard. *How dare you! Trying to pretend like you're playing by the rules when you've committed extortion and kidnapping just this week? Never mind taking files from my implants without my permission. You don't care about a thing but the money. You'd let everyone rot unless you could make a profit otherwise.* Two guards grabbed her arms and pulled her back before she could draw any closer to Sinclair.

He looked annoyed. "Oh, come on, Elya. Sure, people would

be grateful, but charity doesn't hold up in court. Sorry, sweetheart, the world doesn't work that way. I'm not going to risk my company just for some good karma."

Halcyon is killing somebody every five minutes! Don't you care about the risk to your own friends and family? Or did you steal more copies of the antivirus for the people you do care about, leaving everyone else in the dust? The guards' grip tightened as she thrashed against them, her rage increasing.

Sinclair straightened. "Well, I can see my words are wasted on you. No matter. I'll get what I need anyway. Memory-altering implants may be illegal, but if you don't know it's there, no one else will ever find out." Her teeth clenched.

Sinclair nodded at the guards. "Get her out of here." She kicked out ineffectively as the guards turned.

Suddenly, the doors burst open in a rain of gunfire. Inhaling sharply, she tried to duck down underneath the hail of bullets. Guards yelped and cried out as they collapsed around her, blood spraying out from dozens of wounds. She threw herself to the floor as the guard holding her released her to reach for his own pistol, but he was shot down before he could draw the weapon. Within seconds, only Elya and a rattled Sinclair desperately radioing for more security remained standing in the room.

Hesitantly, Elya glanced at the doors into the office. She raised her head with a gasp.

Zander stood at the doors, pistol held out and blood staining his pant leg.

Rising to her feet, she flashed him a welcome smile. His pleased grin disappeared as his gaze rose over her.

"Look out!"

She stopped and spun, but as soon as she glimpsed the gun in Sinclair's hand, a report rang out. She flinched, but it was Sinclair who yelped as the pistol flew out of his hand. Elya turned to face the shooter, standing just inside the room beside Zander. Her eyes enlarged.

Galina stood calmly with her gun held out toward Sinclair.

"It's okay," Zander said, coming up beside Elya. Elya could only glance between Galina and Sinclair as Zander moved behind her. The mercenary caught Elya's gaze from the corner of her eye, her expression unreadable.

"You," Sinclair snarled, standing still beside his desk with his shoulders hunched. Picking up a key from one of the writing guards, Zander unlocked and removed Elya's handcuffs. She sent a quick appreciative look to him as he put his pistol away in its shoulder holster. As his shirt shifted, however, she saw the red-stained bandage on his shoulder, the wound bleeding freshly. She stared at him, concerned, but he merely smiled.

Galina stepped forward, deeper into the room. "I might have been able to overlook your complete disregard for the work and sacrifices that I made for your job. But putting a hit out on me I take personally."

"You failed me!" Sinclair snapped. "The only reason Elya is here now is because she walked in my front door!"

Galina's gaze was implacable as she approached the desk, gun still pointed steadily at Sinclair. "I never told you how long it would take to retrieve her. You're not allowed to arbitrarily assign a cutoff date that was never part of our agreement. And you're certainly not allowed to add a termination clause that involves actual termination. *That's* a breach of contract."

Sinclair's eyes narrowed as he backed away from her. "You attacked me and my employees when you left here."

"*After* you ordered them to kill me, which is a distinction you don't seem to appreciate."

He sneered at her. "Kill me if you can, but inside of thirty seconds this floor's going to be swarming with security. You can't escape."

Galina focused on him intensely. "Oh, I don't intend to kill you, Sinclair. That would be much too easy."

Zander moved Elya toward the doors. "Galina! Come on, while we still have time!"

"My business isn't finished here." The stony calmness in her voice chilled Elya to the bone. Galina reached into a pocket with her free hand and tossed a key ring over her shoulder. "Go ahead." Zander caught the keys, frowning. Her voice hardened. "Go."

Zander turned and began to lead Elya out of the room. Before they walked out the doors, however, a group of security guards turned a corner down the hall and charged toward them. Swearing, Zander slammed the doors shut and locked them. He grabbed a wooden coat tree hanging by the doors, snapped it in half over his knee, and slid the bar through the door handles.

Sinclair laughed. "There's no escape for any of you. They're going to kill you all." His laughter rose as Elya and Zander spun to glare at him.

Suddenly, his laughter cut short with a scream as Galina pulled the trigger. He staggered back, a hand pressed to his shoulder. Blood seeped out between his fingers, staining his sharply tailored suit. Whimpering from pain, he glanced up. He yelped and ducked as Galina fired off four more shots. A large glass pane behind him shattered, wind sweeping into the room and tossing up papers on his desk. Zander grabbed Elya's hand and raced across the room as the security guards banged against the door, the broken coat tree rattling from the effort.

Rounding the desk, Galina kicked Sinclair backward, throwing him to the floor at the edge of the room. He yelped as the night air whipped through his hair. Galina fluidly crouched over him, a knee pressed into his chest, and held her gun outside the window, pointing down at his head. He winced, flinching away from the pistol barrel. Galina fired again. Sinclair yelped as the bullet shot through his hair and the window on the story below shattered. Elya's braid tossed in the wind, strands tearing free and rippling over her face. She glanced down at Sinclair as she and Zander reached the edge of the broken window pane.

Sinclair glared up at all of them. "You'll never get away with this. There are security cameras in every corner. When I show the police what you've done, they'll lock you all away for life!"

"Oh please, you're not going to play that card," Galina remarked. "Not with the testimony of the person who kidnapped an innocent young man for you. One search warrant on your security footage would put an end to your rights."

His eyes widened angrily. "You wouldn't dare. It would ruin you!"

"I hate you just that much, Mr. Sinclair."

"Criminals!" he snapped. "I will personally see to it that you all suffer for this!"

Elya almost pitied him as she looked down on him, so self-absorbed that he still hadn't accepted that the situation was out of his control. She might have, if so many people had not been hurt or died due to his petty posturing or negligence.

Zander slid feet first out the window until he hung by his arms alone. Swinging his lower body, he let go abruptly and dropped into the floor beneath them. Elya barely noticed him leave as she continued gazing at Sinclair.

She kneeled down until her face was inches from his, so close that he could not mistake what she spoke silently to him.

Stay the hell away from me.

"Come on, Elya!" Zander called out from below.

Elya hesitated as she glanced at Galina, crouched over a fuming Sinclair. The mercenary looked up at Elya, her expression still. She held out a hand.

The coat tree holding the doors closed began to crack from the security guards' poundings. Elya gazed down at Sinclair one last time. Thousands of people had died in the past week because the man lying on the floor had refused to offer the antivirus that had already been developed. Now the woman he had hired to recover Elya held a gun to his face. Even without remembering what Sinclair had done with Requiem, knowing only what she had experienced since she lost her memories, she felt a grim satisfaction in seeing him writhe on the floor.

With a nod to Galina, Elya grabbed her hand and stepped out into open air. An enormous expanse of sky spread out before her, the IPD office tower rising higher than many of the other buildings around. Before she had a chance to feel fear from the open space plummeting below her, Zander grabbed her around the waist and lifted her into the room below. He dropped her swiftly to her feet, wincing as he pulled his injured arm away. She gave him another concerned look but he only smiled.

"Let's go," he said, turning to lead her out of the room. They raced around a large conference table stretching across the room and through the doors. "I'm sorry about all this." They passed an entrance to a stairwell on their way down the hall, but they were at least twenty floors above street level and Elya wasn't certain Zander could make it that far down.

Zander pulled out his gun as he pressed the elevator call button. "Get ready to run." She nodded, though she could hear pounding footsteps in the stairwell over the roar of ambient noises in the building. If the elevator was occupied when it arrived, they would more than likely be trapped.

With a pleasant chime, the elevator doors opened. Elya tensed and Zander swung his gun ahead. The doors slid open to an empty car. Releasing a breath, she strode inside after Zander and pressed the button for the first floor.

Elya shifted and heard Zander panting. Turning, she glanced at him. He smiled back at her. Frowning, she leaned forward to examine his shoulder.

He shook his head. "It's nothing. Are you okay?" Smiling, she nodded. She wanted to ask him if he had heard whether the others had been able to recover Chen and what happened with him, but not wanting to mime out her questions, she simply remained quiet as they rode down to street level. It seemed like days had passed since she had last seen him and his presence felt comforting.

Finally, they reached the ground floor and the elevator chimed as the doors slid open. Zander stopped her before they stepped out. Reaching into a pocket, he pulled out his phone and held it just beyond the elevator doors. She could see on the phone's camera that the hall was empty.

He nodded. "All clear." Pocketing his phone, he hurried out into the hall and through the building, Elya following close behind, and soon they escaped through an emergency exit into the night air.

Crossing the parking lot, they had begun to slow their pace when gunshots chipped at the asphalt around their feet. With a groan, Zander started running again, urging Elya along in front of him. He swore as a bullet zipped through his hair just over his ear, Elya echoing him with a gasp as it flew just over her arm. Leaning forward, they pushed themselves faster.

As they rounded the corner of a parking garage next to the IPD towers, the shots finally subsided. She paused, leaning against the wall and panting heavily. Zander looked wild-eyed behind her, almost half of his shirt wet with blood and his jeans stained halfway to the knee. She gave him a worried look.

He smiled faintly. "I'll be fine, don't worry. Let's keep going before they catch up." She squeezed his hand reassuringly and then they ran on. He pulled his cell phone out of its holster as they entered the parking garage and dialed the group connection. "Guys, are you alright?"

Shad's voice came back quickly over the speaker. "Zander! You're okay?"

"I'm fine," Zander responded, his voice hurried and strained as they ran through the parking garage. "Did you get Chen out?"

"Yeah…"

"Great." Zander sounded immensely relieved and seemed to miss the hesitant sound to Shad's voice. Elya sent him a concerned look. "Get out of there now. I've got Elya. We'll meet you guys back at the rendezvous point." Before waiting for a response, he cut the connection and put the phone away. He and

Elya stepped quickly into an elevator and he punched the button for the roof level.

Zander tried to steady his breath as they rode up to the roof. When the doors opened, he darted across the parking garage. The only vehicle on the rooftop was a motorcycle. Elya's eyebrows rose when she recognized the machine.

Pulling Galina's keys out of his pocket, Zander mounted the motorcycle and kicked it to life. Elya slipped on behind him, wrapping her arms around his waist.

Gunning the throttle, they sped over to the ramp down to the lower level and quickly circled down through the quiet parking garage. Elya simply leaned against him, appreciating the warmth of his back as the chilly night air whipped past. When they reached street level, Zander tensed.

"Hang on tight."

Tightening her grip, she chanced a look over his shoulder. Several security guards from IPD crowded the exit from the parking garage. They didn't bother to block the entrance into the garage, but as it was fitted with spikes protruding inward, she supposed it made little difference. Zander sped the motorcycle up as they approached the exit, not wavering from his path even as gunshots pinged off the motorcycle frame. The security guards shuffled uneasily as Zander drove straight toward them, apparently unconcerned about running them down. Elya squeezed her legs around the motorcycle, preparing for an impact.

At the last moment, the guards lunged out of the way with yelps, and Zander tore through the exit, the striped wooden bar blocking the exit smashing as he barreled through. Elya continued holding on as he turned onto the street and sped away from the parking garage, more shots following after them.

Finally, as they began to rejoin the city traffic still passing through the streets, the danger and pursuit ceased, and Elya began to relax. As the sense of danger diminished, however, she focused on their surroundings and found they were moving fast. Too fast. She tried to lean to the side to look at Zander, but she couldn't see his face from where she sat.

At a stoplight, Zander glanced over his shoulder at her. In that moment, she saw the wild look in his eyes, and she inhaled sharply. His pupils were dilated, eyes enlarged with an almost crazed look to them, yet she could see the bloodshot whites and read the exhaustion in his features. She leaned back on the seat, startled.

"Sorry," he said, his voice too deep and faintly raspy. "I'm pretty much running on nothing but endorphins. I'm going to crash, and hard, and I just want to be sure we get there before then." Elya frowned worriedly, leaning forward again. "You okay?" She nodded. He flashed her an encouraging smile, surprisingly warm. Facing forward again, they drove on through the city.

After a stretch of silent driving, a strange tone suddenly came out of his phone. Her eyes widened as he swore at the sound. He turned the motorcycle off onto the next side street and pulled up to a curb.

"That's the emergency ring," he explained as he stretched a foot out, leaning against the curb. He slid the phone out of its holster and glanced at the display screen. He blinked curiously. "It's Tiger." Answering the phone, he held it up to his ear. "Tiger, what's up?"

Elya could just hear the high-pitched, panicky voice coming through the receiver. "Zander, you gotta help me. I finished analyzing the data you sent me, but people are really freaking out over here. Please get me out of here, I'm afraid someone's going to break into my house and steal my food or something."

"Okay, okay," Zander answered quickly. "We'll be there as soon as we can, just hang tight."

"Thank you, thank you so much."

"See you soon." Hanging up, Zander quickly dialed another number, and Elya recognized Squirrel's voice greeting him on the other end. "Squirrel, change of plans. Head over to Tiger's place, pronto."

"Sure thing, boss."

Zander ended the call and began to put the phone away, but paused as he glanced at the screen. Looking over his shoulder, Elya could see the display saying that he had a new text message just as he opened it.

The message was brief: *Call me ASAP.* The sender was "Mom."

A chill settled over Elya at the haunted look on Zander's face. Without a word, he turned off the phone and put it away. Gunning the throttle again, they sped off down the street.

When they arrived at Tiger's apartment, they found him lying dead on the floor.

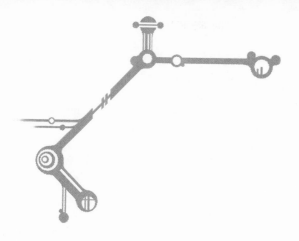

chapter.TWENTYSIX

Two months ago

DWAYNE GLANCED AROUND as he strode out a side door of the office building. His heart raced, but he forced himself to exude nonchalance. He walked down the path beside the building back toward the street and approached a deli down the block.

Halfway there, he paused to wait for the light to change at a crosswalk and glanced at the people crossing back and forth the other way. A few stopped near him to cross when the light changed. One figure stood only a pace away, dressed in an overcoat and a men's flat cap. He couldn't help but favor her with a smile and small nod.

The crosswalk light turned and they and the other people crossed the street. The woman fell a few paces behind, but followed after him into the deli. After Dwayne ordered, he retreated to a table in a quiet corner where she sat.

Elya smiled gratefully as he handed her a sandwich and drink, but she didn't remove her hat. The cat ears were too obvious. "Any problems?"

He sat down across from her with his own sandwich and cup of soup. "I don't think so. The place is dead these days and someone has to monitor the servers with all the engineers from IPD gone. Security barely even notices me anymore."

Nodding, she took a sip of her drink. "Are you sure you're

ready for this?"

He grinned wryly. "I'm ready for this. I'm not ready for the repercussions of it. But you're right. We can't just keep letting people die when we have an antivirus now." He sipped at his soup. "Contracts be damned."

"Whatever happens, you can tell them that this was my fault. My idea."

He chuckled. "I can't pretend like I don't know what I'm doing right now. And I won't let you take the fall for this, anyway, even if they bought it." Reaching out, he laid his hand on hers. "We're a team. I love you, Elya."

A smile spread across her face. "I love you too, Dwayne." She raised his hand to her lips and kissed it. "No regrets."

He nodded. "No regrets." He stood, her hand in his, and she rose to her feet beside him. Leaving their half-eaten meals behind, they left the deli and approached the army offices again. Elya tried to keep in the shadows as Dwayne swung around to the side of the building.

He couldn't help feeling nervous as he flashed his security badge over the scanner and opened the side door for Elya to go inside. She was right about one thing, he had never gone against the rules and breaching a secure building belonging to the army would stay with him the rest of his life. There was no other way to do it, however. The terminals where he had spent the last year and a half working allowed no connection to leave these walls, nor did they allow any external data drives to be plugged in. The only way they could get a copy of his work outside was to install it on someone's implants, and only Elya had the connections required to hook up to the lab's computers.

Silently, they climbed the stairs, not meeting anyone along their way. As they reached their floor, Dwayne quickly looked out into the hall before ushering Elya in and taking a quiet path to the lab. Using his pass to open the door, he hurried Elya inside.

The lab was noticeably warmer and louder than the hall outside. Most of the room was filled with racks of servers, fronted by a workstation with a keyboard and dual screen setup. He and Elya strode over to the workstation and he powered up a wireless implant synchronizer.

"Go ahead and hook yourself up," he said, turning toward his own desk. "I'll get the antivirus ready to transfer."

Elya laid her hand over the synchronizer and looked at the

screens flaring to life as the station recognized the connection.

He sat down at his desk, fingering his computer out of power-saving mode. He tapped out a few commands on the screen. "There, it's transferring over." Rising, he crossed to the workstation where Elya waited. "Installing it now." Silently, they watched the progress bar on the screen as the antivirus was installed in her cybernetics. After a moment, the window changed to a message reading, "Complete."

"There, got it," Dwayne said breathlessly. He began to disconnect the wireless synchronizer from the workstation. "Now let's get the hell—"

The system chimed, cutting off the rest of his words.

Dwayne and Elya exchanged a glance before he enlarged the error message on screen. His eyes widened. "It's Halcyon. It's infecting one of the ghosts."

"Oh my God." She laid her free hand on his shoulder. "We can test the antivirus. Dwayne, if it works, we don't have to worry about finding a way to transmit it throughout the city. We could send it out right now!"

He glanced at the screen uneasily as Halcyon tried to shut down the simulated cybernetics of the workstation. "I don't know. It wouldn't be a very complete beta test, and if something went wrong…"

"Then we're screwed anyway. And wouldn't an imperfect antivirus be better than none at all?"

A progress bar on the screen showed the program's efforts to capture a copy of the virus. It was nearly done.

"You're right. I'm just going to…"

Suddenly, the system flashed several error messages at once and emitted a number of warning sounds. The messages flashed too quickly for Dwayne to read. All he could determine was that Halcyon was scanning the system far more thoroughly than he had expected. It wasn't merely scanning the emulated cybernetics of the single ghost person it infected, it delved into the root system software.

"What the…"

Elya then let out a strangled cry and lurched in place.

"Elya!"

Dwayne reached for her, staggering as she struggled to keep her balance. She pulled the synchronizer off the desk as she stumbled backward, the white dome hanging from her palm where it was still connected. Eyeing the device, he spun around to face the workstation and reached out to disconnect the synchronizer.

His hand was a fraction of an inch from the icon on the screen when a jolt shot through his heart. His entire body went numb for a moment and his hand dropped away from the screen. Then, his heart began beating erratically, too fast and too hard. He struggled to breathe as he could feel his other implants giving out sporadically.

His eyes widened as he realized what was happening. After infecting the artificial implants, Halcyon had gone on to infect both Elya and him. No two infections had ever occurred less than an hour apart or within five miles of each other, yet three had just happened in the same place simultaneously.

As he fell to his knees, desperately grabbing the desk for support, he looked over to Elya. She continued stumbling in place, but she remained standing. Her breathing was ragged as Halcyon battled the antivirus, and the color leached out of her skin and hair before his eyes.

His pulse slowed down, the rest of his body losing strength as the flow of blood slowed within him. He turned toward the dual screens once more. Messages on the display showed the entire system being systematically deleted, as though controlled by an outside source.

It knows, he realized as his own heart stopped beating entirely. *Halcyon knows that we're trying to stop it. It's not just intelligent, it's self-preserving. We'll never be able to stop it with an antivirus without destroying its AI.*

As the last of the software was deleted off the system, he could hear the server cooling systems shutting down and the temperature in the room rose immediately. His strength gave out as the whirring of the servers grew louder, heat pouring out of the motors. He collapsed to the floor while the acrid tang of burning electronics filled the air.

He turned his head one last time, trying to summon the strength to speak Elya's name, but no sound escaped his throat. She gave him a desperate look, trying to speak to him as well, but whether she succeeded, he could no longer hear her.

The last thing he saw was the synchronizer drop out of Elya's hand. Then, there was nothing.

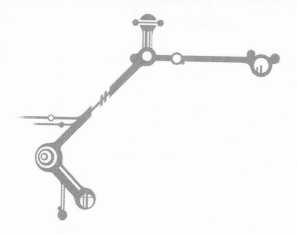

chapter.TWENTYSEVEN

ZANDER STIFLED A yawn as he pulled Galina's motorcycle up to Tiger's home. His whole body was sore, his head throbbed from the pain of it all, and with the endorphins wearing off, his leg seared and tingled where the bullet had grazed it. He knew he had been pushing it to coordinate the infiltration on the IPD offices, but as much as he hurt now, he didn't regret it. Chen and Elya may be hurt, but they were both free and safe. As safe as any of them, anyway.

The urgency had become more apparent when they entered Tiger's neighborhood. Although the streets had grown quiet so late at night, the signs of widespread panic were obvious. Driving down roads lined with businesses topped with apartments, he saw more than his share of broken windows and traffic accidents, and all of the shops were closed. Wrecked cars with shattered windshields lay abandoned in the middle of the street, surrounded by traffic pylons. A heavy weight had settled in the pit of his stomach with the sight. The police were barely keeping up with the injuries, accidents and looting that had occurred since the massive surge by Halcyon and clearly tow trucks were in short supply as well. It was a harrowing sign of the virus's power, forgotten while he was encompassed by the events at IPD, and he didn't want to think about how slim their odds were to stop Halcyon.

He groaned under his breath as he cut the engine and lowered the kickstand of the motorcycle. Elya climbed off and followed him as he swung his leg over the motorcycle and strode down the sidewalk toward an electronics shop. As he approached the door leading into the stairwell that climbed up to the second-story apartment, he understood Tiger's concern. The electronics store looked to have been hit harder than many, the glass storefront completely shattered and all merchandise shelves empty. It looked as if the shop had been abandoned more than a day ago.

Sighing, he opened the door beside the shop and climbed up to Tiger's apartment. He knocked on the door, his right arm hurting from the exertion nearly as much as his injured left. "Tiger! It's Zander."

There was no response.

Zander banged his fist harder against the door. "Tiger! Come on, we're here to get you out." Still no response came from inside. He cast a quick glance at Elya, a line of worry drawn between her brows. Frowning, Zander retrieved his cell phone and dialed Tiger's number. They could hear the phone ringing inside, but the line wasn't answered. Dread settled in Zander as the phone continued to ring, unheeded. At last, he hung up as the familiar sound of Squirrel's van pulled to a stop in front of the building.

Leaning back, Zander kicked at the door, his left leg searing with pain as he put his weight on it. It took three heavy blows before the door swung open. The deadbolt snapped as it broke through, wood chips flying off the door frame, and the chain ripped out of the wall. He drew in a breath as the door banged against the opposite wall and Elya gasped sharply.

Tiger lay sprawled face down on the floor in the middle of the living room, a pool of blood around his head.

Running inside, Zander crouched beside Tiger and checked his pulse, but he could find none. His body was not yet cold, but it was cooler than his own. Zander let out a sigh as he gazed down at the young programmer. The mane of hair running down his back, striped orange, black and white as his namesake, lay limp underneath his worn clothes. Zander rolled Tiger onto his back. Tiger's eyes were solid white and the pool of blood had come out of his mouth, dried blood cracking off from his cheek as his head rolled over. The staircase outside the apartment thumped from footsteps climbing up.

Zander shook his head, feeling weary. "Halcyon. It must have hit him right after he called."

Shad's voice preceded him through the door. "Zander, are you…" He cut himself off with a gasp as he reached the doorway and saw Tiger lying on the floor. "Sean!" He raced to Zander's side, gazing down at Tiger. "Oh shit, no…" He fell to his knees beside Tiger's body.

Zander glanced out the still open apartment door. No other footsteps approached. He turned to Shad. "Where's everyone else?"

Shad seemed to sink in on himself. "I can't believe it. He updated his firewall more than anyone I know. Did he tell you he got infected?"

Zander frowned, his worry about the others growing, but he knew that Tiger had been one of Shad's closest friends. It would do him no good to pressure him about the others. Crouching down, he picked up a data drive lying beside Tiger's fallen hand. "No. He told me he finished analyzing that image file we got." He held the drive out to Shad. "And he was worried about looters." Shad gazed at the drive for a moment, then hung his head with a sigh, tears squeezing out of his eyes.

"It's not fair," he moaned.

Zander swallowed uncomfortably, his concern heightening. "Shad. Where are the others?"

He deflated. "They're in the hospital. Deadeye and Ryn got shot. Deadeye… he didn't look good."

Zander's discomfort grew. "And Chen?"

"He didn't look hurt, but I think they starved him. He could barely stand up."

Zander let out a sigh. From the corner of his eye, he could see Elya, standing nearby with her arms wrapped around her stomach and a weary look on her face. He closed his eyes and his fingers tightened around the data drive he still held.

"Shad." He held the drive out again. "I'm sorry about Tiger. But we might still be able to do something. Please."

Shad shook his head, rage contorting his young features. "What's the point? Everyone's already been infected, including us."

Zander's eyes widened. "What?"

"I got a weird ping, so I checked server logs on the way over. Halcyon's already on every implant in the city. It's probably trying to determine the best way to kill everyone and just hasn't activated yet. There's no escaping it now." He let out a sigh.

"Chen's in no condition to do any programming and even if he was, we lost all his work on the antivirus. It's hopeless."

Zander's shoulders drooped as he sat back, inevitability weighing heavily on him. He pulled his phone out of its holster on his belt, glancing again at the message from his mother. She wasn't concise and his schedule was so erratic that she never insisted on talking to him live. Her three-word message said more than any paragraphs-long e-mail ever had. He knew he should call her now but he didn't feel up to it. It seemed none of them had much time left.

Suddenly, Elya snatched the phone out of his hand. He leaned his head back in surprise as she typed something on the phone. "Elya!" Before he could do anything more, she turned the phone around and shoved the display toward him, a text message entered onto it.

No it's not. I have the complete antivirus.

His eyes enlarged. "Your antivirus works?" Shad lifted his head, a glint of hope alighting in his eyes. "How?" She simply made a dismissive gesture. He shot his gaze over to Shad. "Then we can release it right now!"

Shad straightened, a smile almost forming on his face before he sank in on himself again. "It won't work. Most people have to go to a doctor to get software updates on their implants. There's no way they'd get it in time."

Zander deflated as he realized Shad was right. Most of the people he knew didn't have the connectors or the software to use an implant synchronizer.

Elya perked up, cat ears flicking, then typed another message on Zander's phone.

Unless we transmit it the same way Halcyon does.

Zander followed her eyes to the data drive lying forgotten on the floor between Zander and Shad. Shad's eyes enlarged, a cautiously optimistic look on his face. Picking up the drive, Zander held it out to him once more. This time, Shad took it and plugged it into his palm, the square display flashing against his eye. "There's an ID on the vic. Morrie Deacon, thirty-three years old. Divorced, three kids living with their mother. He was a lawyer."

"That explains the view of real sunlight," Zander said. "What does it have on the infection?"

"Checking now." His eye worked as Zander watched anxiously.

"It's... damn it, it's no use. There's some good stuff here on how it transmits, but it doesn't show how it actually gets onto implants. I still don't know how I can get the antivirus out to people." Zander frowned, but before he could say anything, Shad continued, "Wait, I've got an IP address on the source of infection. Tracing it now." Zander exchanged a look with Elya, quietly focused. "Gateway's a hot spot on first level. Checking the server logs." Shad's eye and fingers worked furiously for a moment, then he inhaled sharply. "It's all here. All the corrupted trace data, the additional activity over the past week and a half, even the spike in the past few hours." Shad glanced up at him. "Zander, *all* the infections are coming from this one place."

Zander's eyebrows rose. "Do you think you can reprogram the system to send out the antivirus instead?"

Shad drew in a breath. "With the data I have here, I think I might be able to whip something up."

For the first time in a while, and despite all his pain and exhaustion, Zander felt hopeful. "We can stop it. We can stop Halcyon right now." Elya stepped forward, squaring her shoulders. Shad turned, glancing miserably at Tiger. Zander grasped his shoulder. "If you want to stay here, you can."

Shad stood, inhaling deeply. "No. Staying here won't bring him back. It'll do more good for me to go with you guys." His eyes glistened as he blinked away the display, but his voice was steady.

Zander laid a hand on his shoulder again, then reached out and placed the other on Elya's shoulder. "It's all up to us now." Shad and Elya looked at him, as exhausted but as determined as he was.

"It's time to end this."

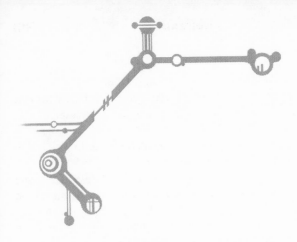

chapter.TWENTYEIGHT

A SOLEMN SILENCE fell over Elya, Zander, Shad and Squirrel as they pulled up to the remains of a factory on ground level. They all stepped out of the van, gazing across the broken parking lot at the decrepit building. As run-down and unassuming as the rest of the ruins marching off into the haze, it didn't even look as though it still had power.

Zander turned to their driver. "Squirrel, I know you weren't as big a part of this as the rest of us. I don't know what's going to happen in here, but there must be some reason this place was never discovered in all these years. You don't have to come in with us."

Squirrel looked as unconcerned as ever as he glanced at the factory. "I'll admit I don't have much experience with this type of action. But it seems to me like none of us have much hope if this fails. I already lost my sister on Tuesday."

Elya, Zander and Shad all sent surprised looks over to him. He gave them a wan smile. "Call it extra incentive to help you guys." Elya reached over to lay a hand on his shoulder with a sympathetic look. He nodded. "Thanks, E."

"Alright," Zander said. And with that one word, they crossed the parking lot toward the doors into the factory.

Shad looked uneasy. "I can't connect to anything. I feel like I'm blind."

Zander grinned at him. "What, you've never gone outside the

quarantine?"

"Not if I can avoid it."

"I'm sure a little unplugging now and then won't hurt you. Just think, this is what people had to deal with before cybernetics."

"And before cell phones?"

Elya watched as Zander pulled his phone out of its holster. She could read the display flashing "No Signal."

"Less distractions," he said as he put the phone away, but she could see the discomfort he tried to hide. They were truly alone down here.

As they drew near to the doors, Squirrel pointed at some broken boards lying beside the entrance, some with nails sticking out of them. "Check it out." The layer of dust and grime over the doors was criss-crossed with clearer strips, within which they could see nail holes.

"The doors were boarded up," Shad remarked.

Zander nodded. "Which means someone has been here recently. Keep your eyes open." Elya inhaled as Zander reached out for the door handles.

The creak of the doors swinging open echoed throughout the building. The cheap daylight bulbs outside threw their shadows far into the large, open room. Beyond it was blackness, and they all paused as they waited for their eyes to adjust.

The doors opened up onto a large assembly floor, most industrial-size machines still whole, if dirty and rusted beyond repair. A few rats skittered away into the darkness. Elya shuddered at the sight. What this factory had once made, she couldn't tell. Even the computer equipment that hooked up to the assembly machines remained, too old and obsolete to be looted.

As she glanced off to the side, her cat ears perked up. She grabbed Zander's arm to get his attention and pointed.

His eyebrows rose in interest. "There's a terminal still on." Zander's voice, though no louder than usual, rang through the immense room. The distant terminal was difficult to see, with the old-fashioned monitor in a power-saving mode and the LED indicators too small to provide any illumination. Yet, the monitor was not the complete black of a shut off unit, but emitted a faint pale light. The system it connected to was a collage of computer parts of various ages and styles, clearly cannibalized from other machines, and trailing up the wall was an old-fashioned network cable.

"That must be it," Shad uttered, clearly afraid to disturb the silence. Zander began leading the way down a row of machinery toward the terminal, Elya falling into step beside him as Shad and Squirrel followed.

Silence laid over the room like a heavy blanket. The huge, open quiet jarred Elya, making her feel as though she was far away from the city, not deep in the thick of it. Few places in the city aside from expensive sound-proofed units completely shut out the noise of people and traffic outside. With ground level so devoid of life, however, only a few creaks from the building settling filled the air.

She flexed her hand, still aching from the bumps of the van as they rode over with her palm connected to Shad's. Zander had thought it prudent that they should all have a copy of the program Shad wrote quickly to override the source computer for Halcyon. Without the ability to control her implants' software like Shad, however, her chances of succeeding alone were questionable.

She began to pick more shapes out of the darkness as they made their way down the rows of machinery. She twitched, thinking she saw a shadow moving from the corner of her eye, but when she focused on it, she saw nothing more. She knew she had little to be concerned about, as she had shared the antivirus with the others before they came, yet she couldn't shake a feeling of trepidation. In this building, Halcyon had remained hidden for years, silently killing people at random, keeping the city locked in fear.

Suddenly, as they neared the end of the row of machines, the ancient lights overhead flared on, illuminating the dusty machines and scuffed floor. By the time they looked down from the lights, two people stood at the end of the row, blocking their path. They stared with vacant expressions, standing still as statues with precisely the same posture.

"You do not have permission to be here," they said in unison.

Zander regarded the strangers warily. "Who are you?"

"No one is allowed on these premises without authorization," came another pair of voices from behind them. They all spun, facing another two people behind them, standing in the same pose and with the same look on their faces, trapping Elya, Zander, Shad and Squirrel between the two long industrial machines. More figures appeared behind those on both sides, most younger than thirty years, but with few other similarities. There were men and women, tall and short, thin and large, of various different races and with vastly differing styles of dress and cosmetic implants. A dozen in total stood around them.

"You do not have permission to be here," the entire group said with perfect symmetry. "No one is allowed on these premises without authorization."

Elya and Zander turned, standing back to back with Shad and Squirrel as they faced the people slowly approaching from both directions. The crowd was too thick to get through easily.

"What is this, some kind of cult?" Shad asked.

"No," Squirrel answered. "Look at their eyes." Elya looked into the people's eyes and her own widened. All of them had eyes of an icy pale blue or red, like an albino, and they had a strange reflective quality to them.

"They all have brain implants," Zander realized. Elya remembered when they discovered Halcyon was aware, that it had specifically targeted the trucks carrying Chen's incomplete antivirus to protect itself, and came to the same conclusion the moment Zander did. "The damn virus is controlling them." Shad swore.

"I had a feeling it wouldn't be so easy," Squirrel remarked casually as Halcyon's defenders drew slowly closer.

"It never is," Zander replied dryly.

"You do not have permission to be here," the group repeated. "No one is allowed on these premises without authorization."

Then, Zander, Shad and Squirrel stumbled or swayed in place. Elya felt it, too. The virus was trying to infect them. Her skin tingled and her throat constricted briefly as Halcyon tried to shut down her implants, but after a moment, the feeling faded and she recovered.

"Everyone okay?" Zander asked.

"All good, boss," Squirrel answered. Elya gave Zander a thumbs-up.

"I guess now we know the antivirus works," Shad said.

The crowd to either side of them stopped, all of them mirrors of the others as they stared emotionlessly. "You cannot resist the infection." Elya could feel the virus attacking again, but now that the antivirus had settled into her implants' software, it was stopped before it even affected her cybernetics.

"We will not fail," the group intoned. Then, without any further warning or change in posture or expression, the crowd charged as one. Shad yelped as the group converged on them. Elya threw her hands forward, prepared to defend herself, but Zander moved in front of her, keeping Halcyon's protectors from reaching her. She glanced between him, Shad and Squirrel, the three of them forming a ring around her and keeping the crowd from getting closer.

Zander, Shad and Squirrel grunted and yelped as they fought, but the crowd remained disturbingly silent, no signs of struggle or pain on their expressionless faces. Their movements were clumsy, easily repelled, though their greater numbers kept Zander, Shad and Squirrel busy. As they fought, Elya noticed, Halcyon's protectors gradually grew more fluid and more successful in their attacks. She flicked her eyes around, wanting to help, but not enough of a gap opened up for her to attack.

"Any ideas, boss?" Squirrel asked over the sounds of fighting. He struggled to merely hold off the blows raining down on him, clearly less experienced with self-defense than the others. "I don't think we're going to wear them down first."

Zander grunted from a punch to the face. "I'm open to suggestions. The kind of control Halcyon has over these guys, I'm not even sure shooting them will slow them down." Elya spun and kicked as one of Halcyon's defenders broke through the line and ran toward her. It was a young woman with a double mohawk, striped in shades of blue and purple. She made no reaction as Elya's kick threw her against the machine beside her and rose immediately to charge again. Elya had barely begun to feel discomfort from the thought of hurting the woman further when Zander grabbed her by the arm and threw her back into the crowd.

Then, all the monitors on the terminal they had approached lit up, alive with activity.

"The virus wave," Shad said. "It's being activated!"

Zander strained to hold back two opponents while kicking out at a third, his eyes wild with endorphins and wounds bleeding freshly. "Elya! You have to get to the console and send out the antivirus now!"

She sent a quick glance to the three of them, struggling harder against their attackers as they learned how to break through Zander, Shad and Squirrel's defenses. Elya hesitated, then climbed up onto one of the machines beside them and leaped over. A few of Halcyon's defenders broke away from the rest of the crowd to move around or over the machines toward her, but she ran for the terminal as fast as she could. Her heart raced as she came near the end of the row of machines, the terminal only a few paces ahead. Time was running out.

Two of Halcyon's protectors appeared ahead of her and a hundred thoughts ran through her mind at once. She didn't want to slow down for fear that those behind her would catch up and she would be trapped, but that left her with less than two seconds to decide what to do about this new threat. She doubted she could fight people who could no longer feel pain and win, but if she tried to swerve around them and continue to the terminal, then they would simply attack her there and likely stop her from sending out the antivirus. Pity, anger, frustration, desperation and worry all tumbled through her mind.

She ran out of time before she had decided what to do. Hunching over, she leaned forward and barreled into the two people, knocking them down. Racing on, she reached the terminal and slapped her palm down on the console, the connectors in her hand emerging and hooking up to it.

Code swirled through her head as Halcyon and Shad's program fought for control of her and the console. Sensing its biggest threat yet, the virus put nearly all its resources into analyzing her implants' software in a nanosecond, searching for a way to shut her down. She stumbled as her cybernetics blinked on and off. Images flashed through her mind, things she realized were memories. People, rooms, feelings, smells. Still the override program fought, trying to overpower Halcyon even as it cut off air passage to her lungs.

Programming filled her mind. Strings, equations and variables rushed through her head at breakneck speed. She could barely catch one character in twenty, but as she studied Halcyon's code, something startling jumped out at her.

Wait a minute... this code is military!

Then, everything went white.

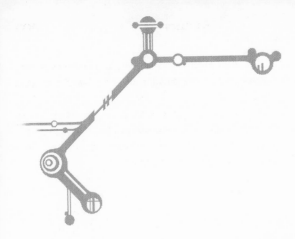

EPILOGUE

ZANDER AWOKE IN pain on a stiff bed in a large, sterilized room, surrounded by gently beeping machines and curtains.

Not this again, he thought.

A nurse soon came to check on him, but she was rushed in her work to the point of terse and didn't answer any of his questions about what had happened. She was gone before he could get any information out of her. He didn't even know which hospital he had been taken to.

From the monitors surrounding him, he could determine that about twelve hours had passed since they went into the ground-level factory to stop Halcyon. That the nurse had enough patients to keep her so busy could be a good sign, or not. He only remembered fighting the people controlled by Halcyon before his endorphins finally depleted and a heavy blow knocked him out.

Three hours passed after he awakened before he was transferred from the ICU into a recovery ward. There his cell phone was returned to him. Swallowing, he finally called his mother back.

She sounded calm enough when she answered the phone, but before their conversation had ended, she was crying and apologizing to Zander for it. He offered her bland reassurances, but his heart felt heavy and he could put no comfort into the words.

His father had been infected while he and the others infiltrated

IPD. Halcyon had sabotaged an implant to regulate his cholesterol and he had died of heart failure before he ever knew anything was wrong.

Feeling empty inside, Zander ended the call and prepared to put the phone away, but it chimed a notification that he had a new e-mail. Blankly gazing at it, his eyes widened as he saw the sender was Elya Renard. He opened the message.

Hi Zander,

I know I shouldn't be doing this through e-mail, but I started regaining my memories after what happened in the factory... like the ones of Dwayne. I just need some time to myself to sort things out before I can see you again. I'm sorry.

It's done now. I was able to send out the antivirus to the entire city. I don't know if Halcyon's actually *gone* yet, but at least it can be tracked down and we're protected in the meantime.

There's one other thing, though. When I was hooked up to the terminal where Halcyon was hosted, I found a military ID in its code. It turns out it was commissioned by the army as a weapon of war. I spoke with the colonel who was in charge of Project Requiem, who I found out was involved in the original project to create Halcyon. In fact, part of the reason Requiem fell apart was because they were locking IPD out too much for the engineers to do their job, because they didn't want anyone finding out that they created Halcyon in the first place. They couldn't stop it because after it got loose and set itself up in that factory, it destroyed the systems where it was created and killed the engineers who worked on it. Just like it destroyed the systems for Requiem and killed Dwayne, and tried to kill me.

The colonel said the army wouldn't go after us for what we did, though she did imply that that's only if we kept silent about what we knew. I shouldn't even be telling you this, and I think she might be writing up an NDA for me even now, but you should know. As for Sinclair, well, who knows. I haven't heard anything yet. We may still get a shit-storm from him, but we have Chen's testimony hanging over his head. I don't think he'd risk his company—or his profits— to indict us on trespassing charges, but he did hire mercenaries before, and he has connections. Be careful.

I want to thank you again for everything that you did. For me, for the antivirus, for the entire city. I really appreciate it, and I'm sorry I'm too cowardly to say it in person right now. It may be a while before I see you again. Trying to pick up my life where I left off when the rest of the world has thought me dead for two and a half months is every bit the pain in the ass I thought it was going to be. My mom's still hysterical and barely wants to let me out of her sight. Reinstating my credit cards and driver's license and stuff could take weeks. I may not even be able to recover some of the stuff from my apartment.

Anyway, I hope you recover soon. Tell the others thanks for me. Take care of yourself. I'll talk to you again… before long, I hope.

Elya

Slowly, he lowered the phone and leaned his head back against the hospital pillow, a range of emotions whirling through his head. All this time, he had thought the army was just trying to do the right thing and IPD was getting in the way of that, but it was almost the other way around. The army was just as guilty of dismantling Requiem, the best hope for creating a working antivirus, and they were solely responsible for Halcyon in the first place. All those deaths through all those years were on the U.S. government's head.

And Elya. He hadn't wanted to admit that he was hoping for more with her, but he knew he was interested in her. The feel of her pressed up against him on the motorcycle the last night lingered with him, sending a shiver up his spine. Yet she couldn't even bear to see him now.

He hadn't even sorted through his emotions before a voice beyond the curtains surrounding his bed said, "Zan?"

He smiled as the curtains parted. "Hey, Shad."

Shad half-shrugged as the curtains opened again behind him. "It's Justin. Justin Singh." Zander nodded, remembering when he had looked that up. The teenager had been pretty thorough in covering his tracks and it had taken a lot of work to uncover his identity, and his meticulousness was part of the reason Zander asked for his help in the first place. The next person to follow him inside, Zander had never even learned more than an alias.

Squirrel nodded with a smile. "Hey, boss. Feeling better?"

"Starting to, and don't call me that." He exchanged a grin with the driver. One last figure followed behind them. Zander's eyes widened. "Chen."

Chen smiled, though he still looked emaciated. "Hey, Zander."

"You alright?"

Chen shrugged. "I'll be okay. You don't look so good, though."

Zander grinned wryly. "Just a few bumps and bruises. I don't think life's going to be as exciting now."

Shad nodded. Justin, Zander corrected internally. "Yeah. It's done." There was a hesitation in his voice.

Zander's heart felt heavy again. "Not everyone was saved, were they?"

Chen looked at the floor, wringing his hands. "Some people were killed almost immediately. The antivirus didn't get to them in time."

Zander closed his eyes. "How many?" There was a pause.

Finally, Squirrel answered, "About two thousand."

Zander bowed his head. There had been that many troops in the base where he was stationed his first deployment overseas. He hadn't even seen a quarter of them.

The army. Those deaths, and thousands more, were all on its hands.

"It would have been millions if Elya hadn't sent out the antivirus when she did," Chen offered quietly.

Zander knew it was true, but it was hard to focus on the countless saved than the ones whose names had filled the obituaries. People like Dwayne. Like Squirrel's sister. His coworker. His father.

The army was the first thing to give him purpose in life and now he couldn't trust it anymore.

He inhaled slowly. "How are Ryn and Deadeye?"

There was another uncomfortable pause. His stomach tightened.

"Ryn said she'd be okay," Chen answered. Zander was already guessing what was coming before Justin spoke.

"Deadeye didn't make it." He frowned. "His name was Tyrone Maddox." Zander let out a sigh, not bothering to tell them that he knew that, and many other things about him besides. "He said he didn't have any regrets."

He may not, Zander thought, *but I do.*

"We all knew what we were getting into," Squirrel said. "None of us questioned you, then or now."

Chen nodded and Justin said, "That's right. And we did what we set out to do. Halcyon's been stopped."

Though it was small comfort at that moment, Zander gave them a smile. "It has. And at least you guys are still okay." They all agreed with him. "Thanks for coming by."

"We're still a team," Justin said with a smile. Zander smiled in return, though he knew it wasn't true. Halcyon had brought them together, and though he didn't doubt they would stay in touch, they would never again be this close. Even as he watched Chen leave, he knew their friendship would never be the same. Chen had needed him and he had needed Chen, but without Halcyon tying them together, Zander had almost nothing in common with the young programmer and doubted they would make very good roommates anymore. Justin had not-so-subtly hinted at a hope that he could move out of his parents' house into their apartment. He and Chen would make much better roommates.

With the number of patients who had suffered illness or trauma before the antivirus was transmitted the last night, hospital staff rushed him out the door that afternoon with a stern warning not to do anything that would require their services again. The staff was so overworked that it took over an hour simply to sign the discharge papers. At last, however, he hobbled out the front doors of the hospital on his cane, his many wounds still aching and a prescription for pain medicine in his pocket.

He ignored the looks he got as he made his way to the nearest train station and climbed down the stairs to the platform. There he stood, staring off at the second city level dropping away through the glass doors on the edge of the platform, wondering what he was going to do with his life now.

Then, a familiar voice spoke up behind him.

"My offer still stands, you know."

His eyebrows raised as he recognized the voice. Galina. He sobered, still facing the doors as the train slid up to the station. "I thought I made my opinion of your ideas of morality clear."

In the reflection from the glass doors, he could see her turn her head away. "It's occurred to me that it might be to my own benefit to be more discerning about which clients I take."

The doors slid open and he strode onto the train, Galina following after him. "So you're looking to me for guidance, is that it? I'm flattered."

"Don't be. I hate searching for a partner slightly more than I resent you. It's easier this way."

Zander smiled, wondering how much of that statement was covering up what she really felt. Switching his cane to his left hand, he reached up with his right to grab one of the overhead bars for balance while she leaned against a pole nearby. Still neither of them met the other's eyes.

"What did you do to Sinclair?"

"He's alive."

He couldn't help but grin at what was left unsaid.

"I meant what I said. Your skills and intuition are worth a hundred times what you make at a hardware store."

"I could get a second job."

The train chimed as it slid up to the next station. "Moving up in the world. Where were you looking next, a grocery store?"

"It was among my options."

"It's refreshing to meet someone who doesn't need pride. Or financial security."

Turning, he finally looked at her, narrowing his eyes. "You're still a stone-hearted bitch."

She faced him levelly. "And you're a quixotic moron. It's a match worthy of song. Now are you going to answer me, or are you just going to blather on all day?"

"Will you promise not to shoot me again?"

About the Author

A perpetual temp who has worked for a number of evil empires, Catherine decided to forgo things like a salary and regular human interaction to start a business. She lives near Toronto, Ontario with her husband, daughter and a black Himalayan with a tendency to slide into walls. Visit her blog at http://thejinx.wordpress.com/

Made in the USA
Charleston, SC
07 July 2012